Amit Siovitz

Where Have You Been?

Éditions
DÉDICACES

First published by Editions Dedicaces in 2016.

Copyright © Amit Siovitz, 2016.

ISBN: 9781770766068

This book was professionally typeset on Reedsy.
Find out more at reedsy.com

1

WHERE HAVE YOU BEEN?

I can't see through the smoke, but that's okay, there's nothing to see. Besides, even if I could see, I'd probably see wrong, or fuzzy, or blurry, and freak out. There are six of us, and we are sitting down in a sort of circle, at least we were when we started. I can hear someone coughing to my left, but he's a bit further off than I remember him to have been. It's only when my bottom gets cold again that I remember I'm sitting on the floor; I gave my seat to Jenny, she's a delicate one. I can't see her now, but she's there and she's grateful. Smoke's becoming thinner and I can make out shapes, I know most of the smoke is in my head, but metaphoric or not, it's clearing. Assuming the shapes are all real, someone must be lying down on the couch. That must be Jimmy, he's new and probably can't handle much; I hope someone will take care of him. There's a coughing again, still from the left, and a slight groan. *Who was sitting to my left?* Maybe Jake? No, then we'd be seven, Jake left early. Someone is fumbling through the smoke, to the right, it's a thin shape immediately next to me so it must be Jenny. She's kind of my girlfriend, but we don't call each other *boyfriend* or *girlfriend*, we just hang out, smoke and sleep together. The shape of Jenny found me and is holding my hand now.

"Johnny, I don't feel well, let's go." She does sound sick, like she just finished a good long cry, but no one cried, as I remember.

"Okay." I agree without realizing, but it takes me forever to stand up; my brain has trouble interacting with my limbs. It's the heroin's fault.

We walk out and I light another cigarette; it tastes like shit. I buy the cheapest kind; the ones they smuggle in from some middle-eastern hell hole. The nicotine levels are very high and the price is low, so it's okay.

Jenny enjoys the fresh air outside, she's not a smoker; she hates smelling of cigarettes and me. We get into the car and realize we are both too wasted to drive, so we just sit there. She falls asleep on my shoulder. She is very sweet, this girl. I don't know why she hangs out with us; all we do is bring her down. She's nineteen, long brown hair, the most amazing green eyes... I could stare at her for days. Once, I took acid and went to visit her, she was clean that day, and I saw her eyes turn into forests, then they were a green ocean with waves that jumped and kissed me. I loved that. I wake up without realizing I was ever asleep and start the car; that scares Jenny awake as well.

"Where are we going?" She retracts herself back to the passenger seat.

"I'm taking you home." She's a good girl, she has a good home.

"Okay, but I want to eat first, and shower so my mom can't smell this on me; can we stop at your place?" Always worried about what her mom might think.

"Sure babe." I kick the car into gear and drive off. My place isn't far off from James's, where we took the Junk and smoked, just a mile or so, maybe less. It's not much of a place, really, a two hundred square feet hovel, with a shower and a hotplate. I've been living there for two years almost.

We get to my hovel and Jenny jumps into the shower, can't wait to get rid of the smell of cigarettes, Junk and my kiss. She takes forever so I spend that time making food. I have spaghetti and a sauce I always buy, it tastes like what an Italian person might throw up, but it goes down sure enough, so I keep on buying it.

We eat together in silence as both our heads start to hurt. Jenny moans and groans about her headache so I stroke her hair and kiss her forehead, now she would have to shower again to get rid of that smell; but she doesn't. After lunch or dinner, I don't have a clock, or a feel for time, Jenny leaves on foot. She lives with her mom and dad about seven minutes' walk from here, and she's safe because no one out there would touch my girlfriend, even if she doesn't admit to being my girlfriend. Even so, I make her call me to make sure she got home safe. She does about ten minutes after leaving my place.

"Did your mom ask you where you've been?" I ask her.

"Yes, of course she did. I told her I went to see a friend and ate there. I'm afraid she might look for marks on me some day." I never thought about that.

"Ohh... Well, no more needles for you, then!" I try to sound responsible, but I just had some hash and I can't stop laughing.

"Not funny, she'd kick me out. Dad will kill me." There is a long pause before she continues– "Then he'd kill you." I never knew her parents knew about me, I fixed their car once, so I know they know I exist, but that I interact (and sleep) with their daughter? That's news. I mean, they knew me when I was little, when my family lived in the neighborhood, but I've grown since then, even have facial hair now.

I can't think of what to say, so I wait. She's also waiting, she's good at that.

"I'm serious, no more needles for you."

"But... I can't stop, you know that." Now she's whimpering; I got her hooked.

"You don't have to have needles, there are other methods."

"They're not as good, not as fast; they're a waste." She's right.

"We'll think of something." I hang up. I can't take this right now.

Jenny is great, but she's very stressed out. She used to have a lot of plans, most of them fell through, but she is still responsible and that is sometimes a drag. For instance, when she started out with us she made rules, Junk rules, have you ever heard of such a thing?

Well, first rule was: No one can lie to her about what she's taking and its effects. Fair enough.

Second rule: No one was to take advantage of her if she passes out.

Third: She will not sell herself for anything.

Fourth: If she wants out, we let her out.

Fifth rule: Nothing that leaves marks. She broke that rule herself.

Sixth rule: If she isn't responding or is in peril, call an ambulance. We never had any intention of doing that.

Seventh rule: if I am not there, she mustn't be given anything unless she asks for it specifically.

Eighth rule: There must always be ventilation for the smoke.

Ninth rule: All new people must be cleared by her as well.

Tenth rule: No one must ever everevereverever tell anyone outside our group that she is a part of our group.

We call these the Ten Commandments of Jenny-Junk. As the person who brought her to the group, I was blamed for bringing in such a drag, but after the first time she took acid with us people saw how much fun she could be. Besides, before her we always did it in such a mess; she even cleans up before we start! Joanna hates Jenny, though. Joanna is James's girlfriend, and she admits to being his girlfriend. I think it's a girl thing; Joanna doesn't like Jenny because Jenny's prettier or something like that. I know somewhere in my brain that it has to be more than that, but I can't see why, then again, Joanna doesn't get to sleep with Jenny, so she is more susceptible to her flaws. At any rate, they fight sometimes; for instance, Joanna would accuse Jenny for being "stuck up" and thinking she is better than the rest of us, or Jenny would sometimes yell and Joanna for making out with James in front of everyone, saying it's "inappropriate". Me and James don't intervene; it's a girl thing, so let the girls sort it out. James and me have been friends since junior high. He was the first person I ever met that was my age and smoked. He offered me a smoke and I took it. I almost threw up. Jake used to be a close friend too, until he started dealing. He became a huge asshole after that. "I can't treat you different than anyone else." He used to say. Asshole. I once saved him by taking the blame for smoking Pot in school, how does he thank me? By charging me full price for that same Pot the next day. Asshole. Not only that; even though we were close friends, just because I'm not rich he always gives me the bad stuff and saves the good stuff for the rich folk. Now, if I were to deal, rich people AND friends would get the good stuff and poor people that I don't know would get the cheap crap; that sounds fair. So now Jake only comes by to hand over the goods and take the money, and it's usually James or Jamal who call him; I don't want to speak to him. Thinking of this makes me upset, so I light up another joint, I have enough to last for the week, all stashed in the intercom's panel; cops rarely take apart electronics during a search unless there's a sniffing dog. I fall asleep after my joint; they always make me sleepy, and call Jenny in the morning. She's all rays of sunshine in the morning.

"Hey there Sweety! How'd you sleep? I slept great, I had another little dinner when I came home and slept like a baby and dreamed of you." She talks so fast in the morning.

"I slept, I also had another something in the evening to help me sleep, but it wasn't dinner." We both laugh a bit.

"Are we going to James's today? I'd rather not, I have plans, but you can join me."

I agree to join her and regret it very quickly, she's going to have a lunch out with her parents and she wants me to come along. *Does that mean I'm finally her boyfriend?*

So I don't smoke anything all day until I have to leave, and I wear good clothes and a ton of aftershave and deodorant.

I am supposed to meet Jenny in front of the café where they wanted to get lunch but I'm late because I couldn't find it. It's a nice place, inspired by the cafes you see in European movies that take place in Paris or Berlin, I think Jenny used to work there; she definitely said something to that effect.

"So, Johnny, what do you do?" Her father is a no horsing around kind of guy and fires his first question before I even sit down. Because I was late, I didn't even get a 'briefing' from Jenny, she just brought me inside and scowled, but I think she is introducing me to her parents as her boyfriend, even though she just said "Mom, Dad, this is the Johnny that I told you about." Of course, they already know me; I'm the guy who fixed their car well and cheap, but am I a boyfriend?

"I fix cars sir, as you know." I try to smile, but I am so nervous it probably looks like an evil grin, like what Jason does under his hockey mask when he kills people.

"Is that all? What about other interests? You don't work in a garage either, a freelance mechanic?" Man, he's good at this.

"I do odd jobs, sir, you know the market... and other interests..." I can't say heroin and acid and cocaine, can I? "I enjoy reading." Where did that come from?

"Who is your favorite author?" That's her mom. Jenny looks just like her mom, just younger; they are both very attractive women. When I was young and before Jenny developed, I had a huge crush on her mom, I even dreamed about her once, but... that's private.

"I like poetry, 'mam, Poe is my favorite." I didn't even know I have a favorite, but Poe sounds respectable, the kind of poet academics write about and young poets get compared to.

"Oh... he had such a way to create a mood!" I think I scored a point with Jenny's mom.

"Odd jobs?" Her dad brings us back to my employment status. Well, I can't tell him that with 'odd jobs' I mean, fix stuff and sell illegal substances, so I stick to fixing things.

"Yes sir, fixing things around the house, cars, busses, yard work, construction when it comes along... odd jobs."

"That doesn't sound like a stable living." He interjects

"You know the market..." I shrug; I just hear people say that a lot all around; the bums and other junkies.... 'You know the market' the magic excuse to not trying to find work.

"I do know the market, very well." I don't know what Jenny's dad does, only that he has a lot of money, maybe he's a stock broker? No, they're all in New York.

"How did you two get to know each other?" Her mom saves the day!

"We met at a friend's house, it was a little party and we stayed together all night, after seeing Jenny and talking to her, I didn't care about anyone else in that stupid party" I heard this in a movie somewhere, thought it might be the kind of thing both Jenny and her mom would want to hear.

"Awww....." Jenny is all red in the face and lowering her gaze. Her mom is making the same noise but looking at us both like we were a painting.

"When was this?" Her dad again with his insistence on the practical.

"Two months ago." I answer without thinking.

"Jenny, you never mentioned Johnny before last week." Her dad turns to her, but I still somehow feel like he's gazing hostilely at me.

"Well... I didn't really know what we were I guess."

"What are we?" I turn to her, trying to imitate her dad's piercing stare, but gravitas is hard to maintain when there's pasta sticking out of your mouth and marinara sauce on your nose.

"Not now." She whispers.

"I want to know." I speak as loudly as would be acceptable among clinking cutlery and fake-porcelain plates.

"Me too." Her dad joins in, the pressuring, overprotective dad of my slightly timid girlfriend is my friend?

"Don't ruin this." She becomes harsh. There are no kisses in her eyes now.

"Fine. Sir, 'mam, me and Jenny, as a couple, started out almost two months ago, after the party I mentioned we went to my apartment, slept together and had a few joints." I really don't know why I said that. It gets so quiet at first, then Jenny starts crying and runs to the bathroom, her mom after her; and I'm left alone with her dad, great.

He's staring at me as if I had killed Jenny. I just noticed he also has the same eyes as Jenny, but they are more... mineral than hers. Jenny's eyes are more like algae, they are alive; his are hard like emeralds.

"Do you think this is funny?" It's like he isn't even blinking; it's making me so uncomfortable I start looking at my plate and play around with what's left of my pasta.

"No sir. It's not funny. I'm just being honest. We met at the party, we really liked each other, she came over to my apartment, we slept together, and then we had some joints and talked." After a moment I think to add "It was the first time she ever smoked, she said." I'm pretty sure that that won't make anything better, but that is also the truth.

"I don't care!" He slams his hand on the table and everybody turns to look at us.

"Sir, she is a good girl."

"I know. It's you that is a problem." He gets up, wipes his mouth with a napkin and walks towards the bathroom where his wife is standing in front of the door to the ladies' room.

I sit alone, everybody around me is taking turns sneaking in a peek at me and I feel like a prisoner on a CCTV monitor when the guards are all taking bets whether he might kill himself in his cell or not.

After a moment longer I get up and leave. I walk out barely able to make use of the door handle; my hands are shaking. I walk around the café to the alley behind it and light up a joint to relax. I haven't smoked a thing since yesterday. One of the waiters from the café joins me, he has his own joint and when I finish mine he lets me have some of his. His name is Diego, but he's not Mexican, he's an American citizen with Spanish heritage, I respect that. When we're done we split up, he walks back inside, and I back around to the front of the café and look through the windows and see if Jenny and her parents are still there. They aren't; the car's gone too. I walk home and have a hit by myself. People say it's dangerous to do that 'Always have someone around in case you OD or something goes wrong', but as I see it, if there's a lot of us, and we all do the same, we'd all OD anyway, so it's useless. The heroin is good, was expensive as hell too. I don't have much, just enough to make the day go away.

When I get back down, it's next morning and I don't know when I fell asleep. The sun's up, but lower than it was when I came home, so it must be tomorrow. The phone rings.

"Hey man, you up to work today?" It's Jeff; he's the one that finds my more legitimate jobs for me.

"Ahh... what's the job and what's the take?" I sound like something out of a Slayer CD, hoarse as a horse, my dad would say, even though it didn't make sense.

"Floor tiling, six bucks an hour." Jeff knows everyone in town and knows who needs what done, when, and where.

"Okay, where do I go and when?"

"Be at Lincoln Road 42 in two hours, be clean!" He also doesn't want his 'clients' to know all his guys are junkies; it's bad PR to tell your costumer his money is going straight to buy Junk.

The job isn't hard, and we work six hours, so it's good money, and we're supposed to come back the next day for another six hours. I come home and check for messages, yes, I have a machine, none. I turn on the TV, it's an old piece of shit I exchanged for some crack last year. This crack-head idiot came to me all jacked up, looking to score for his friends too, but the idiot forgot to bring money, so I came over to his place with the stuff, but no one had money there either, at first I thought they were going to rob me, but they all looked so spindly and weak; they were just new to the game. I left the stuff on the table and said I'm going to take something from the apartment, it was a pretty nice apartment, and they agreed. I regret taking the TV, I should have taken their AC, if I were able carry it. There is NO ventilation in my place, when it gets hot, like it should next month, I can die here. There is nothing to watch, so I zap between things until I find Breaking Bad. Now there's an idea, cook meth in your house and sell it for cash... Too bad I'm too afraid of meth. I know it sounds dumb. I take Junk but think meth is the devil. I never saw anyone enjoy meth. I see everyone enjoy Junk, I enjoy Junk, I need Junk, Jenny enjoys Junk, I need Jenny, Jenny needs Junk, Jenny doesn't need me; except for Junk. Why hasn't Jenny called? I check the machine again; nothing. I turn on my laptop, first time in a week and check emails and messages; nothing except someone wanting some Hash.

I watch some more TV and light a joint, and then call James.

"Man, did you hear from Jenny?"

"Yeah, she came by to buy some stuff, left before I could ask her where you were." James sounds almost asleep. He was also at the Lincoln Road job, 'supervising'. He never lifts a finger when we work, but he always shows up early and leaves late a make sure there's a good atmosphere at work, so no one complains about him not helping and still getting paid; besides, he has stuff, always.

"When was this?"

"Two hours ago, right after I got home." I can hear Joanna in the background; she's singing along with their TV, another thing about her that Jenny hates, she thinks she can sing.

"You two had a fight or something?" He asks me nonchalantly, but I can almost hear Joanna smirking,

"Kind of, I don't know. Can I come over?"

"Not today buddy, me and Joanna have something planned." Selfish bastard, that last hit really was my last, now I only have Hash.

"Okay, but can you bring me something tomorrow to work?"

"Sure buddy, anything for you." He hangs up when his words turn into a yawn, and it takes me a few minutes before I put the phone down and hang up as well. I dial again, Jenny this time.

"Hello?" A woman's voice, Jenny's mom.

"Hello Mrs. Cohen, is Jenny there?"

"Yes, who is this?"

"Johnny."

"Oh... I don't think she wants to speak to you." This sentence is almost whispered.

"I wanted to apologize for my behavior, 'mam, please, let me speak to her, she would understand."

"She can't speak to you." That's her dad probably from another phone in the house.

"Sir... Please, I need to hear her say that."

There's a long pause, I imagine Mrs. Cohen staring at Mr. Cohen, daring him to say the wrong thing. And then–

"Johnny, I need some time apart." Her voice is so weak; she doesn't really believe that. She doesn't sound mad, I think, high maybe, but not mad.

"Okay... I'm sorry." I hang up. I was expecting anger, shouting, but sorrow and vulnerability? How am I supposed to handle that? I could have handled the screaming, but to console? That is not my forte.

It's getting late so I take a shower. While I wait for the water to warm up I take a look at my naked self in the mirror; my bad quality tattoos, and hairy chest, like a bear, all covering a pinkish blob. My face is displeasing when I look at it; not displeased, displeasing. I need a shave. *Why is she with me?* Oh, yeah, the Junk.

The water's hot and pleasing. I couldn't afford soap last time I was at the store because of an impulse buy of some frozen burritos, so I use whatever shampoo I have left as soap as well. I smell like lemon grass and wet skin. I do shave around my beard, leaving my goatee untouched.

I have dinner after my shower, along with a couple of beers and another joint. The TV is supplying background noise while I eat alone. Pizza for one.

The phone rings, a look out the window next to the bed shows me it's morning.

"Johnny, no need to come to work today." It's Jeff.

"Why not?"

"Mr. Berkley caught Jimmy smoking Pot yesterday during work, so he just told me he isn't interested in us tiling his floor. Uptight fuck." Mr. Berkley really is uptight, he was a teacher until three years ago, 'Biology for the Masses' was how he would describe his teaching style. I had him in the twelfth grade, and he was a prick.

"Fuck. Oh well, call me if something else comes up, okay? Will you be at James's today?"

"Yeah, I'm headed there in an hour, you coming? Bringing Jenny with you?" Word spreads really slowly amongst Junkies, unless someone has something good, then it spreads like a wildfire on crack.

"I'll be there later, no Jenny, though."

"See you there man." He hangs up, no questions asked, no one there really cares for Jenny, I think, just that she always has money and that she cleans up before and after.

I get dressed and check emails and wanted ads, maybe a job will come up from the infinite space of the internet. There is something.

"Wanted, help for moving on the 27th of April. Truck supplied, just bring your arms! 8 dollars an hour. Please call (440) 546-5884."

I don't think I know this number. I call and a woman picks up, it's a coincidence, she's also called Jenny. Jenny Everson, she and her husband are moving to a better part of town but they can't afford an actual movers company, so they're hiring anyone who has both arms and can use both legs. I promise to help build up their furniture at the destination for an extra cost. There's still a week for that, so I write it down somewhere and have breakfast: a beer and something that used to be cornflakes. When everything gets boring I head out to James's. He is sitting there all happy holding Joanna's hand; they are both smoking cigarettes and drinking. Jeff, Jimmy, James, Joanna, and me, just five today. Jeff gets up and closes the windows and shutters, then he opens a box and gets his works out, I forgot mine at home, so I borrow a fresh needle from James. His sister is a paramedic, so he has continuous access to this kind of equipment. Joanna gets to go first. "Ladies first" says James and slaps her on the rear, she smiles at him and pouts her lips. Whatever they did last night, they seem closer today. I take second, because James says I just broke up with my girlfriend so I need it more than the rest of the guys. But I didn't break up with her, did I? I don't know, technically, we were girlfriend and boyfriend for the five seconds when she tried to introduce me to her parents, and then I fucked it up. I don't really notice who takes next, I have mine.

The phone rings and Joanna answers, she never sounds high, even when she has a Junk cocktail she could fool a cop, at least with her voice.

"Hello?... Oh, yes, he's here." She sounds irritated, maybe it's

Jenny.

"No, we won't make him do that. Listen, if you want you may come, but don't drag me into your little bullshit fight. Bitch." She's about to hang up and then stops. She starts to listen a lot more carefully and presses the ear piece to her ear.

"You're joking... I'm sorry." Now she hangs up.

There's a few seconds of silence and Joanna comes to sit next to me. She looks contemplative.

"That was Jenny. She told me what happened; she wants to talk to you. Sorry, that's a lie, she needs to talk to you, she's trying to avoid you but she needs you. I can't tell you why, she asked to come here but that we make you leave before she comes. Go talk to her. She's at work." I never heard Joanna use this tone when talking about Jenny, like she was a friend.

"I'm not well enough to drive."

"Walk, you ass." Joanna is a nice girl despite her rough exterior. Her dad owns a little store right in front of the gas station on St. Peter Drive, and when we were all kids he used to give her as much candy as she wanted and told her not to give any to the rest of us, knowing full well that she would, and we all pretended it was a secret; that made him smile. Joanna doesn't really have a mom. Well, she does in the sense that a woman gave birth to her, but that woman is a permanent resident of the Green Meadows Psychiatric Hospital, and in many ways no longer a person. At school some of the girls picked on Joanna for that, saying she'd become crazy too. There weren't a lot of those girls, but everybody else just stood there and let them torture her, only me, James and Jake, when he was still okay, stood up for her. When we were in the twelfth grade and Joanna in the tenth, James got into a fight with Nathan because of that; Nathan was the boyfriend of one of the girls who tortured Joanna. It wasn't a fair fight seeing as

Nathan was in the wrestling team and James in the debate team... James could talk anyone into anything, but he couldn't TALK the shit out of Nathan, so Nathan BEAT the shit out of him. That was around the time he and Joanna became a couple.

I get up and leave, outside the sun is too bright, the air too real. I walk so slowly, I think it would take ages to get there. Jenny works as a receptionist for a law firm, they are small time, but they try to look like one of those Manhattan firms where even the janitor is wearing a three piece suit.

I walk into the building and am immediately greeted by Jenny.

"Are you here to embarrass me at work too?"

"No, Joanna said you... I don't know, she said to come to you." I guess I ruined my opportunity for being the good man who knows when a woman needs him... Real smooth, Johnny.

"Is this man bothering you, Ms. Cohen?" that's Ron, the security guy for the firm. The entrance hall to the building is so tiny that the reception desk is almost placed ON Ron's shoes, Jenny practically has to sit on his lap; bet he'd like that.

"No, Ron, thank you; he's a... an acquaintance." Ron backs off and goes back to reading his book; Harry Potter.

"Johnny, go away. You ruined everything." She whispers at me through her teeth, almost hissing.

"What did I ruin?"

"US! My parents think I'm a pot-head, that I'm a slut."

"So they think you're a pot-head, big deal! You're a junky!" I almost yell this but I swallow the last word, she is at work, after all.

She slaps me; clear across the face, and before I know it, Ron is leading me out by force. Man, he's strong.

I don't know for how long I've been sitting on the curb in front of Cohen & Co, Attorneys at Law, but it must be long, because

Jenny is coming out with her purse, and so are most of the other employs, work day is over.

"Why are you still here?" She sounds cranky.

"I don't know." The maximum range of my smooth talk.

"You call me a junky and a slut and now you think I'm going to forgive you because you've been waiting for a few hours for me?"

"I never called you a slut."

"You didn't say I'm not."

"You're not. Your dad is wrong, you're not a slut. Please let's talk, it's out of my system, I promise I'll be completely there."

"I need time apart, Johnny. My dad doesn't want me to see you anymore."

"You're old enough to decide, you're nineteen."

"But I still work for my dad and uncle." By now she is sitting next to me on the curb, I light a cigarette and give it to her; she takes it and inhales deeply.

"So your dad's a lawyer? I didn't know that." She laughs at that, she always said my cluelessness is cute.

"Yeah, for the area, quite successful." I look at her again, this time mostly sober; she is wearing a nice suit, high heels, her hair is tied tight behind her head except for some unruly little bits floating around her forehead. I never visited her at work before, picked her up from there once, but never came inside.

"Please come home with me, please, I'm sorry." I think I am crying now because people are staring, Jenny looks miserable too, and embarrassed, so she holds me and says okay.

We get to my place on foot since I left my car at James's. We sit on the bed and I can't stop talking.

"I don't want you to hate me, I'm sorry, I'd do anything, I'll tell your dad you're a virgin, that we never smoked, that you're a saint reforming me..." The longer the sentence gets the less sense it makes, and the more it loses from itself acoustically. I completely lose track of it, and am probably talking of apocalyptic visions of Jennysque Valkyries galloping across rainbow skies, lifting me up and rescuing my soul. "I didn't mean to embarrass you, please say you forgive me."

"I forgive you." I just noticed she is holding me, my head is resting in her arms against her bosom, she looks miserable.

"I don't know why I said what I said, I'm an idiot, I'm sorry."

"What's done is done... It's just that... you know my dad, sort of, he panics, he thinks I'm some pot-head slut now. I can't stand the way he looks at me."

"We can quit! Together!" What?

"I can't, I don't want to, I'm fine..." There's a long pause and I notice we are lying down now, in each other's arms.

"I need to be apart for a while, Johnny, I think we need to be apart, at least for a while."

"But I thought you forgave me, please..." I start clambering up her, trying to envelop her with myself, I want to encompass her.

"I do, I just can't do this right now. I have to think." She gets up after giving me a tiny kiss on the forehead. I tried to sneak one on her lips but she was too fast.

"Do you have anything for me? I really need some now; just for a 'pick me up', do you?" She looks down at me; her eyes are moist like the waters of moss covering a cold boulder, softening its harsh sharp surface.

I take some Junk from my back pocket, I can't believe I walked into a law firm with heroin in my pocket, and show her the bag.

"But no needle for you, remember?" I remind her, she has to at least look clean.

"It doesn't matter, my dad would know I'm with you if I didn't come home straight after work... but it's very thoughtful of you."

I get everything ready, it's cheap stuff from James and it liquefies in a heartbeat, we have to share a needle because I've only gotten one from James since I thought I'd be using alone. I let her take first, 'keeping my lady safe' at the very least. Her lips form the widest and prettiest smile of relief, her eyes turn all white from her rolling them up and then the pupils land back down... they are tiny, little marbles, no, like the little dots in the old game... Pong! That was what it was called. I clean the needle with some vodka and then a cloth, then I take my share as well. I love seeing her when we're both high, she's happy, and I get to see her happy.

We metaphorically roll around, not really moving, but our minds do. Sharing some sort of chemical bond unknown to law-abiding citizens. We hold and touch one another in a few moments where nothing can touch us outside what our minds would allow. A sweeping sensation of rolling down something ensues and makes us both smile and shed tears, metaphorical or not, on things words cannot even assay.

When we come down we light one joint after another and drink a bit of beer and some vodka, the cheap kind.

I wake up the next day when the telephone rings. The place smells like vomit.

"Hello?"

"Johnny! How are ya?" It's Jake.

"What do you want numbnuts?" I am at the very least no hypocrite, if I don't like someone, I tell them that.

"Aren't we all hostile today... What crawled up your shorts?"

"Your mom."

"Fuck you."

"Why did you call?"

"I wanted to offer you deal, but now, I might go to someone

else."

"What's the deal?"

"Not one for the phone." That means it's about Junk or something like it.

"I'll meet you at... Northface Park in an hour, 'kay?" He agrees and hangs up.

Jenny is awake and looking at me, she looks like hell.

"Who was that? My dad?" She starts to look worried and looks around for her top. She didn't leave last night, she was too busy getting wasted and now she looks like she hates herself, like the first few times she slept with me after she found out what I do; she felt defiled.

"No, Jake, that turd, I'm going to meet him, he wants to offer me a deal."

"Why? I thought you two aren't friends anymore, especially considering your fond names for each other." She finds her top but it has vomit on it, we both remember that is why she took it off last night.

"Well, it might be a good deal and he doesn't have ANY friends, so that is why he's calling me, I guess." I got into the shower and wait for the water to warm up, Jenny is desperately trying to do some cleaning; she is spraying an entire can of my deodorant where the little mound of puke was. I shower and clear out so she can shower; while she does I make breakfast; Pop tarts and Nutella. She doesn't stay for breakfast and flies out after her shower, wearing one of my T-shirts under her work jacket, if she hurries, she might get to work on time.

The phone rings again, aren't I popular?

"Hello Mrs. Cohen, no 'mam, Jenny isn't here." I hang up before further inquiries; it's family stuff, none of my business, so I get dressed and head out to Northface Park.

Northface Park is, as implied, in the north part of town. It used to be cool there, with a skateboard area with jumps and stuff, but after a short crime spree that was blamed on 'young hooligans' that supposedly hung out there, the skateboard area was cemented– The 'hooligans' were never caught. Northface isn't its real name either. That is what people call it because it's in the north part of town, and it looks like a face on a map.

Jake is sitting on the railing that used to border up the skate-boarding area, now it's just…. A seat for Jake.

"Glad you decided to come."

"Get to it." I try to look cool by lighting a cigarette, even offer him one, he refuses.

"Well, fine, let's skip courtesy. There are those two brothers, Danny and Steve, they're cooking crack up in their granddad's attic, grandpa' has no clue, because you see, he's senile."

"So?"

"So? Have you ever heard of them? Danny and Steve?"

"No."

"Exactly! No one knows them and they don't know anyone, so how can they sell? Through us. We arrange percentages with them and we're golden!" He slaps his hands on my chest like he did back in high school when he was excited.

"How do we know it's not a trick? That they aren't narcs?"

"I tried their stuff, they're the real deal."

"That's how they get you, dumbass, by pretending, but doing it well, then, when you say enough and do enough in front of them, BANG! You're in a squad car." I mime Jake being driven off to county lock-up, I would also mime what his six-foot- eight cell mate might do to him in those cold lonely nights, but that would be too much.

"If that's what you think… just remind me, how much is your

take now? How many crack-heads we've got here? Oh… and did I forget… It's a one-time offer." That's a trick he learned from James, 'put on the pressure', but fuck, it's working.

"Ok, but I want to see them, and their fucking granddad."

"Good, be here again tomorrow at six, okay?" Jake is getting up and starting to leave, he hands me a little bag with a tiny white ball in it.

"A sample, enjoy it." Now he walks off.

I shove the bag into my pocket from instinct and then walk away trying to be invisible, intentionally walking through the crowd.

At home I have a late lunch and a joint. My last frozen pizza is gone so I go to the store. Joanna is there helping her dad, he's old and can't stack the shelves, and James is there too; they are all high. We have a joint together at the back room, even Joanna's dad. His name is Phill but we call him Phillip because we respect him. He tells us about his tour in Iraq in the nineties, yeah, he's a vet, and we tell him about our tours in Afghanistan and Iraq and imaginary planets on our computers and Playstations. I don't own a Playstation, my brother does, but I don't get to see him anymore, so my stories are the real ones, from my tour, it's hard for Phillip to listen to that. After the joints we all get a burrito half price except Joanna who pays nothing. I get some more frozen pizzas and some other stuff like beer and soap and head on home. At around eight in the evening there's a knock on the door.

"Hello?" I try to see through the hole but whoever it is has a hoodie on.

"Yeah, ahhh… You Johnny?"

"Who's asking?"

"Name's Nathan, we were in school together." I barely recognize the voice, I open the door and it's a skinny, pale, hairy, bruised version of the Nathan I went to school with.

"Fuck man, what happened to you?"

"I got robbed outside your house, okay? I was walking through the street looking for someone to help me and I recognized your name on the mailbox so I knocked." He really is bruised and holding to the side of his body like it hurts so I invite him in and show him to the phone.

"Damn, your entire apartment smells like Weed, man."

"I know, I just had some, that's why... and there's poor ventilation" I am a bit embarrassed, this guy used to rule our school, now he's here in my Junk lair.

"I meant what happened to you in general, earlier, you look like shit." I go back to my first line of enquiry

"Oh... yeah, well, after I stopped wrestling I lost my muscle mass, and the bruises are from now... as for my tan... this is the natural me, okay? What you saw in school was Spray on Tan." He doesn't sound or seem ashamed of his transformation.

"So what do you do now?" I ask, *please let it be shit!*

"I wash cars for a living... It's not much, but it's to pay for college, tuition is killing my parents." Shit, he's getting an education.

"What about you?"

"Oh...I... I'm getting ready to go to college next year, saving up now." I am such a bad liar.

"Oh, and what would you be studying? I'm doing Embedded Systems Engineering." He seems to have believed me and taking a real interest.

"English Literature." Only thing I know that you can get a degree in.

"Wow, a real man of books, you are." He smiles like he used to in school and looks around making sniffing noises.

"Wilde used to use so much drugs... he.... That made him write interesting works, Dickens never even saw a drug and he's as boring as hell to read. Poe was a drunk and probably an addict." How do I know that?

"Just pulling your leg Johnny, relax. I'm not judging you; almost everyone at college is on something, even two of my professors." He turns around and dials a number.

"Yes, hello, I would like to report a robbery." I stare at him in surprise; I didn't realize he'd call the cops. When he's put on hold I whisper, "Don't bring them here." He nods at me, I think he understands, but he's definitely judging me now – afraid of cops=Junky. "Yes, I'm... no, 'mam, I am not in any danger now....... Yes... I can wait........" He holds the phone against his shoulder to drown out the waiting music, kind of like elevator music, but for people about to become murder victims.

"What should I tell them, then?"

"I don't know, that you're waiting outside? You can't bring them here."

"Com' on, man... It's cold and everything hurts." I want to help him, I do, but one whiff of the air in my poorly ventilated apartment and I'd have search dogs and fifty five narcs here, no.

"Yeah, I'm still here...yes, the robbery guy." He keeps staring at me, he's trying to decide what to do, I think. I open the door for him, trying to be subtle, but he doesn't budge.

"I'm at 421 Russell Avenue." He sighs deeply and starts shaking his head, "I'll wait outside, I was just using the guy's phone." He steps out after hanging up, looking at me like I were a bubblegum he wiped off of his shoe.

He waits for the officers outside and when they arrive they are so busy with him and no one is even looking at me staring at them through the window. It's kind of a satisfaction to get my works ready when there are two police officers ten meters from my door thinking they are doing their job.

The next day I wait at the park for Jake, it's late, ten past six, and there's no one around anymore but a few people sitting around having a drink, some kids with hoodies and jackets nine times their size. I finally see Jake and he has two guys with him, one older and one about our age, maybe twenty four at most. When we are all face to face there's a short introduction— Danny's the tall older one and Steve is the one our age with the glasses. We all walk to their house on Main Street. It's a big place built in the eighties, a private house with a mortgage and everything, and in the attic— a little stove and lots of different powders. Danny shows me how it works and we discuss profits. Jake is smart about it, I have to give him credit for that, he knows numbers. He projects about two thousand dollars weekly, per seller, which implies it's not just me that'd be working with him, and assures the brothers that they will not be liable if something goes wrong, because only he and I would know about them. They agree for us to distribute, but they want seventy percent of the take, Jake won't have that, so there's a loud argument, so loud that the granddad shouts at us. We agree to give them sixty percent, but agree later between ourselves to actually only give them fifty.

We split with some merchandise to distribute, show off the new brand, we told the brothers not to expect any money from this, this would be free samples, "get them hooked" Jake said. It's annoying because we had to explain to the brothers how things work, they are greenhorns; they are just chemists, we are the pros.

It's like disillusioning a new recruit when he gets his feet on the ground. It's not all Black Hawk Down. Mostly, it's walking around with sand in your shoes and trying to digest SPAM without getting shot.

Jake and I use the first of the samples ourselves, I still have the sample he gave me the day before but I wanted to share that with Jenny. The stuff is good and we both fly. I come down before him and leave. We've done it at his place, his parents are dead so he has the place to himself; it isn't bad. I contact a few crack-heads I know, one of them is desperate and is willing to pay for what SHOULD be a free sample, that goes straight to my own pocket. I make a few bucks that day, a hundred twenty to be exact, but more importantly, I spread the word– there's a new product in town. The next day I go to James's and give everyone some of my samples. Joanna and James love it, they love each other too, and they don't mind showing it. She sits in his lap and lets him touch her as low as her belly button, every now and then they kiss.

I don't enjoy it much but everyone else does so I step outside for a minute to let them enjoy it without me.

In the evening I go home and eat dinner by myself, potato salad that tastes like mayonnaise salad with some bread, then I go to sleep; tomorrow's the moving job so I have to be clean.

The job's really easy; everything they have is light and new, from some DIY shop or something. We're seven guys helping with the move. The husband, Manny, is at work so Mrs. Everson is calling the shots. She is young, about my age, maybe twenty five seeing as women always try to look younger than they actually are. Within three hours the whole apartment is stripped down and only the painting is left to be done, she says that her husband can do it, or if one or two of us would like to volunteer we can come tomorrow again to do the painting– it'd be another four bucks an hour. Two Mexicans jump on the offer and I just carry on working, last few boxes to bring down. I look inside one that's popped open a bit, it's Mrs. Everson's underwear. She has some kinky panties, very sexy, one of them says "welcome" in a nice font, all in red and there's a little kiss drawn on as well, another says "bon appetit" and I can't help imagine her naked waiting for someone to oblige the invitation.

At the new place we unload the truck and bring the things in and build up the furniture, each one takes about half a second. At lunchtime Mrs. Everson brings us pizza and cola, she lets us take a few minutes for a smoke. I light a joint and immediately three students find their way to me from the crowd of movers. They don't have any, one of them has never had any and he wants to try. It's my first joint of the day and I don't want to share; I'm too nervous and stung up from not doing anything all day that I give them another one to share but finish the lit one by myself.

We go back inside and Mrs. Everson smells the weed on us. She doesn't mind much but she frowns. We finish the job and get paid. A total of forty eight dollars because she rounded the last hour up for us, she took over the expenses of the pizza and cola. We thank her and leave one by one. One of the students comes over to me and asks if he can buy weed off me. "Not today, kid, I'm tapped out." I don't know him and rather not mess around with people I don't even know; I'm careful that way.

At home I see I have seventeen messages; my new costumers. I call Jake and we set up a meet with the brothers and tell them we are in business now. During my almost six hours of work today I made forty eight dollars, during two and a half hours of dealing I make eight hundred thirty two dollars, enough for rent, food, a present for Jenny, and enough booze for ages. Me and Jake celebrate with some Junk, it's so much better than crack. Crack is a poor man's drug, we are better than that now.

"Why did we ever fight? We're a good team dude." Jake is

smiling like an idiot.

"Because you were a shit when you started dealing and I hated it, you became a business man and not a friend." Junk makes me too honest.

"Shit man, I needed to make money; my parents are gone, you dick, someone has to pay for the house, for Laura's education, for food and stuff, and I sure wasn't going to make enough money flipping burgers in some shit den." Laura is Jake's younger sister; she is still in school and a model student.

"Don't bullshit me, you dick, you could have let me and James buy for a good price, you could have sold us the good stuff."

"You dense dick are just thinking about what your veins are telling you. I don't have to explain myself to you." He gets up and washes his ugly face.

"I'm going." I get up and head out. It takes me a few seconds to realize where I am, at Jake's.

My car's there, parked up the road a bit, and I get in and have a smoke, just a regular cigarette; it's a good one too, costs a pretty penny, but seeing as I almost made a thousand dollars today, I'm allowed something good.

I call Jenny, yes, I've bought a cellphone, and she answers, all rays of sunshine again.

"Hello?" She doesn't know it's me yet.

"Hi Jenny, it's Johnny. Can we talk?"

"Oh... I don't know."

"Please, let me take you to dinner, somewhere nice." To be honest, we never really go out, unless you count doing Junk at James's as going out; all we ever did was hang out and do drugs together. In the movies and on TV, the women always want to be taken out, shown off, to be shown new things, so I thought I'd give it a whirl.

"I don't know if that's a good idea..."

"Anywhere you'd like, no matter how expensive."

"Really? No matter how expensive? You stole a fifty cents loaf of bread last week, since when is 'money no object'?"

"Since today, for you, every day, please."

"Since you're that desperate, fine. We're going to the Italian place on Riverside Street, I don't know what it's called." I quickly agree and we set up to meet at hers at nine. I drive home and get cleaned up, shower, shave, everything.

We meet in front of her house at nine o'clock sharp. I get out of the car and open the door for her; it just seems natural. Then I see her dad coming down the driveway and I go stiff as a drill sergeant.

"Evening, Johnny." He sits at the back of my car, on my jacket.

"Sir." I sit at the wheel, holding onto it as if for dear life.

"Why is he here?" I ask Jenny in a whisper while he struggles with the seatbelt that hasn't worked since I bought the car.

"He wouldn't let me go otherwise; besides, you two need a second chance."

"But–"

"Johnny, family is important." That ended the discussion. Jenny has some points on which her opinions or ideas are fundamental, absolute, the core of who she is– Family is one of those things.

We get to the restaurant at a quarter past nine, and are seated by a girl with a strong Italian accent at a nice table near a window; unfortunately, the window overlooks a strip-bar and Jenny gets uncomfortable.

"So what's the occasion?" Jenny's dad asks, trying to be polite.

"Ahh... I got a new job. In retail, very lucrative."

"Wow, really??" Jenny sounds a bit sarcastic, she know what I mean, what I'm selling.

"What are you selling?" Her dad always has to ruin things with questions.

"I supply people with something they can't do without, something that makes them feel better, I deal in happiness." I try to sound clever, but I think I am being too honest again, too obvious. "Medication, sir, I sell medication, anti-depressants." A good save, I think.

"I think you have to have some kind of knowledge of the pharmaceutical world to do that..." He sounds doubtful.

"There was a short training period where we're taught what we need to know, it's more about selling; the medical jargon is just decoration. We don't want to sell someone an overdose but that doesn't mean we need a medical degree." I laugh so mechanically I could be Robocop, or better yet, Robojunky.

Mr. Cohen smiles as the waiter arrives, also with a thick Italian accent, either everyone here goes through rigorous acting lessons, or they are all actual Italians.

"I'll have the day's soup as a starter and... the ricotta ravioli, please."

"I'll also have the soup and the tomato and mozzarella salad." Jenny opts for the healthy choice.

"I'll take...uhmm.... The soup and a lasagna." I just need something to sink my teeth into, and honestly, I haven't read the menu, and lasagna is the only Italian dish I know besides pizza.

The food is horrible, Jenny calls it 'authentic', her dad says it's 'elegant'. I think my taste buds are so used to frozen foods I can't enjoy real food anymore; actual vegetables, meat or dough just taste wrong- too intense, too present and imposing. I pretend to like it, though, half listening to Mr. Cohen speak, he goes on and on about Jenny's future education.

"And if she doesn't pass the bar... My Jenny could always work as a legal-aid or maybe even writing court protocols." He has his arm around her and Jenny looks embarrassed.

"Dad... I don't know, Law-School... Aren't we being a bit... I don't know, old fashioned? The daughter following her father's footsteps? The Lawyer Jew?" I never even knew they were Jews, cool.

"Honey, just think about it, you'd get used to the idea."

"No, I won't get used to it, dad. I can choose what I would do with my life." That's her argument voice; a bit of anger, a bit of insult, and loads of intelligence.

"What, you don't want to have a good decent career? You don't want to be respected as a professional working woman?" Her dad's argument voice is different; lots of anger, a ship's load of authority, and a bit of understanding.

"I can be a respected anything! A lawyer is one choice out of a million. Maybe I want to be an actress, or an artist, or maybe an engineer." I know her strategy in a fight, she uses a calm voice, silently sneaking in her opinion turning it into your own too; now, on the other hand, she sounds like a panicked little girl.

"Sweetie, you can't paint or sculpt, but you can convince! That is your strength. As for engineering... do you know what is... the Doppler Effect? Can you even remember long division?" Now that was just mean, Mr. Cohen fights dirty, then again, he is a lawyer.

It's getting really quiet, only the angry clinking of forks, knives and plates. Jenny and her dad are looking at one another with a hopeless kind of 'you'd never understand' expression.

I keep thinking 'this is my chance', 'step in and help her', but I just sit there and enjoy the fact I'm not the center of anger today.

"Aren't we here to celebrate? Come on guys, let's all be nice." I try to lighten the atmosphere anyway.

"I think I should go and let you two enjoy the rest of the evening. Don't worry, I'll call a cab." Mr. Cohen wipes his mouth and leaves after leaving twenty six dollars on the table, for the soup, ravioli and tip.

"You could have said something, you jerk!" That was directed at me, she doesn't miss a second to let me know she's unhappy with me; ever.

"I didn't want to get involved."

"Not get involved? You are involved, you moron."

"Sorry." I just don't know what to say, my head hurts and I feel hot; I need a smoke.

"I need a smoke." I get up and go outside to smoke a cigarette, but when it's finished, I just light another, then a joint.

When I get back she is sitting there all alone with her face hidden behind her hands. The food's been cleared off and everybody is staring at us. Jenny lifts her gaze and I see her mascara is running; she's been crying.

"Can I have some? Please?" She knows I know what she means; her veins are hungry for comfort. None of us can take this; us junkies. We can't argue, we can't win, we can't lose. The world should just let us be.

"Okay, let's go." We walk out after I pay, cash, sixty four dollars, without tip, What Mr. Cohan left would do.

At home we do some Junk, her first, then it's my turn. We have to use the same needle from yesterday, but I clean it first with some vodka and water. Jenny calms down and melts into the bed, she mumbles something, it isn't even English, it might be gibberish. After I take I join her on the bed, and melt onto her.

She is breathing so slowly, so calmly, I touch her face, her nose and her lips. I try to kiss her but can't control my lips right and I almost bite her.

"I can be an artist." That is what she's been mumbling the whole time, now I understand; with my ear right next to her mouth.

"Yeah, you can." I don't know that; I never saw any sketch, or painting, or anything she made, but she is so great, there's nothing she can't do.

I go get her a little block of paper and some pencils and leave it on the bed next to her.

"Draw something."

"Like what?"

"Your heart, your world; you're the artist, whatever you want."

She picks up the block and the pencils, there are only four colors; gray, red, blue, and orange. She goes wild; drawing erratically, switching pencil every second, at time she has two or more in her hand. She twists and turns on the bed as she draws and sketches, drifting with the block of paper with her hair sometimes completely covering her view of what she is doing.

"I'm done. What do you think?" She hands her masterpiece over to me. Her hand is sweating and there are pearls of perspiration on her forehead, she looks as if she has just given birth.

The drawing is so odd, I can't understand it. I think it's an abstract, the shapes are so irregular, like those painting people just stare at dumbly.

The background is all gray and orange, and the main drawing is in blue and red. In orange is an abstract smudge, right at the center, well, not a smudge; it's very symmetrical. Off center is a figure, all in grey, it's more the head, really, than a figure. It's a man, it's... me! The front of the drawing is a grouping of images running together; there are other people, but I don't see any recognizable features. Alongside those people are half words like 'subco', or 'unheal', and 'irrespo', but they blend into another image of deep blue of a window with no view of the outside. At the very bottom of the page there is a girl done with both red and gray; she is crying.

"What do you think Johnny?"

"I... Is that me in the background?"

"What makes you think it's the background?"

"It's in gray."

"That's just what I had to work with. What do you think?"

"It's complex. Like one of those paintings those New York dicks sell for thousands of dollars."

"So it's good? You think it could be worth something?" She sounds so excited now, she doesn't even wait for an answer, she just stands up and walks over to me, stumbling on something on the floor, then she kisses me and drags me into the bed.

I wake up early and Jenny's not there. I listen for the shower but there's no sound. Outside the world is moving, but not a sign of Jenny coming in or stepping out. There's a note on the table.

"Dear Johnny,

Last night was a mistake. Please, stay away for now on, I'll call you when I'm ready to see you again. Please, just keep away from me. What we did, it wasn't passion or even lust last night, it was the Junk, ok? It wasn't me. I'll keep in touch with James, you can ask about me through him, but don't call, don't come and see me,

just back off.
Jenny"

Not me That is what she wrote. *Not even lust,* I think I am crying, it burns my eyes. She really doesn't want to see me anymore.

I take a hit, I just can't think about this. I want to be away, I need something to take me away.

I need something

I need to get away from this

There are silhouettes all around me, plus one bending down right before my face; it's James.

"I think he's okay... Joanna, go get water, Jeff you can let go of his legs. Is Jamal back yet?" Listen to him commanding the troupe of junkies bent on saving me...

"No Babe, he's taking forever... Should I go look for him?" That's Joanna. Why are they all so worried? Oh... I think I ODed...

"You little fuck..." James slaps me across the face. I can barely feel it, it's more like a mute thunder in the distance, cushioned by my near death experience and I want to tell him he hits like a girl.

"You are one lucky bastard you have friends like us... You didn't pick up the phone and here we are, saving your life." James's forehead touches mine; he is a good friend. I think I'm drifting off again.

He slaps me again.

"I'm back, here's everything you asked for." Jamal is emptying a grocery bag next to my head; I am lying on the floor I notice.

"Okay, first we give you some adrenaline to get your circulation going, okay?" I feel the injection then its effect, something in me is sparking up to life... I... I... I throw up to the right, almost on James's hand.

James and Jamal help me to sit up, Joanna immediately gives me some water, I spit it out.

"Jenny..." I mumble it out, then vomit some more.

"She's gone, man, gone." That's Jamal; he's on probation and shouldn't be around us.

Everything is spinning so I close my eyes and lean on James, he keeps me from falling over.

"Is that why you did this much, man? Come on, that's the dumbest thing you ever did, and I've seen you do some dumb shit." Jamal's right. He was in my company in the army, he saw me use a rifle as a pillow and a grenade as a door stop, he saw me run headlong into fire and pull pranks on people that could have sent me into the hornets' nest as punishment.

"No...I just wanted to have a bit and went overboard...I'm sorry guys... You didn't have to come here... I'm sorry... I'm sorry... I'm sorry..." I'm crying again, I can't stop saying sorry, I don't even know for what, or to whom I am apologizing.

Joanna is hugging me, she has taken off my vomit filled shirt and is hugging me close until I stop crying. It takes a while and everyone but her and James leaves. There's a phone call for me, but James answers and says I'm busy and would have to get back to them.

"Was that Jenny?"

"No, some guy, says he's a business associate, wants to buy something from you...Don't worry about it, just get better. I gotta go, work, Joanna, you're taking care of our fallen comrade?"

"Yeah, don't worry babe."

After James leaves Joanna helps me to the bed and makes me a coffee, she says I need fluids and she's right. Sitting against the headboard I look at her in my little 'kitchen corner', every few seconds she throws a look my way; checking I haven't fallen or died again. The coffee does help and I manage to keep it down. Joanna is still fussing over me a bit, but she too is beginning to relax. The thing is... I'm the first of us who came this close to ODing.

Of course you hear about this stuff, every school gives a lecture about this, "No matter what you take, eventually, you might OD and die!" We always thought it was scare-tactics, now...It's a possibility.

"Are you better?" Now she's sitting next to me, half watching the TV, half watching me.

"Much better, thanks. I just... Need to move a bit." I wobble to my feet and start walking around the apartment, trying to skip the mound of vomit. After walking about for fifteen minutes I light a cigarette, then call the number James has written down earlier, of my 'costumer'.

"Hello, yeah, hi, you called me earlier, name's Johnny."

"Oh, yeah..." There's a lot of heavy breathing on the other end; crack heads are so creepy.

"I heard you could help me... get better."

"I can try, but you know, my 'spiritual guidance' isn't free, you sure you can afford it?" With the prospect of a sale my strength comes back to me.

"Yeah, yeah, sure, when?"

"Meet me at seven in front of the café at the promenade, okay?" That's where I embarrassed Jenny in front of her parents; it would satisfy me if the place becomes a hot bed for drug deals now.

He hangs up without anything further, not even asking how much, he's in real need; or he's very experienced.

"What time is it?" I ask Joanna as she comes over to take a beer from the fridge.

"Five to one... Trying to get your bearings?" She smiles at me, no longer worried, just teasing.

"Yeah... plus, I've got business at seven as you heard."

"Yeah, okay...I should get going, okay?" She gives me a hug goodbye. "Take care of yourself Johnny, no Junk today." Then she leaves quietly.

I sit back down on the bed and turn off the TV. There is utter silence in the apartment. Word is going to spread quickly about me almost dying, it has to. Jamal is going to tell his boyfriend, he is going to tell friends, they are going to tell friends, and so on; Jeff is probably going to say something to someone at work, and so on... Only James and Joanna, as an extension of James, can be trusted to keep their mouths shut. Jeff is a nice enough guy... but he's too talkative, knows too many people to shut up; he has to lube up those connections every once in a while with a juicy piece of news. Like a damned teenager. Jamal won't do it on purpose, he loves Terry, so they talk about everything, myself included.

Yeah, as you realized, Jamal is gay. He has been since he left high school, he says. He was a fan of the "Don't ask don't tell" policy, but found it demeaning that he has to HIDE his sexual orientation from the army to be accepted; he's right. What business is it of theirs who he goes to bed with? As long as he does his job, which he did well, who cares? Jamal is two years older than the rest of us, he's 25 and left the army a sergeant, so he also outranks me. You know, the whole "Don't ask don't tell" thing is shit. Everyone knew he's gay. He was caught having sex with a guy from logistics once, so what? Because nobody verbalizes it nothing happened? Besides, as I said, who cares? It doesn't make sense! So he likes cock. Wow, does that mean he can't shoot? He

38

was the best around with an MG. But to be honest, it made me nervous when I first met him, and he saw it; and had fun with it.

He would come into the showers and spend a few moments just silently staring at me; like he's sizing me up for something…Made me stomach go into knots. When I was assigned as his squad-mate for a repair run, he kept touching my hand gently, trying to make me nervous. When we started falling behind the rest of the team he said it was all a joke and that he has a boyfriend waiting for him back home; we've been friends since then.

I notice I am chain smoking; I never did this before. My ashtray is full within half an hour, and I begin to feel dizzy again. I take two aspirin from what Jamal brought earlier and wash them down with a cola.

At six twenty I head out in the direction of the café. It looks strange now, in the dark. The light inside is red, orange, and inviting. I hide my product behind the AC unit of the café and go into the parking lot to wait.

It's very cold now for some reason and my bones feel heavy. From the outside I can still see people inside smiling, laughing, kissing. Women in expensive jewelry half listening to men in cheap suits; wondering if they should let them have some, if they're worth it. Some are couples, judging by their intimacy. They sit sometimes in complete silence, seeing as their lips aren't moving, but their body is relaxed.

"You Johnny?" A voice takes me out of my little day-dream and reminds me of the cold and my heavy bones.

"Yeah." I take a look at him. He's skinny and shivering, but not from the cold, he has a hoodie on the casts a shadow on his face.

"I have money, what you've got?" His accent is odd, like southern; Texas or something like that.

"What you need to stop shivering, that's what I've got." I try to look in charge, but I still feel so weak.

"Good, how much?"

"I think I can give you seventy bucks' worth."

"Fine, where is it?" He is getting nervous, the closeness of his relief is making him erratic.

"Come with me, stay five steps behind me or no deal, got it?" I lead him to the back of the café where the crack is waiting. There are two waiters there, smoking.

"What the fuck, man? Is this a trick?" He freaks out at the sight of the unwelcome company; they freak out more and run inside.

"No man, relax, they work here, I didn't know they might come out, chill the fuck out." I extend my empty palms as a sign of peace; he is still breathing hard, but now I can see his face. He looks pale, wide eyes, but that might be the fright, and no facial hair. His nose is long and scarred over with some kind of rash or skin disease.

"Relax, here." I show him my product; I only take out seventy dollars' worth and leave the rest in.

"Give it!" He signals me with a sharp movement of his hand. When he sees I am waiting for him to take out the money he does so, not missing the chance to show me he has a knife.

We make the exchange and he leaves slowly, a careful slow retreat, and then runs away into whatever sand hill he came from. When he's gone I take out the rest of the stuff and leave as well; best not to come back.

At home I fall onto the bed like it's a recharge station and I am desperate for power. I'm not hungry, so I just have a beer, and then another. I make an improvised seat out of the headboard of my bed and sit against it, my head against the old decaying wooden panel that comprises the headboard. I'm still holding a half-finished beer can in my left hand and I close my eyes, trying to forget today by explaining it away and surmising it as something between a cautionary tale and a waste of time.

I wonder if I was really dead until they saved me.

The thought just jumps at me, an ambush from the back of my mind. I drink the rest of my beer and think about it.

Yes.

I was probably dead. I don't remember it. It was like falling asleep and waking up again, no different; only I wasn't supposed to wake up at all. Jake and Jenny mustn't hear of what happened. Jake won't let me in on his new business, that's for sure and Jenny would never take me back. To make peace with them I have to make peace with my Junk. I walk over to my works still bloody and on the floor. I have to clean them out, blood in the works could kill you, if it clots it's even worse. I clean them out, water, soap and vodka, again and again until I get too tired; I fall asleep on the floor.

In the morning I get a phone call from Jake, he wants to know if I've sold everything I had; I almost have. He wants to meet me so we could give the brothers their share, fifty percent given as sixty. I know you think us frauds, but we aren't; we're just taking care of ourselves. If the police catches us we're fucked, we're the ones taking the risk, so we deserve to get paid well. All the brothers do is mix things in some third grade chemistry set.

We get to the house and Steve greets us. He looks tired and jumpy at the same time; he's been experimenting with his own product. We meet Danny upstairs as he comes down from the attic, he smells like a science teacher or a bomb disposal guy.

"Here you go guys, sixty percent of the take, just from us two in just a couple of days. I really only wanted you to get a taste of the money you'd be making." Jake hands them seven hundred and eighty dollars, all neatly stacked by size of currency.

Jake was going to become an entrepreneur, that's what all the teachers said in school; a head for numbers and the most convincing voice on earth, like James. But in the tenth grade his parents died and after a year he quit school, started dealing full time. That's when we fell out, over him being more of a business man than a friend, James didn't mind that, said he needed the money, but we were all broke, still are. The thing is, Jake is really a good person inside, just when it comes to money he gets serious. When we were friends he stood up for Joanna with the rest of us, he even came to graduation to celebrate with us, brought us some good celebratory Weed too.

The brothers take the money and count it, by their looks they seem pleased, they probably did some projections of their own for the profits, and this answers their expectations, so we are shown the door after getting some more product. I leave but Jake stays; says he needs to discuss something with the brothers.

I don't know what Jake's been doing while I was away in Iraq, probably nothing, he's kind of lazy, but he says he's changed a lot since high school. James agrees with that, they are both rather close, really, but James is close to everyone. James's version of close is the comfortable, lay-back bravado he exemplifies around everybody. Friendship, though, is almost impossible to achieve with people like James.

At home I light my last joint and make some coffee. I don't have milk so I drink it black; I hate that. I call Jeff to see if I have a legit job lined up for me; he doesn't have anything, so I do my rounds at noon selling 'medication' to all the bad boys and girls.

Behind the library is a popular spot, we could always claim to be there for the books and there's open space to run away if necessary, and if anyone gives any trouble it's public enough to get help. I sell half my stash there, make over seven hundred dollars in three hours, and almost get flagged by a cop, but she just walks past in the end.

After dark I head home for a fix of my own, Smack, no Junk. Having just ODed yesterday leaves you with a bad taste. It's kind of a hangover really, but one that's in your arm and not your head. It's probably just fear. Just before I take there's a banging on my door, not a cop's banging so I walk over.

"What?"

"Please let me in" it's a girl, she sounds scared, but I've been tricked before. Once, this girl knocked on my door and I saw through the peep hole she was alone and crying, but when I opened three guys jumped me from the sides and tore the place up, she was their ring leader. So I'm more careful now.

"Who are you, what do you want?"

"Joanna said you could help me, I need some.... Medication." I look closely at her; her skin is ragged, her eyes are surrounded by blackness that is barely hidden by makeup, her hair is frizzy and unwashed– she's a Smack head.

"How do you know Joanna?"

"We went to school together." I don't recognize the girl, but Joanna is younger and I didn't know any of the girls in her class.

"Okay, come in." I open the door and she slides past me, making her way into the main and only room.

She is a short girl with wild brown hair, her eyes are a sewer green and she is way too thin.

"I'm Mary Ann, Johnny, right?" She sits on the bed after looking around.

"Yeah, so it's eighty dollars a pop." I show her my merchandise.

"I don't have that much." She reaches into her purse and pulls

43

out a fifty, showing it to me.

"Not enough darlin', sorry." I put the crack away.

"No, wait, come on, I'm good for it, I'll pay later." She tries to make a cute voice, trying to look sexy, trying to get free Smack.

"Sorry, no credit." If I give this girl credit everyone would want credit, junkies are a dangerous and unreliable lot.

"Come on you asshole, I've been dry for two days!"

"Not my problem."

"Come on!!" She is beginning to panic; her voice is becoming shrill and she is breathing fast.

"Please, Joanna said you would help me. What do you want?"

"I said, eighty dollars." I think I am being fair, eighty isn't much. I hear that in bigger cities a dealer would sometimes give ridiculous prices just because he knows people would pay.

"Come on big guy, I can give you the fifty and we can figure out the rest." She is really close to me by now, her hand in on my shoulder, the other one is in my pants. I've become as stiff as a board, I don't seem to be moving and she is taking it as a sign to go on.

She is on her knees now, in front of me and my pants are around my ankles, and her hands are working their way into my underwear. It's been a while since anyone other than Jenny touched me there. It feels strange.

Her hands are cold and it's uncomfortable. When she puts it in her mouth it gets better but it's still strange. It's better with Jenny. This girl has no method; she just randomly puts it in and out of her mouth, up and down. It takes forever. I keep thinking of how Jenny was always more gentle with me, always more... caring. I try telling her she is good, maybe it would motivate her to do better, but the words get stuck in my diaphragm. I look down at her and she is looking up at me with... me in her mouth;

when Jenny looked up at me I would always feel alive I would feel invincible, I would almost cry with how beautiful she was; this girl is just there. Like some protrusion on my penis. After a while I finish and she spits it out on the floor, gets up, takes the Smack and leaves. I flop down and sit on the floor next to my cum and stay for a while.

I love Jenny.

I can't sleep, so I sit there quietly and listen to the street outside. There's an old man babbling about the government being in league with all sorts of evils; from terrorist organizations to aliens. He knows all.

I reach for the phone and dial instinctively, I know exactly who I'm calling.

"Jenny?" I know she's there, on the other end of the line, sleepy and annoyed.

"Who is this? Johnny? Do you know what time this is? I told you not to call me." I knew she'd say that, but I just wanted to hear her.

"I just wanted to hear your voice, I'm sorry." I hang up and go to sleep.

The next day Jeff shows up at my door; he looks uncomfortable and uneasy. He's here to watch over me. I really did give everyone a scare earlier. Jeff is looking at me as he reads messages on his phone, a top of the line whatever machine; he doesn't want to be here. I only know Jeff through James; he introduced us a week after I came back from my tour in Iraq and I introduced them to Jamal who used to live in Kansas, but moved up north where we're more accepting of his way of life. Jeff is younger than me and

James, but he is good value. He is a father, though he never met his baby. He isn't even sure it was born, the mother might have aborted the baby, or the state might have made her do that, who knows... After she found out she was pregnant she gave herself to the authorities, saying it was what's best for the baby. She was a major junky. Jeff is over it, though. He takes life easy, kind of like James, but he understands the need for money and work outside of dealing. He told me once he wanted to join the army too, but was too afraid when push came to shove and he ran from the recruitment office. He's an okay guy but he has a problem seeing things through. I don't think we ever spent so much time together alone. When Joanna knocks at the door he is visibly relieved.

"Hey guys, my dad gave me some burritos, I told him you're sick; hope you don't mind." Joanna takes out three burritos and puts them on relatively clean plates and hands them out.

After we finish eating James arrives as well, Joanna kisses him and sits in his lap.

"Did you hear from Jenny?" I ask him trying to sound casual.

"Yeah, she stopped by today to buy some Junk, asked to tell you to stop calling." He has a way to make everything sound like it's nothing: 'oh the girl you love hates you, no big deal...'

"I know... I called her last night, she told me to stop."

"Then stop." That was Joanna, she doesn't care for Jenny.

"I love her." That changes the mood in the room.

"Oh... Come on, you've only known her a couple of months... a third of the time you've been in this stalemate. You just think you love her because she's rejecting you. Get over her." As the last of us to finish high school, Joanna always takes on the role of 'the scholar' as if her being fresh out of the education system means she's smarter than us.

"Leave me alone."

"Come on, Joanna, let him be." That's James, taking my side as he should.

"At any rate, she's been buying from me almost every day since you two fell out, I even sold her some of the smack you gave me, when I told her it's from you it made her flinch like it's tainted, but she bought it sure enough. She's been buying a lot, come to think of it." I don't know if he's reporting or trying to cheer me up, but James is at least doing his duty by telling me what Jenny's doing. It's kind of nice to know she's at least using my product.

"Has she been seeing someone?" It gets quiet again and everyone is looking at one another.

"People say she's been sleeping around." It's Joanna that's the first to speak, discrediting my Jenny.

"What people?!" I snap at her without realizing.

"Some of the girls I know, from school and some girls that come to the shop. People." She doesn't seem to care much, but she does, she's loving it; Jenny's downfall.

"Like that Mary Ann girl you sent here? A real pillar of society." I try to sound clever but I sound more like a little kid in an argument with his mom.

"She's just some crack whore, but yeah, she says it too; takes a whore to know a whore." With that she leaves towards the kitchenette, leaving me unable to respond. She just goes on with her own business, as if Jenny is dead, no longer an issue. How dare she? What is wrong with her? Calling Jenny, My Jenny, a whore? This bitch thinks she is so much better? And she acts like nothing has happened? Just standing there making toast?!

"Shut the fuck up you bitch! Get out of my house! All of you!" I think I snapped again, I find myself pushing everyone out, even James. Joanna looks afraid of me, she's standing outside my window looking in, her eyes are... hurt. I take out the drawing Jenny made and look into it, rub it against my face. I take a hit, a big one and stare at the drawing again. The lines are so much clearer now, so fluid and alive, like I'm seeing what it was that Jenny tried to capture here. The words are whole now, "Unheal me" and "Irresponsible" melt into the images to their right, a cop car driving away and a tower called "Tomorrowland" being burnt to the ground by a syringe-like dragon. All the while I am in the background, in gray; sitting alone with my hand covering most of my face with an orange fire coming out of my eye leaping into the image of the girl crying at the bottom of the page. It isn't Jenny at the bottom of the page, it's her mom. At least I think it is they look so much alike.

In the morning I go and take a shower and a shave, then have breakfast, pop tarts and honey. I have a joint and start on my apology phone calls; first James:

"Yeah, I know why you freaked out, no sweat, but me and Joanna would stay away for a while, come by for business, but no social calls; Joanna is really upset about this." I knew he would understand, and I knew he would say that about Joanna, she just isn't as cool about these things as he is; women never are, they just can't swallow their pride and see things from someone else's perspective.

Second is Jeff. He isn't as cool about this as James, he say "fuck you" a lot, but eventually he calms down and says it'd be fine, just to stay out of his way for a while I promise him some discount on my next supply of Smack and he lets bygones be bygones.

Last and least is Joanna, she isn't cool at all and doesn't want to speak to me, at least that's what she says, in reality she doesn't stop talking for fifty minutes, going on and on with things like "You know what your problem is?" and "If you would just..." I keep saying sorry whenever she stops to breathe and eventually we hang up, but I don't think we're okay just yet.

With all this bullshit I didn't even have time to think. My Jenny, is she really sleeping around? I know at least ten guys that said they'd "do her" but they didn't because she was mine. Did she let them have her? It's all just rumor, never trust rumors spread by girls about girls; that is as true today as it was in high school. I remember the girl who took my virginity; she was a real slut, and everyone knew it. She slept with at least 5 other guys from my platoon, seven others from around the company and her sergeant, and there was a rumor she had lesbian sex with one of the female officers, that's the only story about her I didn't believe; because it was a rumor. But if it's true? If Jenny really is sleeping around with strange men? The idea makes me sick. I light a cigarette just to ease myself away from it and have a couple of beers. I decide to do my rounds again today, sell as much as I can and buy Jenny a big gift, something to wow her pants off, figuratively speaking.

I make only a hundred and fifty dollars, a poor make, but it's a Tuesday, so I'm not surprised. You must think this rather stupid, but yes, Tuesdays are always slow for dealers. It's too far from either weekend, so people don't need to 'come down' nor are they in need for party drugs. It's also not as depressing as Mondays or Wednesdays, so we sell a lot less. Drug 'rush hour' is always Friday. People want to go out and party and they need cocaine or heroin or something to help them; have you ever tried dancing to dubstep without acid or ecstasy? You can't not look like a cock. Modern music needs chemicals to be enjoyed. So I guess Jenny's present would have to wait until the weekend then.

At the apartment it's really quiet; I end up shooting up all on my own. It takes forever to take hold because I keep thinking about Jenny, and Jenny with other men. Let's get one thing straight,

I am not jealous and I am not possessive, but this is wrong. We are technically still... You know, sort of together. And you know what? If it were one guy I'd understand, but sleeping around? Jenny? No. However, James did say she's been using a lot, maybe someone took advantage of her? Maybe she doesn't know what she's doing? She's still a rookie, more so than Jimmy. Maybe I should call? No... Maybe... Maybe... The heroin is making my thoughts... scratchy. Like they are peeling off of the walls of my skull like paint from the wall. I can't think anymore and that's a good thing. I wobble over to the computer and turn it on but the screen is all blurry so I put it back down. I go to eat something and end up emptying the bottle of ketchup between the floor and my mouth.

In the morning Jake calls, he wants to discuss something with me and other distributors. I didn't even know he found others already.

We all meet at Bud's, it's a little Cowboy style bar right at the edge of town. Someone once told me Bud's an ex-con, convicted for murder and let out on a technicality, and that he's actually guilty, but as I said, I don't believe in rumors.

Jake's other distributors are all serious junkies. Skinny, jumpy, erratic little dicks; some look too young. We talk about the usual stuff; Jake's using higher terminology to seem in charge and better than us; he's saying "Place of Transaction" instead of "turf", or "Cash-flow" instead of "take", "Product" instead of "Smack"; but in the end we each know our assigned location to sell, I get to keep the library, and how much we get to keep from the sales. When everyone leaves I stay to talk to Jake but we end up fighting again, so I go home pissed off and drunk.

At the library I make some good money, two hundred and seventy dollars, better than yesterday. I even see Nathan, but I have to avoid him; no use in him seeing me peddling crack. In the evening I call James and ask if I can come by to buy some stuff from him, he agrees since Joanna is helping her dad close the shop.

"You know, we are very serious, I thought you might be serious about Jenny, I've never seen you with a girl like you were with her." Don't get the wrong impression, James is really not the sentimental 'let's talk' kind of guy, but he knows when a friend needs a 'heart to heart', he's good that way.

"I was."

"So what happened? Why'd she give you the boot?"

"I didn't get along with her dad, I think."

"Bull crap."

"yeah... I don't know man I don't understand women, man. I mean, someday Joanna is going to dump you, or you are going to dump her and you won't know why."

"I'm afraid you're wrong, my friend, me and Joanna are in for the long haul, we're getting married."

"What? When did you decide that?"

"A month ago, just after you and Jenny broke up. Yeah, I know, it's weird, marriage." He's smiling like a retard; content with his little thoughts of his little wife and little house and little life.

"You can't get married, man, who ever heard of a couple of junkies getting married to each other?"

"Why the hell not? We've been together for five years, and just because we like to get high every now and then doesn't mean we can't start a life together. I already asked Phillip as well, we have his blessing." He is really serious about this.

"You are really serious about this, aren't you?" I admit I am shocked, I never thought one of us might get married.

"I am." There's a long pause and I hear something he never

said to me in private without Joanna listening in.

"I really love her, we are ready to quit so we could really be together, especially when we decide to have kids, and I want her to have my babies." He's a bit choked up by the end of the sentence, but it's really obvious he means it. I really don't know what to say, I can't handle this so I get out to get some air and smoke, when James follows me outside I realize I'm chain smoking again.

"Big news huh?" He's all smiles and cheers again.

"Yeah, I should get going, oh, I also need some needles." He gives me my 'order' and sends me off, warns me of an approaching 'dry period' when he quits. I sort of accept it, sort of shrug it away and I can't wait to get home and take a hit; James getting married has me rattled. I am happy for him, it's just weird. When I left for training, he was going to break up with Joanna. He said he had enough, back then she was doing really bad because of her mom, plus he didn't want to date a high school girl. When I came back they were still together. In his letters, yes James wrote, he explained he couldn't leave her when her life was so hard, a few months later it was because he cared about her, two months more he didn't even want to anymore. To be honest, Joanna is a great catch. She's pretty, she's really nice inside, and also really strong, but most of all she's nurturing. This is something people don't realize about junkies, we are also people. And we can be nurturing, and we need to be nurtured. Not every junkie girl is a whore who sells her pussy for a hit, or more. Not every dealer is a complete ass-wipe. Not every dealer demands a girl to suck his cock for Smack; that other night was the first time for me and it wasn't even my idea, I just... went along with it. It even made me feel uncomfortable; I didn't know what to do; she had obviously done it before. Joanna never did anything of the sort. She's not with James for the Junk; Jenny was with me for the Junk. I never had what James has.

I've never been in love.

I think I am in love with Jenny.

Jenny is definitely not in love with me.

No one has ever been in love with me.

I need another hit.

As soon as I get through the door I find my works, open a new needle and get some Junk into me. Then I spread the Hash James sold me and decide on where to stash it. Junk goes under the bathroom tiles, the Hash has no permanent place. I end up stashing it under the microwave, regret it, and put it inside the mattress. I pretend to be busy by rearranging my room; bed, closet, dresser, all get moved around just so I won't have to think.

I find Jenny's drawing on the ground after I move the dresser and start crying. I can't stop crying until it hurts in my throat and eyes. Why can't she see me now; how sorry I am? I am in love with her.

This is so new to me. I admit to not being experienced with women. I lost my virginity at eighteen and a half to a complete stranger in a bathroom stall. I only had one real girlfriend, Jenny, and she hates me now. How do I make her love me? I call James.

"How did you do it? How did you get Joanna to love you?"

"Man, are you high?"

"Answer me, please!"

"Forget Jenny, man, move on. Or at least ask me when you're on this planet again, okay? No more drunken phone calls for you man." He hangs up. I trust his judgment, if James says I'm not okay enough now to learn this then I'm not. Tomorrow I'll be sober enough to learn how to make a woman love me.

The next day I come over and both James and Joanna are sitting together; she is wearing an engagement ring.

"I heard James told you the good news!" She comes over and hugs me, too happy about getting married to remember me pushing her out of my apartment.

"Yeah congratulations, I guess. James, I thought we'd talk alone."

"There is no more alone for me, I'm getting married, everything I know, Joanna can know, and vice versa."

"Sure... whatever." I am still hesitant but I take a seat and wait for one of them to speak; they don't, they just sit there holding hands.

"So James..." I start my question but he cuts me off.

"Na-ah, observe how a real couple interacts, that is all." Now that just sounds stupid and condescending, but I can't tell them that.

"I don't have time for observation, I need quick answers."

"There are no quick answers, a woman's heart is a complex and INDIVIDUAL thing." They both speak almost simultaneously, it's kind of creepy.

"With all seriousness, I think you should drop it. Jenny is past you she's going too fast and too hard these days." That's just Joanna now, not using her snarky, mean voice, but the serious one, so it's not just out of Jenny-hate.

"What do you mean?"

"She's doing too much, she's here a lot to buy and she's buying Smack off some kid around the pool, and Meth from some whore near the old mall." Meth? That's news. I told her that was bad, that that is too much. She was curious, she thought it was like Junk, but it's not.

"Who's this kid, or this whore? Since when does she go to people she doesn't know? Come on those are just rumors...right?" they look at me with a mix of concern and pity.

"Just promise me you won't OD because of her again, okay?" That's Joanna with her best 'adult voice'; she does sound very motherly when she uses it, even though she's younger than me.

"I won't, just tell me how to get her back."

"I agree with Joanna, she's too far gone, man. Get over her. Even to me, she's just a client now." James is no longer holding Joanna's hand, he's by me with his hand on my shoulder and I notice I'm crying again. Joanna also walks over and gives me a hug; I never noticed it, but she's using the same perfume as Jenny.

I go home an hour later, feeling slow and heavy. I'm clean at the moment. After getting home I go to the library to do my rounds, make five hundred dollars and almost get stabbed. Nathan saved me from getting stabbed. He saw the guy attack me and ran over to help; he can still throw a punch despite his diminished size. It really was nothing, I was just too absent to notice things getting out of hand, I didn't care he didn't want to pay, I didn't care he was willing to kill me for his hit. I just didn't care. Nathan saw what I was selling, he told me to get lost.

When I get home again I turn on the TV and cry again. I take some Smack but it doesn't help me, so I have some left over cocaine as well, but it still doesn't help so I keep crying until there's a banging on my door; my next door neighbor wants me to turn off the TV; he says it's late so I go to sleep.

Every day looks like a copy of the one before, every day I sink deeper into my little rut. I don't care anymore how pathetic everybody thinks I am right now. I see how they look at me, I saw how Jake looked at me when he "fired" me. He says I can't be selling his product in my state. I remember shouting at him and calling him names again, I think I tried to punch him. He was stronger than me and beat me up. He's just an asshole, like I told you. He's just concerned about his business, his money, not his friend. I walk around with a knife now since everybody seems to be armed with something these days. There are also so many new addicts going about in town. Smack, Junk, Meth, circulating in human form through my street, like TV zombies. Within two hours, everyone knew I don't have anything to sell anymore and my phone and Email went dead. No product, no friends.

James still calls. So does Joanna, and Jeff when he needs an extra pair of hands at work. I haven't heard from Jenny for over a month. James and Joanna still tell me rumors about her; that she's going too fast, doing too many drugs, too much Meth, too many men. Jamal informed me she is selling now. I did my own snooping around and it's true. She's selling Meth and Junk; I don't know who she's getting it from, but she is selling. She also quit her job and moved out of her parents' house. I don't know where she is. James and Joanna are getting married in two weeks. A quick wedding, they wanted it because Joanna is pregnant. They are quitting Junk together.

They found out last week, about the baby I mean. It was so weird to hear. First James tells me he's getting married and a month later that he's having a baby. Jeff went really weird when they told him. He looked at Joanna like she's a witch. But when they convinced him they will quit and raise the baby together he became super psyched. I am really happy for them, but it means that I can't go there anymore; James is out of the game. I hope they make it. Jamal is still on probation and Jeff can never score, so getting anything is hard. Jake won't even sell me anything; he says to keep away from him. Jeff buys from him and we split it, but it's a bad way to do it because what if there's an emergency and I need to score quickly?

Jimmy is out too, arrested. He was picked up three days ago.

Possession charges are nothing, though, so he'll be out again soon, unless they get something else on him. The cops here aren't dirty, I think, so it's not likely they'd make something up, but they might actually find something on Jimmy. He was always a bit shady on what he did before we met him. He's a friend of Terry's, and Terry is Jamal's boyfriend, and Jamal is my friend, that's how Jimmy found his way to us, but I don't really know him.

I don't really know how they got him; I would have thought they'd be after me; selling crack and everything. The DEA is really cracking down on the area. The news also has a story about drug users and dealers every night. It's somewhere between "raising awareness" and downright scare tactics. It's hard to watch sometimes. Well, anyway, Jimmy came home to find two squad cars waiting for him. He tried to run, but they had other cops waiting a bit further away. He called his mom who works at city hall, but she left him out to dry. At least she had the decency to let Jamal know since she trusts him because he's a vet. We tried to bail him out but bail was set on five thousand dollars and we just don't have that kind of money. We told James too, even if we barely talk to him now. I went to visit Jimmy earlier; he looked depressed. There was no fiberglass, no little phone, no orange jumpsuit; our station is too small for that kind of stuff. We sat and talked for a long time, he was a surprisingly good listener. It was odd because we talked more about me than about him; it was my fault really. But it seemed to cheer him up to see other people have problems.

At any rate, Jimmy is surprisingly tough, not ratting out anyone. He says the cops are treating him okay, but they are also pushing him for information on me and James. He says they know a lot about me already, that that Marry Ann girl said I molested her when they picked her up too. Jimmy stood up for me and said there's no way I did that because I'm in love with Jenny. It'll be my word against hers, and she has a reputation, so Jimmy says it'll be okay; but I'm digressing again and talking about myself. It's hard to concentrate on others when my own life is such a mess. I don't have work, I don't have money, I don't have my friends, I don't have Jenny.

Jimmy is getting three meals a day, all the coffee he can drink, and some books. He's a bit scared because of his trial next month, but until then he's staying in lock up and not an actual prison, which is better. He's alone there, because they're keeping him away from the real messed up junkies. Jimmy's a nice guy, yeah, he does take drugs, yes, but he isn't a junky. He doesn't shake and doesn't do anything stupid. He's got a head on his shoulders, and he isn't dangerous to anyone. The others in lock up are real screw heads. The guy that tried to stab me was there too, along with Marry Ann and a few others I wouldn't trust with a sharp object. In their defense, they are probably all in withdrawal, but so is Jimmy and he's okay.

Terry also went to visit him and came back home all upset for seeing him like that; they have kind of a 'big brother-little brother' thing going on, which leads me to think they've known each other for a lot longer than I had first thought. Jamal was also upset about Jimmy getting arrested, he started getting really worked up and lectured me about jail and the law and stuff; he used his "sergeant voice". He kept saying that that is the best result we could expect from our way of life, kept referring to me ODing and stuff. I remember when Jamal introduced me to Terry. They were both clean at the time but Terry was a former addict, he was our first contact.

Terry used to do a lot of Weed and acid, but while Jamal was in Iraq he got into cocaine and stuff. When Jamal came back he quit and only did Weed, they did it together, no institutions, no rehab. Terry gave us a few numbers, mostly Mexican guys, Terry's Mexican, and we called them and got set up. I only made a rule of not buying from Arab guys or Persians, because I had a bad feeling about anything we got from them. I once got something from this guy in a village and it was horrible. Well, at any rate Terry is a former addict and he didn't like Jimmy being in jail and Jamal was in jail for a few months and he doesn't like seeing anyone going away.

Jamal was arrested last year and sentenced ten months ago. It was for possession with intent to sell, but because Jamal is a sergeant in the US army with an Iraq tour on his record and one commendation the judge released him after five months and put him on probation. I probably would get a similar deal if I get pulled up. I'm just a corporal, but I guess it'd work too.

I have two commendations, one for a rescue operation, and one for "calm in the line of fire". Technically I was under fire for both cases, the rescue thing was a downed tank, hit by an AT missile, we had to get it out and there were mortars coming down everywhere and sniper fire. The second thing was on a convoy to another job, a routine checkup, but we were ambushed. I was the first one of the technical team to return fire. We had escort, and they were tough SOBs from the second battalion but they couldn't do it alone.

Well, now I keep thinking of stuff I don't want to think about because I'm all dried up. That's worse than the withdrawal, the headaches, the cramps, everything. Jamal also started out when he came back, just a bit of weed, just a bit of this, a bit of that. When Terry said they should quit and go back to the way they used to be he was in, all the way, body and soul. That's probably where James and Joanna got the idea they can do it.

I see Joanna around her dad's shop, helping out. She's working as a cashier now, with her dad smiling from ear to ear at the prospect of having his little girl there with him and engaged to be married. Phillip never doubted Joanna for a second; he knew she wouldn't end up like so many other girls, ignorant as to the identity of the father of her baby, or with a man who would leave her as soon as the little test thingy turns blue. He has a pretty good idea as to what Joanna has been doing until now, the Junk and other drugs, he wouldn't say anything because when he came back from Iraq when we were kids he drank a lot and beat Joanna's mom, so who's he to judge? He made his amends, he was really sorry, went to AA meetings and everything. Joanna forgave him, that is why they are cool now. She has no resentment for him, if anything, she hates her mom. I don't fully understand this whole family resentment thing. Her mom's mentally ill, not consciously avoiding her, she's not consciously anything. My own family, they threw me out. No grief, no pain, no shouting; just a 'get out' and that's it.

Damn it.

I don't want to think about this. See what happens when I'm dry? I have some codeine in the cabinet, I took it from James's sister's medic bag the last time I was there. I have a bit of that to ease me to sleep and hope I could score some tomorrow.

The next morning I go to work with Jeff. We're redoing someone's bathroom; it's a big job and we have it for a few weeks with a bonus if we finish quickly. It's eight hours a day with ten dollars an hour. It's getting harder and harder to get out of bed and function one hundred percent with all my limbs but the money helps me get on with it. I started buying Weed from a student that works with us. He's a nice kid, twenty years old and really smart. He's doing English literature as his major and we talk a lot about poetry and I amaze myself with my knowledge. He keeps comparing me to Wilfred Owen after I showed him some stuff I wrote while in Iraq; to be honest, I have no idea who Wilfred Owen is, so I looked it up when I came home that day. The job is fun when I think about it; there's always something to do and keep my mind off... my mind. The kid's name is Henry... or Barry or something like that. He's just some college kid looking to make some money. His stuff is cheap Mexican Weed, but it's all I've got.

Jeff's got things figured rather well for the next few weeks, well, moneywise he does. As for Junk and other forms of "recreation" he's counting on me and Jake. Today after work, me and Jeff gathered up two hundred dollars between us and we bought some Smack with it. It's not as good as Junk, but it'll do. Jake delivered to Jeff's place and then Jeff came to my place to smoke it. We get wasted together a lot now, me and Jeff. He confided in me to have bought a bit of Meth from Jenny, "Just to try it" he said. He said she looked good, and that she sounded like she knew what she was doing. She was clean and well-dressed according to Jeff, she even hugged him hello, but they didn't talk.

I still don't like meth and I don't approve of it and I don't like Jeff taking it. He suggested I call Jenny and set up a buy, just to see her, he understands my need to see her. Problem is, I don't want to be associated with that crap. I know what Jenny would think, even if it's just to meet her she'd mock me and I'd never get her back.

Jeff says the Meth wasn't as good as Junk too, he said the rush was too quick, the crash too intense. He had the shakes and hot and cold flashes the day after, does that sounds like fun to you? I don't know why Jenny keeps using this thing, I know she does. I found that whore she bought from near the old mall. She's so young I felt horrible; I gave her a hundred dollars for the information she gave me. Jenny bought from her up until two weeks ago, Meth and Weed mostly, sometimes Speed, but she stopped, and the whore, Carla, doesn't know why. But Carla knew to tell me that Jenny's still using because she sees her at parties and with other Meth users. I am genuinely concerned about Jenny. I know some people might think of me as obsessed or something, but I am just concerned; I got her into this, I feel responsible for her. If only I could see her one more time...

I get off the Smack and Jeff is still here. He's raiding my fridge. When he comes back to sit by me he has a soda can for us both, but we're both too far gone to get anything into our stomachs. Our heads are throbbing and our eyes feel too big for their sockets. Coming down with Jeff isn't as much fun as it was with James or Jenny. We also talked about what Jeff thinks about his kid; if it was born or not, boy or girl. He's sure the girl went through with the pregnancy, and that it's a girl. He drew a sketch of a baby and she looked cute and real. He talked more about the mother, though. I didn't know the mother, I only know who she is because I've seen her around town and school, but we never actually met. She wasn't very attractive, or very nice, but Jeff was in love with her through and through, well, as in love as a seventeen year-old gets. Jeff was into heavy drugs way before me, James, and Joanna. He and that girl, Tammy, were doing cocaine when the guys and I still thought weed and beer are the coolest things ever. He doesn't have her address or phone number now, he can't even look into it, he says, so he gave up on ever knowing; he just hopes that if he does have a kid out there, it would someday ask its mom about its dad.

I think we fell asleep rather late. The soda cans are on the bed, tipped over and their content is all over my mattress. Jeff is also not a morning person and we both take forever getting out of bed. No, we didn't sleep together in the bed, we put up a partition. I make us both breakfast and then we go to work on the bathroom job. On the way there we keep quiet and to ourselves. Our heads still hurt, but other than that we're fine. At work we're rolling around like logs, stumbling through any task. It's lucky Jeff is practically the boss and I am kind of a senior at work, so nobody can complain about us being slow today.

After work we each go our separate ways; Jeff tells me he'd try to score some Junk for us for next time and I go to visit Jimmy in lock up again. It's like a therapy session with Jimmy, he sits and listens, absorbing everything I have to say and then he releases all his fears, and doubts, and regrets on me; it's mutual therapy. Neither of us judges, neither of us speaks out of turn. We nod, we agree, we encourage when the other's courage fails him and he can no longer speak. That is invaluable, I find; having someone to just sit there, shut up, and listen.

Jimmy has a new friend in lock up, a girl he never saw, but she's one cell over, and they talk deep into the night. The other junkies are all gone, sent away with assault charges and B&Es, Jimmy and that girl are in for possession, so their cases aren't "priority". He talks about her like she's the "angel of music" and he's Christine, it's a voice from the wall that helps him. He drew what he thinks she looks like, she did describe herself to him, and he's a good artist so she looks cute in the picture, though the breasts look disproportional.

I tell him about Jeff and work, and James and Joanna, but mostly about Jenny and my plan to call her for a fake deal and to swoop her off her feet. I tell him I'm jealous of what James and Joanna have, the love not the baby, and how depressing it is that everyone has someone, even him, but not me. He tells me I shouldn't worry, that I should look for someone other than Jenny, but I can't, but I don't tell him that. An officer tells us I have to leave and I do without a fuss.

At home I turn on the TV and stare at it until it's time to go to sleep, but I can't fall asleep without Weed. It's been a problem for a while now, so I just automatically light up another joint and try to relax. Everybody is telling me to stop thinking about Jenny, but it's hard. I've tried it, to stop thinking of her, I actively tried to stop loving her, but how do you do that? I had arguments with her in my head I told her in my head, that I don't love her anymore, but at the end of the day, literally before I go to sleep, she is the last thing I think about and the first thing I think about in the morning. I've more or less found a job, with Jeff, he even thought of going legit and setting up a proper contractor company, him and me, but nothing seems right as long as Jenny is far away. She's fallen into Meth and sex, more Junk, Smack, too far away from me to watch out for her; that is what we fight about in my head. When we argue in my head, I sound like her father, Mr. Cohen, Attorney at Law. I call Jenny.

"Hello?" She sounds like she's sad, slow, tired; high.

"Jenny? It's Johnny, are you there?" I lose courage; my heart is pounding so hard I can feel it in my ears.

"Oh Johnny? It's been ages! How are you?" She doesn't sound mad, she sounds genuinely happy to hear from me.

"Good, have a more or less legit job going on with Jeff."

"So I've heard, I also heard about Jimmy, and James and Joanna." She's killing off possible topics to talk about, leaving only me, or us.

"Yeah, amazing... a baby in our midst... Can we meet?" It doesn't feel like the first time we met, the first time I asked her out; when she was the little innocent girl and me the big bad guy who does drugs and had seen the world. She knows me, she knows more than me.

"Yeah, sure." After a pause she continues, "Business or pleasure?"

I take a long time with the answer; I think of her body, her lips, and get all excited and anxious to touch her.

"Business." I have to play it cool. "You see, I'm kind of in a dry spell here with everyone gone or hating me."

"Hmmm... a dry spell can also be interpreted in several ways." She laughs lightly, flirtatiously, she is not the Jenny I know; she is so much more comfortable with seduction.

"You know what I mean, I'll see you tomorrow night, at eight, okay? My place?"

"My place, it's near Northface, Parker Boulevard 532, buzz at Cohen. Don't be late." She hangs up and I'm happy with how the conversation went, with my ambiguous reference to 'dry spell'. Yesterday's Smack was the first real high I had in a long time, and the closest thing I had to sex since Jenny was that Marry Ann girl sucking me off back then, and all I did was think of Jenny. I doubt she'd sleep with me, but being around her, rekindling the old spark, would satisfy me a great deal; I still love her, even if she's a different Jenny.

The next day after work I go straight home and have a joint and then a shower, then another joint. It's been three months since I've last seen Jenny and I am incredibly nervous. I want to win her back, save her from Meth, get her away from this. I want us to do what James and Joanna are doing, quitting, not the baby.

At eight I'm at her door, I buzzed at Cohen and she buzzes me in. the building is old, built in the seventies when tons of blacks moved to the area and needed cheap housing. She lives on the fifth floor and across the hall is another apartment. The inside is nice, green carpets and exposed brick, the nice kind, for the walls. I'm not sure it's the actual brick though, it might be decorative. The elevator is small and slow, and I get tired of waiting for it so I climb up the stairs.

Jenny's door is open, she knows I'm here, of course, I buzzed. 5A; that's her apartment. She greets me after I enter. She is beautiful as ever. She's wearing more makeup now, and her pose is a lot more relaxed, but her smile is still her smile and her eyes, beneath the makeup, are still her eyes. I get a hug and a kiss on the cheek and I take another look at her; she looks happy. She's wearing a long skirt, black, and a purple and dark pink baggy top that exposes her shoulders decorated with two red bra straps. She is bare footed and her hair is packed in a nice little pony tail. On her left ankle is a new tattoo of a bird and her nose is pierced. The apartment is cozy, bigger than mine and less cluttered, but that doesn't go to say it's orderly. There are underwear and dishes on the floor and on furniture, and other clothes are on the floor by the closet. She has a big TV, a flat screen, and a nice looking kitchen. Her furniture is cheap looking, but in good taste. After the little tour she sits me down and puts out drinks, vodka and juices, and we start to talk; and I'm afraid I'll make a mess of it.

"So how are you, you look like you're doing well, I like the tattoo."

"Thanks Johnny, I just wanted one and got one; it was a mistake, though, it was just me enjoying my freedom."

"I heard that financially, you are doing well too."

"Yeah, I'm selling Smack and Junk, from Jake." That little bastard, if she tells me he slept with her I'd kill him.

"Oh you two are close?"

"No, just business. I wanted to do him." She smiles weirdly and examines my reaction "but he said he prefers not to, us being in business together and all... We both know it's his loss." She smiles in that weird way again and I know she wants me to react.

"Good, he's not your type, I mean, you're too good for him, I mean..." I force myself to shut up and I see how she's smiling, this time a real smile, she's enjoying it.

"That's sweet of you."

"Jenny, I can't stop thinking about you." I throw it out there and everything goes quiet.

"Johnny, I've moved on. I don't know if we could work things out. I'm happy now, I have money, I finally know what it's like to be free."

"I brought you this." I give her the drawing she did at my place, it has some smudges from my tears, but I thought she might like having it.

"That is really sweet. You know, out of all the men I've been with lately, you were by far the sweetest." That's a good thing right? Girls like a sweet guy...

"But, I need something else. I don't know. You said you were going through a dry spell?" This doesn't sound promising for me, she is looking around her as she speaks, like she's already searching for a date to come and replace me.

"Yeah, I just can't score Junk, only Smack."

"I could help you." At that sentence, it all goes blank, every word she says becomes irrelevant. I can almost smell my next hit, another relief from the earth. She hands me a bag of Junk and asks me if I need a needle; of course I say yes. She sets everything up; this girl who five months ago didn't have the courage to light up a joint, a girl who didn't know how to do a chase, or find a vein. She is quick and proficient now, like James or me.

67

After we take we cuddle as we come down, we don't crash because she has weed and vodka, and cigarettes. She holds on to me and it feels like before. I see our reflection in the TV screen and realize it isn't like before; I am different.

I've lost weight and am starting to look ragged. There are black circles around my eyes, and my cheekbones are jutted now. I am more muscular than before because I have been working more with my hands. I look at her in my arms and the difference is that it doesn't look like she would break if I let her go. Her confidence is so obvious and that is disconcerting. When did she get like that and I became the little lamb? I like the new Jenny, but I loved the old one; the old one needed me, the new Jenny doesn't, she wants me to need her.

I'm at the hospital with James and Joanna. They invited me to join them for the sonogram, me being James's best friend. Joanna is a bit embarrassed being in the robe in front of me. I don't know why, pretty much everyone in our group saw her naked at least once. She tried to take Jamal shopping once as a "gay friend". I think that's stereotyping. He's a US army sergeant, he's a real tough guy, even Terry who is a bit more feminine wouldn't be interested. Well, Joanna undressed in front of him, so he saw her naked. Jimmy saw her topless when he walked into James's place unannounced. I once walked in on James and her having sex and when he rolled off of her I saw her completely naked. To be honest, she is pretty, but her body isn't that great. I see a picture of the fetus. It's beautiful. Just a tiny lump in Joanna's belly but it was beautiful. It's hard to imagine that that is something they made together. The doctor asks questions and they tell him they used to take drugs but that they quit; they even let a nurse look for marks on them and she finds nothing, well, nothing new.

Joanna is really excited and happy. She looks great, radiant. I think that the phrase "pregnancy agrees with her" really suits her. James is all over her, like TV dads in the fifties. He fusses over her even though she is still small, her stomach has still not come out. She doesn't need help walking or sitting down or getting up.

They look so happy as I drive them back to Joanna and Phillip's place. They invite me in and we all have a coffee together; Joanna has herbal tea. They function like a family and I am jealous of them. Joanna and James are holding hands while Phillip looks at them in pride. I sit there and try not to sulk. The happy couple is trying to find a way to afford a place of their own. James is working in personnel for some small company in the area. They make paper and stationary, but James is a small time clerk there in personnel. Joanna isn't even looking for anything outside her dad's shop; who would hire a pregnant woman? So they live with Phillip in the spare room above the shop. James's mom and dad and sister aren't happy with him being married. He told me his mom said she won't help him until he proves he's responsible enough to start a family for real. James's family is nice, and they didn't care about the drugs as long as no one got hurt, but pregnancy? That was too much for them; they ignored the part that Joanna has been James's girlfriend for five years and that they love each other, they blamed the Junk. When I say "didn't mind" I oversimplify. They knew they couldn't do anything about it so they tried to be loving enough to motivate James to quit; "if he knows he has a family that loves him we won't lose him," that's what his mom said over and over. Well, a baby was the straw that broke the camel's back. That's why Phillip has to pick up all the slack. It's a bit cruel of James's family, to let Phillip do it all. He's a local businessman; he can't afford to support a young family too. His store is small and he doesn't make a lot of money. He and James together do manage to pay all the bills, but if James's family would agree to help it would make it a lot easier.

"I saw Jenny last night." A change of subject might be nice.

"What?" That was Joanna, she doesn't look too happy with me now.

"Yeah, it was Jeff's idea... she looked good, happy." Excuses.

"That was dumb, man, you know what she does now; I thought you were following our footsteps; cleaning up. She would only drag you deeper." James is looking sympathetic, but he always does, but I really think he understands.

"I'll leave you kids to talk of stuff that can get the Corporal here arrested." Phillip always calls me "the Corporal", he's a gunnery sergeant.

"You know it's stupid. What did you guys do?" Joanna is still curious; I think she started feeling sorry for Jenny.

"She had Junk, I hadn't had any for so long..." I start rubbing my eyes again and again. My head starts to hurt, it's like talking to a cop; but it's just James and Joanna, I don't know why I'm so nervous.

"We talked, and cuddled a bit; it was different."

"Well, she is on Meth and fucking around now..."

"No, me, I'm different."

"How so?"

"I don't know." This conversation is going nowhere.

"I missed her, that's all. She... she's my Joanna. She's my girl... I can't stop thinking of her, I just can't."

"Well, play it safe." James knows he can't get me off of her, he knows it's useless; I've always been the dumb guy of the group.

We say goodbye and my adult time over coffee and tea is over, back to being a dumb fuck out to destroy himself. I have a beer at home and have a smoke; back to smuggled cigarettes for me. I have a message from Jenny.

"Hey Johnny, I had a great time with you, like back in the day. Maybe we could patch things up. Let me buy you dinner, you look really thin. I made you another sketch, made it flying, I think you'd like it. Meet me at Café Romana tomorrow at nine, okay?"

She sounds a bit like Old Jenny, but there is so much flirtation in her voice it makes it different; it's almost like she is talking with her vagina. This mixture of Old Jenny and New Jenny is scaring me. I don't know her anymore, I don't know what she wants anymore, who she was with; who she is. Things are just out of place, Jenny, everything. Of course I'll go to see her.

At the café, the same café I met her parents at, she is waiting for me at a table. She is wearing an elegant black dress that is probably new, and a lot of makeup. She is drinking wine and there is a glass there for me as well. I sit down in front of her and try to smile.

"You look nice." I did try to play 'dress up' for her, a nice shirt, a nice jacket, everything I could.

"Thanks... You look beautiful... is the dress new?"

"Yes, bought it last month so not new per se, but new. Have whatever you want, my treat." She smiles, moving confidently, her hands move and caress everything, her chin her wine glass, my hand. It's like she is a child exploring the world through the sense of touch. I look at her, this beautiful woman, and I feel only sexual attraction, no love anymore. She reminds me of so many whory girls I met in my life; so many girls that play this game but not to find "a nice guy" but to find a guy to fuck them, to pleasure them without meaning. But it's still her inside, I can bring out the Old jenny, I see her every so often in a smile, a shy look that seeps through and doesn't just want to get me naked.

"I want to know what happened to you since we stopped seeing each other." I try to catch up in this race of seduction, to use a voice, look at her like those guys in the movies do. She looks immune to my efforts, or maybe she has a good poker-face.

"You don't, besides, I've learned to appreciate the need to have a bit of mystery about me." I'm in over my head. She knows what she's doing, the right gesture, the right tone of voice, the right pose, the right clothes. I'm just trying to keep my head above water.

"Fine, have your secrets. When did you move out on your own?"

"Hmm, two months ago. I just wanted a place to go every night without my parents checking everyone with me for tattoos or needle marks, and where I wouldn't have to get guys to climb out my window when I'm done with them. I saw, after everyone cut me off, that I have to, and can, make it on my own. I started making so much money selling that I didn't even need the job from my dad and uncle, so I quit; getting rid of my dad's last means to control me." She isn't happy with that question. Her gestures and pose indicate this. She is looking away from me, fidgeting with her fingers.

"I think I know what you mean... Well, I'm very happy for you. I'm working with Jeff on some home-improvement, we're thinking of going legit. Still living in that dump."

"As long as you're happy."

"I'm not." Why am I saying that? "Ever since you left, nothing is going right... I fell out with Jake and don't work with him anymore, some guy tried to stab me, people are getting arrested, people are going away... I almost ODed." How is this helping Johnny? Huh? How? She already knew you're a screw up, now you're trying to show her you're not... dumbass.

"I heard about the Jake thing, but ODing? That's news to me, are you alright? How did it happen? You are always so careful." She looks sincere in her concern. She is looking at me with Old Jenny eyes, deep and alive, and her hand is covering her mouth.

"Forget it, it's not important." I try to turn it into a mystery, like her little secrets.

"No, it's important!" She looks like a scared little girl, like my Jenny.

"I was just... I was thinking about..." Wait, how do I tell her ODed because of her?

"I had no idea Johnny, I wish someone had told me."

"I think they wanted to protect my privacy. They're kind of nice like that, and besides, I was still in business with Jake and I was afraid he wouldn't let me work with him."

"But he doesn't work with you anyway." She's back to her snarky voice.

"Let's talk about something else; I don't want to talk about this." Choose your battles. She looks at me and is obviously thinking of something to say, I think I caught her off guard, thrown her off her little game of seduction where I am unarmed now that I don't have any drugs to tempt anyone with. Maybe I can use pity? Maybe I can be mysterious? How do I go on?

We are both sipping on red wine and having something that smells of mushrooms and is smothered in butter, the wine is good but the food is horrible. We look at each other and no one says a thing for a long time.

"I think I understand your drawing now." I try to interrupt the sound of clinking dishes and cutlery.

"Oh, that... I almost forgot about it until the other day." She is embarrassed by me mentioning the drawing, that's a good thing, right? Temptresses don't get embarrassed.

"It's fear, isn't it? About fear and disappointment."

"I suppose. I made it high, and angry, I don't know what I was thinking anymore." She is avoiding the issue, but I know I was right; she drew her fears.

"I really loved it; it was honest. Are you giving thought about what you want to do, other than deal?"

"Not really. I make money, I have friends, I have a place of my own. I don't need anything more right now."

"Right now, but eventually." I sound like her dad.

"Johnny, please, let's not talk about stuff like that. Are you seeing anyone?" Is that a trick question? I already told her I want her back.

"No, I couldn't bear the thought of anyone but you, Jenny." I try to be sweet again, I leave out the fact that some smack-head sucked me off. I did think of Jenny the entire time, I did wish Jenny was the one doing it. I know it's not the same as not being with anyone, it's a poor excuse having thought of her while getting a blowjob from someone else.

"That's sweet of you. I... I've been with others Johnny." I don't know if that is merely a report, a factual statement, a test, a remorseful recollection, but she doesn't look happy.

"I know. It doesn't matter, I never stopped caring for you." It's time to bite into this- "I am worried about you taking Meth." Yeah, I finally said it. I hope she won't freak out over this, won't think I'm controlling.

"Johnny, I'm fine, I appreciate your concern, but it's fine. Meth is actually not as bad as you said it is; only in the long run, and I'm just toying with it, that's all." Yeah, that's how it gets you. 'just toying with it' and before you know it you look like... Keith Richards.

"Well, I'm not one to preach..."

"Yeah, you're not. You who taught me how to do a chase, or find a vein, or roll a joint..." She is smiling playfully now, another mixture of Old and New Jennys.

"You mentioned another drawing."

"Yes, later, it's a present."

"I can't wait to see it." I take her hand now, trying to be romantic, but I feel I'm sweating too much for it to count, but she is still looking me in the eyes and smiling, not noticing the clammy sweaty hands.

"I love you Jenny; I loved you before and I still do." I'm afraid of what she might say, or think. I start to imagine her laughing hard and heartily at the idea, then I imagine her throwing her drink at me and yelling "How dare you!" and storming out. I'm so busy imagining her reaction I fail to notice her reaction. She is looking right at me, her eyes are wide open and one hand is on her chin, the other is over her heart. She is smiling the most beautiful smile I have ever seen; you can see gratitude, relief, sorrow, surprise, they are all mixed together in her lips and eyes. It's the most beautiful thing I have ever seen. Why have I waited until now to tell her this? Why? Look at her! She is not laughing, not running, not rejecting, she is just smiling.

She gets up and takes me by the hand, she leads me to the ladies' room and then into a stall, closes the door, looks at me intently. She unbuttons my shirt, leads me to unzip her dress, it happens slowly, or it looks that way to me. She's not wearing a bra and the sight of her brings me out of slow-motion. I lunge at her and surprise her, but in the good way; we smash into the stall's door and hear someone outside coming closer.

" Are you okay in there?"

"Fuck off!" That was Jenny talking, her breath coming in

short gasps already, her hand inside my pants and me getting comfortable under the skirt of her dress as well. The woman outside walks away and we move faster, moving closer to what we want. She lets me do anything I want with her, but all I want is to love her, to please her. She is wearing her dress more like a belt now, her back is like a desert landscape before me as she is bent forward, leaning on the stall's walls, shifting sands moving with me, soft skin that sends jolts through me; she smells of Junk and perfume.

We get back to our table and spend the rest of the evening in an intimate silence. As we part, she gives me her drawing. It's on an A3 paper and enclosed in an envelope. I drive her to her place and we kiss good night, I ask if I can call her and she says yes. I get home and do a stupid little "victory dance" I got my Jenny back; now I only have to make sure she is My Jenny. The key is the Junk, if I get the Junk she would need me again.

The next day I go to visit Jimmy in lock up. I can't stop talking about myself and how I got Jenny back, but I think Jimmy understands. He knows how much I love her and how much she means to me, so he understands. He says I should go slow, let her go back to Old Jenny nice and easy and not force anything on her, or I'd be driving her away; he's right. He laughs a lot and says he knew I'd ignore what everyone said and try to win her back, he just knew it. Jimmy doesn't know Jenny well; he joined us shortly before I met her at that party, but they never talked. He had no quarrel with her and she had no quarrel with him. They stayed out of each other's way.

As for him, he met his little lady friend yesterday. He said she was very pretty and that he wants to find her when they get out. They kind of had "letter sex" by throwing little notes to each other's cells, kind of like Amish cybersex. He looked happy. His lawyer said he'd be getting out next week due to Lack of Public Interest; no bail, nothing, just patience.

I showed him a copy of Joanna's and James's sonogram, he was fascinated. He tried to find a head or something, but it was kind of a blur. As you can imagine, James and Joanna don't have insurance, so their treatment isn't what you'd call "the best". They throw as much money as they have for baby things, but they can't afford to go to the doctor with the best equipment, so their sonogram is older and less detailed.

I say goodbye to Jimmy too and head home, my place smells like cheese and feet, so I decide to clean. On the bed I see Jenny's drawing so I put the cleaning on hold and open the envelope.

The drawing is much more erratic than the last and much more colorful. There are waves of blue and green and a shade of purple that run along the middle of the page, segmenting it to two halves. In each half there is a Jenny, with a different colored hair; in the top half it's red and orange, in the bottom half it's black and brown. The top Jenny is asleep and smiling, surrounded by other smaller figures that look like they're dancing the bottom Jenny is afraid of the same figures. Across this segmenting line, crossing it to "touch" the worlds of both Jennys are the figures of two men. One is skinny and straight, his eyes are fixed and hard, like emeralds; the other is rounder, looser, kinder. Each of the men has his head in the world of a different Jenny and the feet are at the world of the other Jenny. The straight one's head is with the Jenny who is afraid the other one is with the happy Jenny.

The more I sit and look at this, the more I find striking how much less heart she put into this, how much more thought and pain, but less heart. Her first drawing was full of virgin creation; this is mimicry of something she could grasp, less raw. It's more coherent, yes, but she knew what she was doing here, not exploring. I look and try to decipher some hidden message, in the colors, in the image, in the very existence and giving of the drawing might be a hidden message to me; a call for help from Old Jenny, or from My Jenny. I stay sober to look more closely, but my eyes begin to itch and my head begins to hurt, so I lubricate my brain with some Weed and hope for clarity; instead I fall asleep.

I am woken at six in the morning by a call from Jeff, he asks me to come in early to the bathroom job, says it's really important. When I get there he is waiting for me along with the house owner, a Mr. de Silva. Mr. de Silva tells us he changed his mind about the color of the tiles for one of the walls and that he wants them in a bright blue now, and we are trying to haggle as much money out of him for this change. Jeff introduced me as his "senior partner and consultant" and I try to step in and squeeze as much money as possible, but Mr. de Silva is a crafty bastard, he keeps saying he can find day workers to do the job instead of us and he would probably get it done cheaper and faster, so we should be grateful. In the end we get and extra week and a half for the job plus the costs of the material, and an extra one hundred for the trouble. He actually tells us to get an extra guy and calculates those costs at around one hundred, but we thought it would be best to keep the guys we have and make everyone work harder, and keep the hundred dollars. During our lunch break, after I have some weed with my new student friend, whose name is Omri and not Barry or Harry, I call Jenny. She sounds tired, sleepy and sluggish.

"Hey there, babe, how are you?"

"Great, squeezed a bit more money from the bathroom job with Jeff."

"Good to hear, I don't want you mooching off of me the whole time." It's like I can hear her smiling; I imagine it's her Old Jenny smile.

"Sure..." I try to chuckle but it comes out in flood of uneven laughs and giggles.

"I hear you're having fun at work, I can almost smell you laughter from here." She's very quick to realize I'm high.

"Yeah, you know, it might be the chemicals in the paint and glues..." I laugh again and so does she.

"Okay, babe, try not to saw your hand off."

"I love you."

"I know." She hangs up, and now I picture her going back under the blanket, turning over and smiling herself back to sleep.

I get back to work happy as a... I don't know, something really happy, who cares what? I have my Jenny back, sort of, I have a job, for a while. And another thing, Jimmy gets out on Monday! Sweet freedom. I go see him after work, Jeff stays behind to talk to Mr. de Silva again, so I go to Jimmy alone.

Jimmy seems in a good mood, he is also very friendly with the officers there now and they even go out to get him stuff if he asks nice. By stuff I mean coffee and some food, doughnuts or he says one guy once agreed to get him Chinese food from across the street; I guess not all cops are bastards. Jimmy already gave his little lady friend his number and address so she can find him when she gets out. By the way, her name is Joyce, and she works at the same company James does, in the mail room. Jimmy is so excited, more about being with Joyce than about his freedom. Jimmy says jail-time did him good; put him in perspective. We obviously don't talk about our... recreation, we are surrounded by cops, and nice as they act around us now, they are still pigs inside.

I tell Jimmy everything too, about Jenny and how I told her I love her. He was more confused than impressed. He wasn't mean or anything, just confused. I don't think he understands love;

he's just infatuated with Joyce, not in love. He says it's too soon for me to have done that. He thinks I should have waited, because of me being a wreck and Jenny being not that much better inside than me.

I say goodbye and promise to pick him up on Monday, at eleven. I have to say I'm disappointed at him not understanding me. The whole time he was inside he just listened, sometimes gave advice, but never judgment. I suppose that now that he's coming back out he's going back to his own mysterious old quiet self. It doesn't matter, I already told her and I can't take it back, I don't want to; it was a moment of non-drug-induced honesty. At home, I sit down and watch TV in a sort of a sober high-on-life feeling, self-contentment, to be more accurate. During the second episode of the Law and Order marathon Jamal calls.

"Hey man, I heard Jimmy's getting out on Monday and that you're picking him up, could Terry come along?"

"Sure, I'm picking Jimmy up in the morning, about eleven-ish... If that's okay for Terry he can come along, where do I pick him up?"

"At work, you know the place." I do know it, the worst kind of place in this stupid town; an art gallery.

Terry isn't an artist but he fancies himself one, so he wanted to work somewhere where he could 'absorb art', the only reason I didn't punch him for saying it like that is because his boyfriend is stronger than me. Terry works there as an English-Spanish translator for guests and the written material, as well as some artists (one guy from Mexico sells his paintings exclusively to that gallery.)

"Okay, tell him to be ready by ten to eleven, got it?"

"Sure, thanks man." He hangs up at that.

To say the truth, ever since we got back from the damn desert, me and Jamal hardly get along. You know what it's like when a friendship works at one place but not another? There, we were forced together into a shitty situation, and what holds a company together is the company itself. But I don't know, not being there anymore, not having to rely on one another for safety and sanity... that's when you start seeing how little you care for that person in regular situations, how different you are, how little you have in common to talk about. Before Jamal quit, which was only shortly after he started using, we hung out a lot. We went to parties, he helped me hook up, I saw him almost cheat on Terry (eventually he remembered he has a boyfriend and detached his mouth from the other guy and told him to fuck off.) but when the smoke and haze cleared, we have nothing more in common; not the uniform of the US army and not the uniform of the junky.

The morning hits me like a ton of bricks. If I don't smoke something before I sleep I wake up slowly and raggedly. My system is far too used to substance "abuse", and last night I was so pleased with life that I didn't smoke anything.

The room smells weird. Not of weed of Junk or Smack smoke, just weird, like a wet sock you left under the bed. I check under the bed for the source and find nothing substantial, but the smell is definitely strong there. I abandon the search and head to Philipp's shop. Joanna is the only one in the shop today and she looks like she'd prefer to be elsewhere, anywhere really.

"Hey, morning." A shallow greeting in a distant spongy voice.

"Morning, just came in for some beer and stuff, be out of your way in no-time." I try to smile but I feel like she sounds; spongy.

"Oh, no, take your time; I'm just a bit sick."

She doesn't look like she wants to talk so I just grab a few beers and a frozen pizza and some rum, a special today, almost a dollar off.

Joanna takes the cash really slowly, her stomach is obviously swollen with the kid by now, not immense, but you can't mistake it for putting on weight. I leave and drive to Jenny's, but she doesn't answer the door bell, so I call her.

"Hey..."

"Did I wake you?"

"Yeah, sort of, I was not really there, you know?"

"Alone? You know better." Again, I sound more like a Junky parent.

"Don't worry, I'm fine, it's not what you think. There's no real danger in that."

I don't understand her cryptic talk now, she's moved on to Terra Incognita as far as I'm concerned, but it's my job to bring her back to... Terra Cognita? Is that a thing?

"Can you buzz me up?"

"Sure, didn't really hear the thing... hold on." I hear a bunch of stuff crashing in the background, and the buzzer sounds and the door opens. I climb up, and as I do, a guy is coming down. He seems kind of familiar, and has an air of self-satisfaction about him, and he smells of something, something powdery. I reach her door, it's open but she isn't there. I walk in and smell something in the air, weird and unfamiliar, maybe there's something wrong with my nose, everywhere I am today, I smell stuff. I can hear music form inside, Eric Clapton, Delilah, and then a toilet flush.

"Well, what are you waiting for?" She sees me as she leave the bathroom and asks, smiling to me as a sign that there is no danger.

"Nothing.".

"What's that smell?"

"Oh, never mind that." She clears her coffee table of various powders and papers and we sit on the couch. I hold on to a piece of paper in my hand, a gift for her. I can't draw, or paint, so I can't give her something like what she gave me, but I do have something.

"This is for you." I hand it over. It's a small piece of recycled paper, stained by coffee, and wet tobacco. On it, in my bad handwriting and in a cheap military issue ball-point pen, is a poem, my first ever poem.

"A soul that's dark
And a heart that's torn apart
A spirit full of dreams that will never see light
That is all I can give to you
All that I am and all I seem, is a dream that will never come true."

"It's just something I wrote when I was away... It's just stupid, but it's my first one ever, so I want you to have it. Original copy..." She reads it through and smiles embarrassed, then give me a kiss and let me hold her; this was a good idea.

"You never told me anything about what happened there, neither did Jamal..."

"It's behind us." Yes, now it's US again, me and Jamal, the soldiers, this and only this topic brings us together.

"I want to know."

"Let's change the subject." I struggle for a minute, then, "I saw some really weird looking guy coming down as I came up... He smelled just like your apartment..." I try to make it sound like an anecdote, a weird story, but this is me water-boarding her.

"Who, Mike? Yeah, he was here; gave me a little present." She gives me one of those weird girlish smiles and displays her bounty; a little bag of Meth.

"I don't like you using that."

"I know, but it's my body."

"How much did it cost?"

"It was a present."

"Are you sleeping with him?"

"Fuck you." She gets up and leaves the living-room, then comes back, takes the Meth and a pipe and leaves again.

I don't have time for this, I lie to myself, so I get up and leave as well; she'll calm down soon enough.

"Fuck you!!! I haven't touched anyone since our date!" She calls out from another room as I leave.

"I believe you." I hope she heard me. It's impossible for me to stay mad, I don't know why. She could do the worst thing in the universe, she could hurt me any way she could, but all it takes is for her to say something, anything to counter it and I turn like a little puppy and somehow feel I'm the bad-guy. It's weird, an irrational but also rational fear of upsetting her, setting off another departure and long absence..

Sitting in my car now, I better scan her street; it looks poor and every wall is covered in graffiti, but the people walking about don't look like what you'd expect. They're well dressed and walk straight and upright, a few look like skin-heads but not the dangerous kind.

It's like the opposite from where me and Jenny came from. Our neighborhood used to be really nice, very middle class, well, not my street, but that's new. Now the whole neighborhood's gone to shit, full of junkies and crime. I shouldn't judge, being a junky myself, but I never robbed or assaulted anyone. Jenny's neighborhood used to be a den of cut-throats and negro-junkies, now it's middle class and has only "Street-Art" graffiti, not the gang kind.

When I start the car people start staring. I have to admit, it's a piece of trash, my car, I bought it when coming back from Iraq, using whatever money I saved up being cut from civilization and commerce. The radio didn't work, but I fixed it, and I sort of re-welded a piece of the front axle together; it might not be "up to code", but I get from A to B.

I get home and drown the world in a random stream of TV ambience. Another episode of Breaking Bad is on, some guy gets taken out, his head is chopped off, I haven't been following enough to tell why. I fall asleep to TV gun-shots and screams.

I head off to work without having breakfast because I have woken up late, Jeff is already there tearing open the nylon off a shipment of bathroom tile. The others come in in a trickle until we are all there and can get to work.

At a quarter past eleven I leave to pick up Terry and the Jimmy, it would be the first time I've ever been alone with Terry for more than two minutes.

"How do you like it? I made it myself!" Terry shows me the small twenty inch cake with the word "FREEDOM!" written on it with frosting and a tiny marzipan Scottish, Mel Gibson-like figure.

"Really cool, did you do the little William Wallace yourself too?"

"Kind of, I got it as a person and added the hair and kilt."

"Impressive" He puts the cake back under its plastic cover; it still smells of chocolate and banana in the car.

"How long have you known Jimmy for?"

"Wow... Twelve years. He was such a sweet kid, and a very handsome teenager, my first crush."

"Really? So not the sibling-like- relationship I thought it was."

"At first, maybe, but after I turned sixteen and came out of the

85

closet, he was fourteen at the time... No."

"Because you had a crush on him."

"He also had a phase, don't tell Jamal."

"You and Jimmy?" I almost stop the car just for dramatic effect.

"It was brief and innocent, I touched it, and he realized he'd rather I were a girl."

"But no hard feelings? Ahh... No pun intended."

"Not at all, and it was a great pun." Terry is smiling so sincerely it's impossible not to believe him.

We get to the police station and after a debate about whether we should go inside with or without the cake we go in cake-less.

"Wait here please." A really pretty police officer tell us after we inquire about Jimmy, she walks off and I find myself disappointed at how loose and baggy her uniform is on her, one can only guess about her figure. One cop comes up to Terry and they start speaking in Spanish, I can only understand those words Spanish and English have in common, but the general drift of the conversation eludes me.

The pretty cop comes back escorting Jimmy, he looks smug and happy, with a bit of the convict walk in the way he carries himself now, but I know it's an act, besides, he's never been convicted of anything. We all go to the car and have the cake together after stopping for coffee as well. Jimmy and Terry put some whiskey in their coffee, but I don't, I have to go to back to working with Jeff later, and odds are, I'll be in charge of the belt-sander. Jeff thinks that because I'm an army tech, I can work any piece of machinery, big, small, electrical, pneumatic, or gas powered. To be honest, yes, in the army, if you're a tech for one thing, you're a tech for everything, but I'm a civilian now, leave me alone.

Back at work, I really do get left in charge of the belt-sander, but it's not a hard machine to operate, so I'm okay with that.

Omri, the literature buff, hangs out around me all day, asking me questions and shares some weed with me on the break we decide we deserve. He's an okay kid, a bit naïve, though. He says he has this girlfriend in Michigan, and he's one hundred percent sure they are making it work long-distance, but he also says she is spending way too much time with one of her male friends.

"But girls, you know, they aren't like us, they aren't as likely to cheat as men." Omri professes his gender philosophy, driven by a conviction only weed can provide.

"I'm sorry to tell you this, but they are just as likely. Women enjoy sex just as much as we do, maybe more, and if something is in itself enjoyable, then that is reason enough to do it. The only thing that MIGHT hold them back is that they wouldn't want to get a reputation, or feel bad." I haven't smoked as much as he did, so I make more sense.

"Nahh... Inbal wouldn't cheat, she knows I care about her."

"Inbal? What kind of fucked up name is that?" I start laughing, maybe I did smoke enough.

"Well... It means... okay, it is kind of a weird name, it means uvula, in Hebrew."

"Still fucked up."

"Whatever, man, my point is that she won't cheat."

"Sure, keep telling yourself that." I go back to work. It's monotonous work and takes a very specific part of my brain to concentrate, the rest of me can wonder off in thought, and I think of Omri's problem, which is in a sense, my problem as well. Was Jenny sleeping with that Mike guy?

I know where I recognized him from; he's the bartender in that Café Jenny likes, the one we had our date at. He kept checking her out the whole evening, but I thought that is just because she is really pretty, was he just reminiscing about fucking her? Was he making plans? I dial Jenny's number.

"Hey, I just wanted to apologize for yesterday, it was out of line."

"I really don't understand you Johnny, I don't know why I came back to you, for you... One minute you're super nice and all, and the next, you're a jealous asshole. We said what happened when we were apart is behind us, not important, Mike is just a friend now." She hangs up.

Now. Just a friend, now. What was he before? This was so much easier when those guys she slept with were faceless.

When work is done me and Jeff stay last to talk to Mr. de Silva again. He wants to know how much longer and Jeff is doing most of the talking, calling me for support only when Mr. de Silva asks why we didn't hire another guy with the extra money he gave us.

When we're done talking to him we go to Jeff's place and have some Junk he bought from Jake, who has become quite a drug baron in town. The Junk is top notch, like the smack Jake sells, I must admit, when he does something, he does it right; like being an ass.

"So, whatcha' gonna do about it?" Jeff asks with a cigarette drooping from his mouth, he always goes a bit limp and weird when on Junk, and it always starts with his jaw. We've been half talking about the Mike-thing, about how he must have fucked Jenny when we were apart, and he might be fucking her still. Jeff is very touchy when it comes to women, seeing as the mother of his child left him.

"I don't know man... I think I'm going to... do nothing." I'm also smoking, one after the other, I've lost track at what number cigarette I am.

"Nothing??? Pussy."

"Fuck you, what would you do?"

"Kill him." I hope that's the Junk talking. "Go G.I. Joe on his ass, man, come on"

"Go G.I. Joe? How fucking high ARE you? Look at me!" I look down at my body and am surprised to see I am rather tout, the belly is gone, the arms are bigger.

"I can't beat someone up with no reason."

"You have a reason. Okay, get up, we're going, you're driving."

Without leaving me room for an argument he walks to my car and we drive off.

"Where to?"

"Café Romana." Jeff looks like some kind of James Dean or Jack Kerouac; someone cool, anyway.

We get to the café and stay in the car, inconspicuously parked across the street from the parking lot; the only car there... so not that inconspicuous. We must look like two rookie cops at a stake-out. We're only missing the doughnuts and coffee. The patrons are starting to leave the café, in pairs or threes, third wheels saying goodbye and driving off. Inside, the staff is starting to clean up the place, collecting their tips and distributing them.

We step outside of the car and walk over to the back entrance, where I once sold some smack to a weird guy, and wait for 'Mike'.

"Can I help you guys?" A young girl comes out of the back door and asks us, she's carrying large garbage bags and it's obviously her turn to take care of the recycling and waste.

"Yes, ahhmm... Cindy" Jeff reads her name-tag and smiles at her like she's the only person in the world. "We're waiting for Mike, we have something for him, he's not expecting us, but tell him we're friends of Jenny's, he'll know." He winks at this Cindy girl and taps her on her behind, she flushes but is obviously enjoying the attention.

"Sure, I'll tell him to come out, he's done for today anyway."

She winks back and walks back inside.

Within a minute this 'Mike' guy walks out the back door and meets us, Jeff is all charm and joy, putting his arm around Mike's shoulders and talking to him in a tone that would make anyone do anything. We take Mike in the car and drive off; he thinks we're going to sell him some Meth, so he's up for anything.

We get to an area out of town people used to call "Cunt-de-Suc" because everyone used to go there to have sex without their parents knowing. Now, the place is used for big drug deals and some minor criminal activities.

We get out of the car, there's no one else around, just a few dogs rummaging around. Mike looks at me and Jeff, taking out his wallet.

"I got a lot of tips tonight, I can buy a lot."

I don't waste any time, this guy is too much of an addict, all he can think of is Meth, there's no future for him.

"What the hell?!!" He yell as he hits the ground. I was never much of a fighter, but I can throw a punch, and this one landed well, right on the temple. I kick him in the chest when he tries to get up, then again in the face when he's down.

"Fuck you!" I kick him again, and Jeff takes a shot as well, kicking his back. We let him stand up again, blood is coming down his nose and mouth, I think I broke some of his teeth. He puts up his fists for a fight, you've got to commend this, he fights despite the odds.

I feign a low kick and punch him again in his breast-bone, then a left hook to the jaw, then I grab his arm, twist it, and hit his elbow through, breaking it, a little army trick for you there. He screams so loud, and he starts crying, a sort of sad wail one cannot ignore.

"Take it... Take my money! Please!!!" He thinks this is a robbery, he thinks this is about money. I throw his wallet back at him and spit in his face, I grab a rock and want to hit his face, I don't know why, I just do. Jeff stops me before I kill him, I remember how Corporal Washington, rifleman, killed an Al Quida operative with a rock when we were ambushed, the guy managed to get close, wanted to take hostages, as the investigation slash debriefing committee declared.

"Let's go, we made our point." Jeff gets in the car, he looks nervous.

I follow him into the car and we sit there smoking before I start the car. We both stay silent as we're driving back into town, only talking if we need a smoke or a light. When I drop him off he gets out of the car and looks at me weird.

"You have blood on you shirt, you might want to get rid of that, evidence." He walks into the building and I can see him going up the stairs through the windows at the stairwell, he stops every now and then, sometimes in the middle of the stairs and just stands there, thinking, I suppose. I don't think Jeff has ever been exposed to real violence, and I think I scared him. To be honest, I scared myself. I haven't done anything like that before; I am rather ashamed, when I think about it.

At home I smoke a bit of weed to relax; my hands and shaking, and I am sweating like a pig, but that might be the result of bad ventilation. There are so many witnesses, so much evidence against me. What now? I fall asleep thinking of a way to get out of this, to avoid arrest.

The phone rings, it's really early, I'm not sure how early but it is. I pick up.

"Yeah?"

"Hey, don't come to work today, okay? I think it would be best if you stay indoors today." It's Jeff, he sounds like major Schuster, telling me I'm being discharged, honorably.

"Uhm, okay, I guess." I go back to sleep and have a little breakfast, toast with jelly, along with a bit of coffee and some gin. I call James, but he's at work, Jimmy is at the police station, getting Joyce out along with Terry and Jamal. Jeff is at work and Johanna too, so I'm alone; aside from Jenny.

I do nothing much the whole day, I call Jeff a few times but he's not happy to hear from me, but says we'll talk tomorrow. I call Jenny too and we talk for a bit about nothing, she already knows about the beating, but not that it was me, for the moment, it's just "some guy".

I go and visit her in the evening, she is sitting on the couch in shorts and a bra, surfing on her laptop looking like some scene from a porno. The whole apartment smells of weed and canned goulash, the little ceiling fan doing well to spread the smell evenly in the apartment.

I sit and join her on the couch and make myself at home with her weed. She has a bong shaped like a genie's lamp, and every time we get high, or take acid, and it's around she keeps playing with it "trying to get people to understand the joke" even though we all did already, and it wasn't that funny.

We sit in silence for a while, with her surfing and texting and me just smoking and eating the canned goulash. We start watching a movie, something stupid with Josh Hartnett in it, but the action makes up for the lame story-line.

"Tell me something... Is it hard killing someone?" After Eric Bana kills seven people, she looks at me and asks, looking almost sober and very curious, her eyes distract me from looking at her breasts.

"Don't know."

"Bullshit." She comes close, her words and expression seeming independent from each other.

"Let's just watch the damn movie." She goes quiet for a while after that but keeps looking at me funny, like a kid would look at a Kinder-surprise egg.

"They don't really fly around like in the movies, right?"

"From explosions." Got to give her something.

"Did you see that happening?"

"This movie sucks, let's watch something else." She goes quiet again and we keep watching the movie.

"Oh! Wait here!! I have something for you, it's stupid I know, but... hold on" She leaves the room all excited and I hear her fumbling around in the bedroom while Hartnett keeps shooting, now at a bunch of people sporting AK 47s, I don't know why, but it looks very intense.

"Here, it's the last in the set of three." She hands me another drawing, this one done with shades of gray and a deep, deep black. It's very good, she improved a lot, but it's also disturbing.

It's a woman, tied to a bed and blindfolded; around her are... gargoyle type creatures with long snouts. You can tell the woman is naked, but you can't see any of her private areas. One of the gargoyles is pulling her hair, another is starting to climb the bed, the others watch. The background looks like some cave, but has Colonial architecture windows. At the foot of the bed is a man lying down, he looks afraid, like in a nightmare. He is in uniform, army uniform I mean, and he is covering his head.

"Is that me?"

"Yeah... Do you like it? It's a birthday gift." Yes, it's my birthday today, I am 24 now.

She kisses me and keeps saying "happy birthday", in the background the credits are playing as we lay down on the sofa and she say she's going to give me my "real birthday gift". I close my eyes and get ready, but feel she is no longer on top of me so I open my eyes and she is not in the room. Within a few seconds she comes back with needles and a plastic bag of Junk, it looks rather brownish.

"We can fuck any time, this is your gift." She is staring at my crotch and smiles, seeing what I was thinking. "It's the best money can buy, from Columbia or some such shit hole."

I put sex out of my mind and get my works ready. This is a better birthday gift than sex. Yes, you heard me, this is better than sex with Jenny, hell, it's better than sex with anyone!

I let her go first, and spend a second just looking at her eyes when she gets it in her, then she closes her eyes and drifts on pure joy. My turn. I put it in. The room stops moving, warmth envelops me and squeezes me in. Me and Jenny fall down where we were, sort of entwined like weeds or vines. Her hair is right in my face, and my hand is on her belly. Her breathing is slow but short, making it quicker, she grabs on to the armrest of the sofa like it were going to fall, then she rolls over to face me. We try to kiss again but miss; I kiss her chin and she my nose. It's not even a kiss, more of a lick, really. We smile a little, I'm not sure I am, but she is, then we try again. I hit the mark. It's the shortest kiss I ever had because her head then falls and her lips escape me. We tumble to the floor and roll around. We start a sort of a laugh that turns into a pant and then to a moan. We try to wriggle around each other but lock in even tighter. We move against one another, again, and again, and again, and again, and then—

We throw up.

Almost simultaneously we both lose it and throw up on her floor. We are both too drained to clean it; our eyes hurt and our mouths feel both parched and liquid, there is a pain right behind my left eye and above my nose. We lie down on the couch after spraying two cans of air freshener and just stay put. That was some good stuff.

"Was it a good gift?"

"Yeah, babe... the best." I smile, though she can't see it; her head is resting on my chest and I am stroking her hair. There's a piece of half-digested tomato caught in it.

"Do you ever get scared that this is how you'd die?" She curls up around herself like some puppy, her head still resting on me, but now so are her knees.

"No, why?"

"I saw someone almost die like that... and... Well, you said you almost ODed."

"What happened to that person?"

"He took some Meth, then started dancing, fell and hit his head on something, I think it was the table, and we called an ambulance and ran away. He's okay now, just... well... Blind. It was horrible to watch, so much blood."

"Yeah." I think I was shivering as I answered, probably coming down.

"Are you okay?"

"Yeah, babe... Fine."

"Did you ever see something like that?"

"I think I've seen worse." I have a headache, everything is killing me, I don't have the energy to lie, or talk, or do anything, why doesn't she shut up?

"Like what? Wait, do you mean there?" There means Iraq for her, basically, for Jenny, anything outside of Ohio is "There".

"Yep, now please drop it." I know she won't, I'm just covering my ass so I can remind her I told her to drop it.

"I want to know."

"Why? I don't want to, and I don't want you to, so let's drop it." I try to get up but nothing responds, the little people in my brain have to sit down and re-wire everything, and that's going to take a while.

"Someone who got shot?"

"He wishes." Shut up, Johnny, shut up Jenny, just drop it!

"What do you mean?"

"Fine, if you have to know: there was a guy, afterwards I learned his name was Darren... something, he was a tank mechanic, or more specifically, the turret of the tank. Now, he was stationed in a little workshop for tanks, not big, but they had cranes and everything. There's a standing order for mechanics never to work on anything suspended from a crane, but he... ohh... Darren knew better, so he had someone lift the turret on the crane and started working on it from below while everyone went for chow. Me, I was there to catch some R&R and hide from my CO, and I'm half watching Darren fix the turret and half sleeping, and then BOOM!!!!" I manage to gesticulate for effect. "I open my eyes and... no Darren. And the turret is on the ground. Then the blood starts flowing. I alert people, and we manage to get two crane APCs, borrowed from the British, and lift the turret. Now... You remember those Willy Coyote cartoons, when an anvil, or some boulder falls on him and he goes flat? That's how dear old Darren looked like, only when it happens to a real live human being, all the blood, the guts, the brains, the internal organs, they have to go somewhere, so they just explode out of you. And the worst part... The worst of it was his left eye. Because, you know the eye is basically jelly, right? Well it, from the force and weight of the turret, kind of fused to it, the heat probably helped, and as they lifted the turret back up the eye was stuck to it and it ripped out of the face." I stop for a moment and realize how fast

I was talking, and try to catch my breath. "And you could see the inside of his flat skull, the bone, everything. Then, to make things worse, it, the eye, kind of... flopped back down with an indifferent inanimate THOMP." I throw up again and stop talking. I notice I am shaking still and that my headache got worse.

"I should go." I get up and look for my car keys until I find them in my pocket, and make for the door before she has a chance to say anything.

The air outside helps me relax a bit, well... I say outside but I'm sitting in the hallway leaning against Jenny's front door. I feel sick again and get back into the apartment, into the toilet and throw up.

"Are you okay?" She's there, seeming sympathetic or scared, I'm not sure.

"Leave me alone." I manage to spout out between heaves.

"I'll order us some pizza."

Happy birthday Johnny.

I don't wait for pizza and leave for real now, start the car and head for home, making a detour at Jeff's and regret it half way there. After deciding to head directly home I stop only to get some food on the way at a Mexican place Terry once recommended.

At home I go straight to sleep, waiting for Jeff's approval to join him again at work the next day, instead, I find out I am his one phone call in the morning.

He sounds confused and still sleepy, but he talks quickly in quarter sentences.

"...died in the hospital...", "Waitress gave descriptions...", "tire tracks...", "Prior offenses involving violence.".

I tell him to calm down and set out to the police station, taking the bus; if they found tire tracks, coming in the car that has made those tire tracks sounds way too stupid.

On my way there Jenny calls me in half panic half rage:

"Mike's dead! They say Jeff killed him! Oh my God! Say something you asshole!" She is crying a bit, but mostly she is angry, I think.

"What can I say, babe? Jeff didn't do it, they are wrong."

"What the fuck?!!" She is screaming and straining the loud-speaker on my phone, "If he did it I want you to kill him! Mike was such a nice guy..." Now she's calming down again, memories of the fallen curbing her anger, hopefully not memories of love. "He never once treated me bad, he was so shy..." I don't like where this is going, so I say I have to go and hang up, I'm almost there anyway.

It's the same station where they had Jimmy locked up, a big brick house built in the fifties and renovated once in the eighties, there is a grotesque above the door we used to say was the first Chief of Police in town. I inquire about Jeff and they say I can't see him yet, he's being interrogated for murder in the second degree, whatever that is. I explain I was his phone call and that he has no family, and I just want to see he's okay.

They put me in someone's office and tell me to wait a moment, a cute cop, the one I saw last time, offers me coffee and I take it. After a moment a fat guy in a suit walks into the room and starts asking me questions, "Where were you two nights ago?", "How do you know Mr. Hunter?", "Has he ever shown signs of violence around you, or indication to drug connections?".

I stick to a version of the truth that won't get me a seat next to Jeff, and try to get the cop to let me see Jeff. When all his questions have at least been given a response if not an answer, he takes me to the interrogation room.

Jeff is handcuffed to the chair and is kind of wobbling from side to side, spittle is coming from the side of his mouth. I look at the fat cop and tell him we used to do stuff like that in the desert when we didn't get any answers.

"He tried to bite off officer Macintyre's ear, we had to restrain him and taser him." Jeff, you moron, but hey, right on, pigs don't really need ears, do they?

"Jeff, come one, you're not a violent person, you couldn't beat up anybody, right? Remember, you only met Mike for a second, then we left after giving him a ride somewhere, right? Remember?" I improvise an alibi, I go at it for several minutes, try to "remind" him what "happened". Every once in a while he groans and grunts a yes, or a right, and slowly, he get control over his mouth back and starts talking to me.

He tells me how they offered him a deal, his daughter. They will trace her, if it is a her, he still just assumes that and they went with it. Slowly I realize, he is going to confess just to see his daughter, who might be a son.

He is jumping on the judicial grenade for me.

Wow.

"I want to see my daughter."

"You don't know it's a girl."

"Then I want to see my son."

And that was that. I leave the station more than a bit bewildered, like there is a ringing in my ear after a grenade went off. I start walking as far away from the station as I can before my heart explodes. Fuck it, I keep walking to Northface Park, another mile or so and sit on a bench at the east side of it, directly in front of where I first met up with Jake and his two Crack producers.

I light a joint and try to relax, only now I realize how relieved I am that this whole thing is being blamed on someone else, and that he is walking into it happy as a... Well, maybe happy isn't the word for it, resigned.

My phone rings.

"You fuck-wad! Don't you see I'm having a crisis here!! You hang up on me! You son of a bitch!!" It's Jenny, it sounds like she's on Speed or something, maybe she is, though, last time she took Speed she just act like well, a fast Jenny.

"Yeah, I know, I just wanted to give you some time to cool off, not much I can do anyway, right?"

"You could listen to me." Laconic and true.

"Sorry, I went to see Jeff, I was his one phone call, figured I owed him a visit. He didn't do it, but he confessed anyway, they're gonna help him find his kid in exchange for a confession, or something like that."

"Please, he probably feels guilty, the little ass-wipe. Don't you know they don't give you that kind of deal for confessions? My dad's a lawyer, I heard of some deals, and this is a deal for a squealer, a snitch. A rat." We both go quiet, I can hear my joint burning in my hand.

"You think he's a rat?"

"I'm telling you, they threaten him with murder charges, and he goes spilling SOMEONE's beans." She sounds like the way Joanna used to talk about her.

"I'm going to work, make sure everyone know we're still in business and that Mr. De Silva hasn't hired some Mexicans to finish the job, okay? I'll come by in the evening." I send her a phone kiss and she hangs up, passive-aggressively signaling her displeasure.

At work everybody asks where Jeff is, and seeing as they are going to see it in the paper or news anyways, I tell them the truth, the one he and I agreed on. It's kind of like those scenes from cheap TV-movies from the nineties, the chief giving the inspirational speech to the troops, telling them how they are all going to move on, to get through this; even if he has no clue as to the reality of his words.

At five Mr. De Silva comes home and immediately guns for me as I say goodbye to the guys and put the tools away, looking forward to an evening of hanging out with Jenny and her fine quality Junk.

"Arrested? I'm employing criminals?" He gets right to the point, I can at least appreciate that.

"Yes and no. He got arrested, but it's bogus, Jeff is a stand up citizen."

"Bull-crap, I know you're all on drugs, yeah, I know." He's sharp, me and Jeff knew this, but we didn't think he'd notice that, not to mention talking about it. "I can smell the pot on all of you." Oh, he meant pot... Well, woopty doo, weed... If only you knew...

"That's just some of the guys, and only after work, Jeff is cool. Besides, the charges are of assault, and yeah, he didn't do anything."

"You can all fuck off until I see he's been released and all charges cleared. I don't want even the place I shit in to have anything to do with criminals. Here's the money I owe you, now fuck off." He hands me a wad of cash, hundreds and fifties, mostly. It's supposed to be everything for the work already done; I guess we're fired. It isn't as bad as I thought it might have been. De Silva's accent lends itself so well to drama, and so does his consistently half-open buttoned shirt, in either pale green or sky blue, but I rather just pick up my things and head off to Jenny's than to stick around and hope for hi to change his mind and go on with his self-righteous tirade.

I set aside what we need to pay the guys, a total of one thousand three hundred and seven dollars, and count our profit, four hundred sixty each, me and Jeff. We've worked for four weeks like damn mules, and all that for four hundred dollars? God damn it. Jenny makes that much selling in an hour.

I drive over to her after calling all of the guys telling them to meet me next day to collect their pay, I need something to forget this mess, and Jenny has just the thing.

At her place we smoke in silence for a while, her apartment smells of pizza this time, and mango for some reason. We're on the bed this time, just sitting there smoking, her bedroom is a very clean kind of messy. Things pile up in some kind of thematic order, clothes, food packaging, stuff thrown in anger, dirty tissues, underwear, used up needles and lighters.

About half an hour goes by and we don't say a word, she sits on one end of the bed, leaning on her pillows, and I am sitting at the ledge, not really facing her, just in an over-the-shoulder kind of way. Finally she comes over to me and wraps her arms around me.

"I miss Mike."

"I know, babe, everyone misses someone when they lose them." I turn to her and hug her, putting her head on my chest. "Were you too close?"

"kind of, he was sweet. The only one out there that was kind of like you. He didn't touch me, or at least always waited for... I don't know, permission? Yeah... something like that. He was kind of like a teenage boy, you know? Super-excited by a kiss." Stop telling me about him touching you, or kissing you, he's dead, I'm here.

"Sweet teenage boy on Meth." I think I am allowed to remind her that.

"Stop being an asshole."

"Sorry."

"let's smoke one for Mike."

"Okay." She then takes out a pipe, a really small one, like what I have for Smack, but she takes Meth and puts it in.

"Ahh... Not what I meant.

"This was his favorite, he gave me this pipe, and the content, so we are smoking it for him. Smoke it." How the hell did that happen? How did I get to be forced to smoke Meth? No.

"No."

"Then fuck off." She starts smoking. It smells almost like Crack, but odder, like cough medicine on Crack. "Are you taking it or not?" In her own special way, it is like she is letting me in on something, a gesture that can kill you; everything needs to have an edge to it when you're numbing your mind as a recreational activity. I see she isn't backing down, so I take a puff or two, it's not that bad, actually. It tastes of some kind of rancid air, like if you leave mold to fester in your room for too long, but the effect is like Crack, but much stronger, direct.

She takes another puff as well and starts smiling, like she's teasing me.

"You took Me-e-eth...... Haha, got you!" It's like she just won something, a kid's game of catch, or hop-scotch. Her smile is different this way, very different from the way she smile in the café when I told her I love her for the first time, when I told anyone I love her for the first time. Now, she is smiling like it isn't her, like someone else is smiling through her. We start to feel a bit misty, like we're floating to each other.

"Not so bad, is it? Not as strong as Junk, but you know, it's a different kind of kick." She's talking, I know that, I just can't tell from where exactly.

"You're funny, where's that from Johnny? Sounds like some-thing they made us read in school." I don't remember having spoken just now, but she seems to be responding to something I said. I start thinking of King Lear for some reason, then I find myself quoting Shakespeare to her, then it gets even weirder.

"Shall I compare thee to a summer's day?
You wouldn't listen anyway...
Words and metaphors are fluid in your eyes
You don't see my surprise
When it all falls short before the crass
acts of fools referring only to your "ass"
You'd mock and scorn and jeer
You'd call them stupid and queer.
But I have no interest in you
for you have already forgotten
for you the heart is through
And you remain a version rotten
of a nostalgic world of words
One I never lived in but miss nonetheless."

I have no idea where that came from, but it sounded good so I write it down before I forget it.

"Wow, that was kind of beautiful, like a poem. Wait, fuck you, I'm rotten?" I don't even listen to her now, I just keep writing, another poem or two, at some point she gives up on talking to me and smokes some more Meth, I stay on the floor and write.

At some point I must have fallen asleep, because I wake up in the morning, it's almost time to meet everyone from work and give them their money, which is at my place, so I have to get there, fast. Jenny isn't home, she left a note next to me on the floor.

"Dear Johnny,
Sorry for getting mad at your poems, they were really nice when

I read them again, not high (too early in the morning for Junk or Meth, right?), I'm off to "work", might be back at around 1 for something to eat. Enjoy your day, babe.

Yours, Jenny."

"Yours"

She is mine.

She admitted it now, it wasn't just sex, it wasn't just getting high together, she said "Yours".

On the bed are some papers, my poems, I guess, it's all in my bad handwriting, well, my Meth handwriting; my Junk handwriting is also horrible, my Crack handwriting is better than my sober handwriting. My sober handwriting is not messy, just small, like I had written it properly and then compressed every letter together to make more space on the paper.

I gather everything and leave, getting into the car and trying to get home less than ten minutes behind schedule.

When I get there, Mr. De Silva is speaking to Jeff enthusiastically, while all our guys take turns shaking hands with Jeff, I just pull up and can't stop staring at Jeff.

"It was all a show, man, they said they can't find her, and seeing as they had no evidence, they had to cut me loose, so fuck them."

"Damn straight, young man! Those pigs..." That's Mr. De Silva, he's shaking his head and holding onto Jeff's shoulder. If there is one thing Mr. De Silva hates more than criminals, it's the cops. "I knew you were innocent, Jeff, hombre, I knew it, and that you come to work the next day... wow, man. Take the day off, let your boys get things done."

I agree with Mr. De Silva and let Jeff go home after giving him his cut of what Mr. De Silva gave me yesterday, some spending money.

Me and the boys labor all day, during our breaks I read what I've written last night, it's mostly twisted shit.

"A marionette with but one string.
Tied down inanimate
with no puppeteer him to celebrate.
A string to the chest, and an eternal frown.
Jumping as he saw you, and right again he flopped back down.
Arms are stale, eyes that are so long faded.
Pull the string of my heart again, and see an old and tired existence elated."

That's the only good one I find, there are others with potential, but nothing I'd let anyone but myself and Jenny see.

After work I drive over to Jeff's but he doesn't answer the doorbell, so I ring his neighbor's bell, Ms. Levine, she's an old Jewish lady from Germany, but after the war and all, always talks about how Germans are better than Americans, but she's harmless and has Jeff's extra key.

"Sure thing, honey, I'll get Jeff's key, hold on." She disappears back into her musty apartment, which ironically enough smells like a Meth-Lab, I guess.

"Here" She hands me the key. "You know, in Berlin, we never even locked the doors! We trusted one another... Yes, one break-in in the whole neighborhood in sixteen years. So much crime here. Is Jeff in trouble? The police brought him home today."

I try to reassure her but slide away at a step-per-word kind of way, retreating towards her neighbor across the hall: Jeff.

I open the door and Jeff is right there hanging. Literally, hanging.

He is somewhere between blue and gray, slightly swinging on

the rope, good quality rope for lifting cargo of up to four tons. He's still in his work clothes, even the stains from this morning's coffee are there, everything is the same, just colder. I fall. I fall to the ground and run to Jeff's bathroom to throw up, then leave. I come back, yes, I saw the note, it was in his hand:

To whomever it may concern,

My name is Jeff Hunter, I am a drug addict, I am an unlicensed contractor, I have one conviction for aggravated assault, but six years ago I did one good thing: I made a baby. I did not know what happened to the baby because the mother, Tammy Jensen, was also a drug addict, and becoming pregnant made her turn herself to the authorities for help. For six years I looked for my baby, I just knew it was a daughter, but in vain. Yesterday, I was arrested for the suspicion of murder, the police offered me to find my daughter in exchange for either a confession, or giving up the culprit; I agreed. The police found my daughter, yes, I was right, daughter, Samantha, they told me she was born in Albany, Georgia, and buried in Atlanta. She died at nine months because Tammy relapsed and forgot about her. She died because she didn't have a father to look out for her. The police probably knew that from the first moment, they have those computers, right? They used this to get information, and I can't give them the satisfaction, so I retracted my statement, and I do so here as well. I AM NOT INVOLVED IN THE DEATH OF MICHAEL POPE. I met him for a transaction of illegal narcotics, but there was no violence, so fuck you, pigs. Now, killing myself will be so much easier, at home and not in a prison cell. I have nothing left, I failed my daughter completely. Bye now.
    ACAB, Jeff Hunter.

Jeff has a beautiful handwriting.

I need to call someone, not Ms. Levine. I call Jenny first, I don't know why.

"Jeff is dead." There is nothing on the line, not even breathing. "Jenny, are you there? Jeff is dead."

"Did you do it?" She's on Meth, I can tell. I can smell it on her voice.

"No, he did it."

"You mean he killed Mike?"

"No, listen! He killed himself." It's quiet again.

"Did he leave a note? Did he say anything about killing Mike?"

"Aren't you listening? My friend, Jeff, hung himself!"

"Well, I didn't know Jeff so well, and I want to make sure... you know."

"Whatever."

"Are the cops there yet?"

"No... I called you first."

"Why? Call 911!"

"I wanted you to calm me down. Never mind." I hang up and call 911, the operator asks "What is your emergency?" and I tell her everything, from the moment Jeff was arrested to now, she must be so confused.

I light a cigarette and wait for the cops to arrive. The rope Jeff is hanging by is creaking and making strange stretching sounds as Jeff swings in the evening breeze. I consider letting Ms. Levine in when she knocks to ask if she could have her key back, but the sight of the young man hanging in the hallway might kill her, so I tell her to wait a few more minutes; this is when I see the police lights in the street. They're here.

Within a minute or two the apartment is occupied by people in uniform, civilian clothing with a badge as a belt buckle, or guys with "Coroner's office" on the back of their jackets; they move and prod Jeff's body, take pictures and wait for some kind of "all green" from the cops to take Jeff away. The cops are also taking pictures, looking under stuff, in stuff, over stuff, behind stuff. Looking for stuff.

Finally a young cop in uniform comes over to me with a notepad. He looks like that guy from that movie, "The Untouchables", not Sean Connery, the other one.

"Hello sir, are you the one that made the 911 call?" Kevin Costner, that's who he reminds me of.

"Did anyone ever tell you that you look like Kevin Costner when he was young?"

"Uhhm… yeah, sir, did you make the call?"

"Yes. Yes, I did, I found him."

"How did you get into the apartment, sir?"

"It was a great movie, Sean Connery was a real bad-ass in it."

"Sir?"

"Ms. Levine from across the hall has a spare key, I lent it from her to come see Jeff."

"okay, what's your name, sir?"

"Johnny."

"You have a last name, Johnny?"

"Milaowic."

"Okay Mr. Milaowic, I know this is hard for you, but I'm going to have to ask you a few questions."

"Death is always hard." He nods his consent. "especially when it's pointless."

"Sir, did… uhh…" He checks his notes for the name. "Mr. Hunter mention anything prior to his death about regretting something? Maybe a Mike, or Michael?" I can't believe it, they are still fishing about that asshole Mike when Jeff's dead body is hanging right in front of them!

"Who? Who gives a fuck?!"

"Sir, calm down. As you probably know, Mr. Hunter was a suspect in a murder case."

"Fuck you! Fuck all of you!" I get up and point to every cop, telling them off, I leave out the Coroner's Office guys; they are just here to take care of the body.

"Sir, I need you to calm down and take a seat." I sit back down, no use getting myself into trouble.

Another, older cop, the one I met while visiting Jeff in lock-up, walks over and pulls the young cop away so that he stands in front of me.

"Hello Mr. Milaowic, I remember you, you came to visit Mr. Hunter at the station." He starts off all smug, but slowly, his voice becomes more and more sympathetic; cop trick. "How about we drive over there now, huh? Talk this over away from the smell of death, okay? Give you a chance to gather yourself. You can follow us in your own car."

After the drive I am shown in, all courtesy in the cops' eyes now. I get seated in a big chair in a tiny room, the walls a khaki or shit color, the door is puss green. The table is a colorless kind of mass that is either plastic or metal, I can't tell.

The old cop comes back in with two cups of coffee, one a normal mug and the other is those little brown plastic ones you get from any vending machine; he hands me that one.

"Describe your relationship with Mr. Hunter." He looks a suspicious kind of indifferent, the kind of indifferent that should make you uncomfortable enough to be afraid, but comfortable enough to talk.

"We worked together, we were friends."

"Worked together as unlicensed contractors?"

"Yes... ahhmm..."

"Don't worry, I'm not the IRS." He smiles a bit.

"Come on, we just try to get by, you know the market." The magic excuse, again.

"Yes, I do. When did you see Mr. Hunter last."

"Hanging from the ceiling."

"Before that, I mean. Last time you saw him alive?"

"This morning, he came to work, looked happy about something."

"That is common, he had already made his decision." He doesn't even sound apologetic. "And were you with him on the night Mr. Pope was attacked?"

"No, I mean yes, we met Mike at the café, picked him up, drove with him to the Cunt-de-Suc, Jeff and Mike talked and exchanged something, I waited in the car."

"So the tire tracks, they are from your vehicle?"

"I suppose." Who gives a fuck? I am here about Jeff, and the pigs' involvement in his death.

"You waited in the car, you say... We found spittle on Mr. Pope, it did not match to Mr. Hunter's, would you object to a test?"

"What?"

"Will you voluntarily do a test to see if your spittle matches the spittle found on Mr. Pope, probably being the spittle of his assailant, or do I need to go get a court order?"

"What? What does this have to do with anything? I am here about Jeff! He's dead because you guys gave him a dead daughter!" I start breathing fast; I have to get out of here.

"Calm down, Mr. Milaowic, this isn't helping." He's so calm, like he's watching me on TV.

"Fuck you! I want out of here! I want to go home."

"You're free to go, you are not here as a suspect of anything,

111

yet, but you know... Your name is tossed about the station, I know, for instance, that you are involved with former Daddy's Girl Ms. Jenny Cohen, or with high-school-dropout Jake Cole. It's not that far of a stretch to assume you know they are both drug dealers, and that you are a client. I can arrest you right now for involvement in drug distribution, but I don't, I don't give a fuck what you and your junky girlfriend do" Don't hit him, Don't hit him, Don't hit him, Don't hit him. "I'm just trying to figure out what happened to Mr. Pope and Mr. Hunter."

"You killed him! You bastards promised him things and gave him nothing!" I start hyperventilating, but feel like I'm not getting air at all. "You just wanted a confession, that's it! Wrap up the case!" I sort of start sobbing, maybe that way they'd let me go, I have to get out of here. "You killed my friend." God, that sentence tastes familiar.

"Sir, I have no idea what you're talking about." Smug asshole.

"Let me out of here!! Fuck you! I can't breathe... I"

I wake up in a room, next to a desk, it's an office with lots of books and an old looking computer under the desk with fans that make more noise than the sirens outside. There's a woman to my right, checking my pulse. She's short, a bit chubby and blond, wearing a crisp white shirt with a little red cross on it. I keep staring at the little red cross, I don't know why. Then I jump. I duck for cover, and reach for my gun, but it isn't there, I can't even find my tool-box. The lady with the red cross gets up and walks over to me, saying something, but I can't hear her; the first Hummer's been hit, it's on fire and there's some secondaries from the ammo. Someone from Second Battalion is yelling something, and there's a lot of shouting in Arabic "Katalahum! Katalahum!" The lady keeps talking, but a grenade explodes close by so I can't hear her. I reach for my gun; it isn't there. I roll away from the body, some second battalion boy, faced down in the sand. My heart is racing, they have us surrounded, I reach for my gun; it isn't there. The lady with the little red cross takes out a syringe, I start calming down. The shouting stops. She injects me with something. I come back into a real sleep.

I wake up in a smaller room, a snotty green room with a coffee machine and a fridge. Two uniformed cops are there, having a coffee and eating some kind of pastry. I'm the subject of their conversation.

"I'm telling 'ya, he's fucked in the head or something."

"Then send him packing, I have enough shit on my plate."

"Since when do you use plates, you fucking pig? Look at yer' shirt!" Cop B has mustard on his uniform shit, as well as a little stain on his pants that was not yet mentioned.

"Did he knock someone around?"

"Na, lost it in an interview, passed out, woke up in the lieutenant's office and had another fit, medic said it was a flashback. Now, get this, LT checked, he's a vet."

"What, like an animal doctor?"

"No, dumbass, V E T E R A N. He was in Iraq or some such shit."

"Ohh, we should cut him loose."

"When he wakes up he gets a coffee, a Danish, and a goodbye. LT's orders." Sounds fair, I'm starving.

"I take my coffee with three sugars." I decided to announce the end of my 'stupor'.

"Holy crap!" They both kind of jump up. "Don't do that, you little fuck. You scared me shitless." The fat one, cop B looks like he has just had a heart attack.

"Sorry. And a Danish, I'm starving."

After my little midnight snack they send me home, the sun is coming up as I pull into my spot and park.

The inside of the apartment smells of ten days old soda, yes, it's a familiar and distinct smell to me. I sit on the bed twenty two seconds before I decide to tap into my "emergency stash". Mine is hidden outside, in the creepiest garden-gnome I've ever seen. I hid it there because when I came back home from a party, jacked up on Speed and Acid, that gnome was the only thing I remembered from the walk home, so I thought I'd never forget it, no matter how fucked I am, I will always remember that gnome. I actually stole it from Mr. and Mrs. O'Shane's yard and cut a hole in it, put in some Junk and closed it back up, and presto! An emergency stash.

So I go outside to Mr. and Mrs. O'Shane's yard and look for the gnome; it isn't there! In its place is some stupid looking smiling gnome with a stupid blue pointy-hat. That is not the right gnome! It's smiling at some untold, bad joke, like it knows something I don't. I kick it several times and go around the garden ten times in hope that the gnome was simply put elsewhere, but it's gone. They probably threw it away, fucking Irish retards.

I go back indoors and light a joint to relax and help me think straight. I know what to do. I get into the car and drive over to Jenny's, she can be my new emergency stash; she'll give me what I want, she'll do it, she cares.

Her lights are out even though there's barely enough light to see outside. I ring the bell and wait for a few minutes before ringing again, no answer. I jimmy the lock and get through the front door and start climbing the stairs; at her door I stop and wait, after a few minutes I knock and wait again; not a sound from the inside. Do I keep waiting? Fuck! Why can't she hear me knock? I don't want to wake her and piss her off, should I break in? She wouldn't mind.

I pick her lock, it's really cheap and a bit rusty, but I get it to open after a few minutes.

It's still dark inside, the TV light is blinking a bit, but other than that I can't see a thing so I turn on the light. The living room is cleaner than it was last time; only the ashtray on the table is still messy and full. I go into the bathroom and take Jenny's stash from behind the mirror; she has tons left over and some fresh needles. I get to work and prepare everything in the living-room, within seconds I make my escape, all is well.

I don't have to think anymore, my flashes are gone, the soldiers are gone, the militants are gone, there's only me and the Junk, only me and myself, only me and my peace, only me. I don't need to be afraid; it's all in my head, none of it is real, the soldiers, the militants; this joy, everything, life, it's all in my head. I can make my own version of reality as long as I have Junk running through me. There were no cops, there was no hanging, no dead daughters. Jeff is at home, asleep, waiting to go to work and improvise solid-looking toilets to some guy's house.

"Johnny? You scared the shit out of me!" There's a voice coming through the fog in my head, I don't really care. "Johnny, hello!!!!!" I am being shaken a bit, but I don't really care. "Is that my Junk? You selfish asshole! Who said you can use it! You owe me eighty bucks! How the fuck did you get it?"

"I think I broke in." I get my voice started.

"What? This is my home! Mine!!" I don't care.

She is prying into my pockets and looking for money. Of course she finds my wallet and takes some bills out of it. I don't really care.

"Fuck you." She's going somewhere.

"Jeff is dead."

"I know, you told me." She's in the kitchen.

"He hung himself."

"And that means you're allowed to break into my house?"

"His daughter is dead too." I can't feel myself.

She isn't saying anything. I can hear something getting hot, on the verge of boiling, probably coming from her coffee maker.

"I was at the station, they wanted to pin that thing with Mike on Jeff, but I didn't let them; he didn't do it."

"How do we KNOW that?" She's sitting next to me with a cup of coffee, preparing a hit for herself while drinking. "I mean, he's been at it for longer than we have; who knows what's he REALLY like."

"He's dead, isn't that enough?"

"Yeah, but really, you can't KNOW he didn't kill Mike."

"How about some loyalty? He was one of us!"

"And Mike was MY friend, he was sweet, and he cared about me."

"He was a fucking Meth-head." She slaps me a bit.

"Don't call us that. Fuck you."

"Jeff didn't do it, I did." I feel good; confessing feels good, showing her what I think of her Meth-head friend feels amazing!

She's yelling, hitting me, I think. I just stare ahead and think of Jeff's letter. I realize at some point I'm outside her apartment, but I can't tell if I got tired of her yelling and hitting or if she managed to get me out herself. I'm sitting on the floor two stories below her apartment, judging by the numbers on the doors, and leaning against the wall, surrounded by shattered glass.

There's a kid, a girl, about seven years old I think, she's standing in front of me while chewing on something.

"Are you okay, mister?" She's kind of sweet, but I can't help but stare at her teeth; they kind of bulge.

"Yeah, I think I fell."

"That girl from upstairs was yelling at you a lot."

"Yeah, she's mad at me for some reason." I finally start to slowly stand up and realize my legs hurt.

"Mom says she needs Jesus. That she's bad and that I'm not allowed to talk to her."

"Your mom is wrong, Jenny's a good person, she just makes a mistake here and there." I get the last of the glass shards out of my clothes, they always get stuck in the folds, hiding there until you throw the clothes on the floor so they could later on dig into your feet when you step on them.

"She gave me some candy once, and a pretty ring, see?" She shows me a little ring on her index finger, it's pink plastic and has a little picture of Jessica Rabbit on it instead of some precious gem.

"That's nice." I check my pockets to see if I left anything at Jenny's place, which I didn't so I start going down the stairs.

"Are you going?"

"Yes, I have to be at work."

"Okay." She scampers back down the hall and behind the door.

I get into the car and readjust the mirrors. It seems like every time I get into the car the mirrors are different from how I had them earlier. Either that or I am constantly shrinking, growing, and becoming cross-eyed.

I drive over to de Silva's house and most of the guys are already there, several might be inside, actually. Luckily, Mr. de Silva himself isn't around, so I just sink into whatever work my arms allow me to sink into, mostly though, I just check to see that everyone is doing something useful, and doing it right, well, besides me. At lunch we stop and I decide it's a good a time as any to tell the guys that Jeff is dead.

I gather them in Mr. de Silva's kitchen, which is quite large, and has lots of chairs for us, and give them the news. Most look sad, one guy even looks upset, but none actually know what to say. After a minute or two that no one says anything I realize I'm still talking, that I just haven't given them the opportunity to speak. I give up on realizing what I'm talking about and go on with my speech on auto-pilot, only paying attention insomuch as to make sure I don't digress into something too irrelevant.

"That's it guys, I'm going to give you a minute to let it all sink in, but... yeah. Jeff's gone, I'm in charge, and we ARE going to finish this job, get paid and see what happens, because Jeff promised we'd finish, got it?" No, I didn't copy some 'let's do it for Private Bla Bla' speech, I really don't want to break Jeff's word. I mean, what does he have left? Confession or not, he's going to be forever associated with that Mike guy's death, even though he didn't do it.

After work I try to call Jenny, but she won't pick up, probably still mad. I was hoping we could work it out over a hit, it's not like I meant to kill Mike, it isn't my fault he died, why isn't anyone arresting the doctors for... for being shit doctors? Couldn't they patch him up from a little beat-down? Isn't that Negligence or something?

I go home and wish I still had my emergency stash, but lacking that, I find some weed I had left over from last week and smoke a bit to relax. After an hour or so, and halfway through Disney's Lion King I give up on Jenny calling me back, so I bite the bullet and call her again, when she doesn't answer I decide to bite an even bigger bullet and call Jake.

"What?"

"Hello to you too, dipshit."

"What?"

"Have you talked to Jenny today?"

"Yeah, I did."

"Is she okay?"

"She is now."

"What do you mean?"

"Not your fucking business."

"What did you do?"

"Fucked her."

"Fuck you! She wouldn't do that, or you for that matter."

"Well, she did, so screw you."

"If you're lying, I'll kill you." If he's telling the truth I'd do that same.

"Fine, fine, fine, I didn't. But fuck you anyway." I can hear, or feel, he's about to hang up.

"Wait! I need something."

"Of course, why else would you call." He sounds smug, like Hannibal Smith with the cigar in his mouth.

"Come on, I am still a costumer, right? Not a friend, okay, but... a costumer?" I hate being this pathetic, this needy, but Jenny won't pick up, James is out, and Jimmy's in the wind.

"You're the most unreliable person I've ever met Johnny, give me a reason."

"I have money."

"So do I."

"Come on, man, help me out."

"Fine, you can get some of my... help. Meet me.... at your old vending area." He means the library. "in about two hours, okay?

119

And bring a decent amount of cash."

"Sure, no problem, thanks, I owe you."

"Yeah, you do. Oh, and I did talk to Jenny, when she was able to talk at least; I don't know what you did to her, but she is deep in it, man, won't even let herself come down." At least she didn't tell him.

"Yeah, I fucked up again."

"Doing what comes natural, see you." He hangs up.

I try to wallow my time by reading something, I have some old books my mom's uncle gave me, some of them were borrowed from the library of Boston in 1850 and simply never returned. The one I like best is a collection of short stories called "12 Short Stories", and is a translation from German. No, I haven't read all of them just yet, and in fact, I'm not really reading it right now, I just enjoy holding something this old and grounded in my hand, that's all. Eventually I get bored and watch some more TV; there's a documentary about Hitler's grooming habits and love of jazz, I turn it off half way through an interview with some would-be expert.

When it's time to leave I head for the library, it's nice and sunny out so I walk. My feet are kind of shaking though, so I end up taking the bus. Jake is already there waiting, and he looks as smug as he sounded which pisses me off again. I get off the bus and light a joint, trying to play it cool, but it really is just downplaying the symptoms.

"Look what the cat shat and dragged in." He is a real jerk sometimes.

"Fuck you." I take one big drag and offer Jake the joint, he takes it and gives me a mock salute with it.

"So, can I buy off you?"

"Sure, if you have money."

"Yeah, hold on." I dig in my pockets and show a nice little wad of bills, the ones visible are fifties, but there are other denominations as well, it gives the illusion of being a lot, though. "I don't need a lot, just to last me until Jenny cools off." He's making a strange face at that, a bit uncomfortable looking.

"That might be more than you think, though, big J..."

"Fine, give me... three grams."

"Fuck, man. You stacking up for the apocalypse?" He starts laughing.

"Fine, fine... How about... one and a half?"

"More reasonable." He reaches into his pocket and takes out a small scale and two bags, weighs one and a half grams and give me the bag. I briefly think of running with it, but for old time's sake I give him the money.

"Good, all done and said. Hey, I heard about Jeff, man. That you found him and all." I don't know what's his angle, but I don't like the way this is going.

"He was already dead."

"Yeah, I know. The police took you for questioning?"

"Yeah, but I faked a seizure so they cut me loose."

"Ah... Good thinking."

"I wasn't going to say anything." I think I have an idea on how to get more from him for free. "You know, they did mention you." That got his attention.

"Oh?" I can see him getting real tense, wondering if I was the one who brought up his name.

"Yeah, the one who questioned me said something." I try to give him a wily smile, like George Clooney in that movie, pretending to be the Man with the Plan.

"What'd he say?" He's getting a bit aggressive, his chest is all pumped up, it's becoming obvious even with all he's got on that he's been working out.

"Can't remember."

"Trying to shake me down is not a good idea, Johnny." I remember his little intimidation routine, still the same from school. First the whole standing around like Stallone, then the hints, next he's going to 'narrow' the space between us.

"This isn't a shakedown; I'm trying to help you."

"Then just say it." The chest is deflating, the tone is back to normal.

"I'm just looking for some gratitude first." That came out a little too much on the pathetic side.

"Ohh... So that's the reason for the 'Memory Lapse', I see now." He takes out some money.

"Nahh... I just thought, you know... cut the middle man..." I can taste it.

"Fine, here's another half gram, now out with it." I tell him what the detective said, and make some stuff up to make it sound like it was worth half a gram of Junk, and then I hurry to leave.

Back home I take one hit, a small one. I take my phone and dial Jenny's number again for the millionth time, no answer. I don't know any of her Meth-head friends so I can't call anyone and ask, only Jake, and he's just her supplier. I try to stave off the nausea by staying still, Jake's stuff is shit and wears off too quickly. He still sells the bad stuff to 'normal people', even friends and old partners. On the other hand, I have to admit, he looked like he's doing well; nice jacket, despite the heat, fine ironed pants, a nice shirt, Armani sunglasses... Dickhead's got money.

Seeing that staying still isn't helping I head for the bathroom, preparing to throw up, but after ten minutes nothing comes, so I got to the kitchenette and heat up a pie and drink a beer.

My pie is done and I can start eating, I feel like I haven't eaten in days. It's one of those pre-made frozen cherry pies you can get anywhere, so it's not that great, in fact, it falls apart before the fork actually touches it. That makes a poor combination with beer too, so I end up throwing away half the pie and have another beer instead of eating.

Out of boredom, emptiness, or simply habit, I take another hit, also small. It usually isn't a good idea to have multiple hits on one day, but I'm glad I did, it gave me a brilliant idea.

I am going to get Jenny to forgive me, I get to the phone and call The Crier, our local newspaper, and tell them I want to make an obituary. The lady on the line, Amanda, takes down my obituary and tells me where to transfer the money to, which I do online within a few minutes. I spend the next two hours trying to fall asleep, already imagining Jenny forgiving me.

The next day comes, I had to help it out by taking some Ketamine I had left from a party last year, but here is the new day. I drive to work and get it over with as soon as possible.

When I can finally get away, at lunch break, I head out to Jenny's picking up a copy of The Crier on the way. I wait outside until someone goes into the building and just walk in after them and up the stairs I go. When I get to her door slide the paper under it, open on the obituaries page. And now I wait. I can hear movement from inside, something being lifted off the ground, paper being folded and crackling around as fingers run on it.

"What the fuck is this?" Well, at least she's talking to me.

"It's my way of saying 'Sorry'." There's a long silence, and then,

"Fuck off! I hate you."

"Have you read it?"

"I don't want to."

"Please." There's another long silence.

"This doesn't make up for anything."

"I know, but it's something." She finally opens the door. She's standing there with a tank-top and shorts, no makeup, and flip-flops. Her skin looks almost scaly around the eyes and her lips are cracked in places, I can see the small mole under her chin, the one she's been hiding for a while with aggressive application of makeup.

"So you wrote him an obituary, big fucking deal."

"Not just, it's more than that; it's unique, not the usual little 'bla bla, will be missed, bla bla'." I take the paper and read out my obituary for Mike.

"Senseless fate of ours, senseless death of thine,
Kind heart so young taken, trust, your only crime.
They cry for you still, those you loved and left behind,
They love you still, you see? You never really left their mind.
A young girl is crying, wondering where you are,
She looks but finds no comfort, with you gone so far.
Tell her you are better, tell her you found peace,
Tell her to find comfort, in a lover's kiss."

I wasn't expecting anything dramatic, for her to fall into my arms or kiss me... I just thought it would somehow make things better... It sounded, no, felt better in my head. Now I am standing here in the hallway like an idiot holding a fifth-rate newspaper in my hand looking pleadingly at the woman I love. Shit.

She isn't looking as aggressively at me as earlier, I think she is just as confused as I am. I have to be the first to speak.

"What do you think?"

"I told you, big fucking deal."

"I spent an hour coming up with that." Not pathetic at all Johnny, well done.

"You should get out more." Wait... was that a joke? She's

grinning... does that mean I'm in on the joke and not just the subject of it?

"Probably..." I try to smile at her, but I think it's too transparent of a smile, too eager, so I try to soften it and end up with a face like a Frankenstein movie.

"It was an accident." Still silence. "I know this doesn't fix everything, I just wanted to show you I'm sorry." Still not much of a response, but she is at least paying attention.

"It was stupid, I admit it, but it wasn't really me; the doctors, come on, can't they patch up someone after a bit of a beat-down? They were reckless!" She's looking at me funny, but she isn't sending me away.

"Please." I take her hand, she kind of recoils from me, but I hold tight. "Let me in, let's talk, I am so sorry, I don't want to lose you again."

There are a few tears, maybe hearing me say that finally got her. I try to hug her but she pushed me away. I don't know what else to do so I stand there and wait for her to gather herself. After a moment or two she steps aside in the doorway and signals me to come in. We go into the living room and sit at on the couch. She wipes her nose after finding some tissues under her needle and some lighters.

She basically looks very confused, but I expected that, I didn't expect utter forgiveness 'on the spot'. We sit in silence and alternate from her holding my hand and taking as much distance between us as possible. I roll us a joint when I have both hands free, and let her have the first few drags; she kind of hogs it, but I know better than to complain.

"You look like you haven't eaten in days, come on, I'll make you something."

"There's nothing in the fridge." It speaks! Finally, she reacts.

"Ok, I'll just pop to Philipp's ok? Any requests?"

"Just go."

I head out full speed ahead to Philipp's, on the way I call Bart, one of the guys from work and put him in charge for the day. I feel revitalized, mended in some way.

Philipp himself is at the cash register today, looking quite tired, but it's a Tuesday, so he just did stock, so of course he's tired.

"Hey there Corporal, how is everything?" Yes, I am still Corporal to him.

"Not bad." I place three bags of chips, two instant noodles, one chicken flavored and one pork flavored, and a bottle of rum, the good kind.

"Okay, that'll be twelve dollars fifty please." I pay the man and hurry back to the car.

I get back to Jenny's. She left the door open and she looks like she just used, so no use talking to her now, or feeding her for that matter. I sit next to her and watch TV. Hers is much bigger than mine, it's also not one of those with an extra ten feet of elctro-gizmoes at the back, it's a flat screen, a knock off Toshiba, so a knock off of a knock off. Weeds is on. There are so many shows about drugs these days, somehow, we, Junkies, have become rather popular; granted we are good looking, friendly, and far away. The image of drugs there is rather friendly, "Small Time" Jake would say. I get kind of annoyed so I change the channel to one of those I-couldn't-care less-what-is-on-as-long-as-you-provide-me-with-background-noise-channels.

"Turn it off." She didn't so much say that, more like a grunt and a general noise of displeasure, so I turn off the TV. I start petting her hair, letting her know I'm here. You have to be careful with junkies sometimes; if they come to and not know you're there and catch you asleep or unaware as well they might jump you, or throw up on you.

After a few minutes I get a phone call from Bart. I go to the other room to answer where I wouldn't disturb Jenny in her state; she's happy, let her be.

"What, man?"

"Police came by looking for you, everyone's super nervous." Bart sounds like he's more than a bit on edge too.

"Well, fuck 'em!"

"Yeah, I know, but still." What the hell is he getting at?

"We didn't know where you are, so everyone's suspicious and a bit... you know."

"Scared like a bunch of chicken-shits?" I try to be helpful.

"Wouldn't put it that way... but yeah."

"Tell everyone it's just a follow up, nothing to worry." That sounds like something someone reasonable might say, someone who has their shit together.

"Ok, anything else?" He sounds like a little kid, I hate it when someone you think is confident and independent turns out to be just as confused and lost as I am in life.

"Yeah, get the fuck on with it." I hang up, which isn't as dramatic as I intended it to be on a cellphone, but still, he got the hint, I think.

Back in the living room Jenny is throwing up; it's mostly liquids so I go to the kitchen to cook her lunch. The poor girl barely knows how to take care of herself; it's just one death, she's going to have to learn to deal with that better.

I try to remember my first death.

It was in my first day in Iraq, on the way to meet my CO in my new "home". It wasn't super dramatic... We ran over a civi... it looked like he was a beggar. The medic pronounced him dead, against protocol since only a proper doctor can do that, but it was better than waiting two hours for one. We handed him over to local "police" and kept driving. I don't know what Jenny's problem is; she never even saw the body. I always thought that's the hard part; the lifeless eyes... or even worse, eyeless sockets. But yeah, I can't complain that she is better than me.

The noodles are done, I didn't use the flavor–powder–packet, so it's just noodles. She won't be able to taste it anyway. When you're on Junk, or just coming off, flavor is the last thing your brain has time for, so it all just registers as: Generally Paper Flavored Goop; so don't bother having a steak dinner after a hit.

She eats it half a fork at a time, the other half falling back to the bowel in a splash of colorless soup. I try to feed her but get too much spit, noodles and soup on me, so I let her be. She heaves again, but keeps it down.

And now there is quiet.

Again.

We kind of look at each other, she is looking a bit beyond me, but I can see she is trying. I think we're both trying to find something to say, and I have every intention of winning this arms race.

"Was the food okay?"

"Yeah... thanks Johnny." She's massaging her temples with her eyes closed, making semi circles with her head, trying to recover more and more of herself.

I just sit there and watch her for a moment, I watch her massage her temples, I watch her light a cigarette, I watch her watching me. I can tell she is trying to make some kind of decision, about me, I suppose. To cut me off, to leave me, to forgive me, to turn me in.

She puts out the cigarette and I light one, we both drink from the rum, in turns right out of the bottle.

"Do you swear it was a mistake?" She made a decision.

"Yes, I was just... I don't know. It was stupid."

"It was." We go quiet again and drink."

"I want things to go back to how they were before."

"Before what?" She resumes eating the noodle-soup, but now she looks like she is missing the flavoring packet.

"When we sat at James's and were just having fun, all of us." I lean against her, letting my head drop all the way to her lap, feeling rather vindicated when lets me. "I miss not being the fucked up one." She leans down and kisses my cheek; at least I can invoke pity in her.

"Johnny... You're not that bad." She feeds me some of the noodles, like I was some kind of overgrown baby.

"I miss it when you loved me."

"I miss that too."

"Can you please give me some?" She has enough; let her make a hit for me for once.

"Want to try something new?" She sounds encouraging.

"I don't care." I wait until she finds it under all the crap on her coffee table. I admit to being in the way, which is why it's taking so long; I just don't want to be physically separated from her now.

"It's Morphine, should be good, should be just as good as Junk, but not as dangerous." I let her do it all; finding the vein, injecting the Morphine into it, making sure I don't die of the euphoria that takes me.

It isn't as intense as Junk, but similar. I feel weightless, but the feeling of something dirty, something wrong, travelling up and down my veins, entering my brain and making it blotchy is missing, and that is what I like about Junk. I don't like Morphine, it feels like medicine.

"I like it." I lie to Jenny, though. I think she wants to feel she is taking care of me.

"I'm glad to hear it." She kisses me again on the cheek.

The phone rings in my pocket, but my fingers are unable to grab hold, feeling more like one of those claw-hands rather than a palm. Jenny gets it for me.

"Hello?... No, he's... indisposed. No, he's in the shower." She pets my head as she says this; she always loved us sharing a lie together. "yeah, I'll tell him. Bye now, take care." She hangs up after saying goodbye in her best receptionist-voice.

"That was some guy called Bart, wanted to let you know that other than what he called 'The Thing' the day went smooth." Thank God for that.

"That would be forty dollars please."

"What?"

"For the Morphine." Is she charging me?

"What do you mean?" I get up and look at her, maybe she's kidding.

"I can't afford giveaways, Johnny, so, yeah, we're still... but you're also a costumer and I try to keep... business as clean as possible."

"So every time we are going to get high together you're going to give me a bill?" This is just wrong, I never charged her.

"Not exactly, but for some things, that Columbian stuff was a gift, for instance, but Morphine is hard to get, so it's expensive, and Jake sold me that like... really overpriced, so... I can't give it away."

"So why did you give it to me? You could have given me the regular stuff, damn it." I suddenly get really mad at her, but I keep it down, I know I shouldn't. I should swallow my damn pride. Maybe that is what went wrong all along, my damn pride; a Deadly Sin.

"I thought you'd like it, is all." She's trying to be nice, or she feels sorry for me, that bitch.

"Okay, okay... The money isn't important, here." I put a twenty dollar bill on the table and get up. "I don't have the rest right now, I spent the rest of what I had on the rum and noodles."

"We'll call it even, then." She's putting the money in what looks like a purse; a small little lump of denim and zippers.

"I won't charge you all the time Johnny." I don't really answer, I just wave and leave, it isn't rude per se, but it makes ME feel like I made a statement.

Either she is learning from Jake how to only think of herself or he is really charging her a lot for her merchandise, forcing her to charge me as well. Yeah, that would be it. I get into my car and see the little black girl from before, from when Jenny threw me out. She's standing in the street, with friends, well, other girls, I don't know if they're friends, and they're all smoking.

That kind of pisses me off. I know, I'm not one to judge, but still; why can't kids just be kids anymore?

When I was her age all I cared about was football, or wrestling, or where I could get cheap candy and who isn't talking to whom and why. Smoking was something for adults. Mom told me when I was seven that her friends smoke because their kids ruined their bodies already, so why bother? Took me ages to get it. I caught my brother smoking when he was 11, I was just 15, I beat him up a bit for it, and then told our dad. Our dad made us both watch a video about lung cancer, then had us dissect a lung (pig lung) to "familiarize us with what goes on in there, with what we were destroying."

"Sir?" It's a cop; a black cop is bending over and looking at me through the driver window, tapping it with his night-stick.

"Yes officer?" Trick number one in dealing with cops when

high: #1 be polite, but not lavishly so, just nervous enough to be a law-abiding citizen.

"We got reports of a strange man sitting in a car staring at a group of little girls... What are you doing, sir?" He looks more bored than concerned; I think he knows I'm just pissed off seeing them smoke, he gets it, he has a wedding ring, he probably has a kid or two, he's also troubled about these things.

"They're smoking."

"I see that, sir. I'm going to have to ask you to leave, you're making the parents upset."

"Sure."

I put the car in gear and drive off, going straight home.

I have two messages on the machine, both police; a detective Berger. Judging by the voice it's the fat-ass cop who questioned me, he says I should call him back, and I feel like showing him a more in-control version of me, so I do.

"Hello?"

"Detective Berger? It's John Milaowic, you were looking for me?"

"Ah, yes, Mr. Milaowic, you're still there."

"As opposed to?"

"Oh, I don't know, Kansas? Well, anyway, I was told I should apologize for my...conduct."

"I suppose you were trying to do your job."

"Would you mind coming to the station tomorrow? We still have some questions."

"I need to work."

"You weren't at work today."

"Emergency; my girl was ill."

"Sure... Let's do it at around five, then, you guys usually finish at around four." They've been watching us?

132

"Okay, I'll be there at around five." I hang up, try to remain calm, but end up throwing a soda can against the wall. It kind of explodes and the whole place is probably going to smell of orange soda for weeks.

I light a joint and try to reenact how that bastard roped me into meeting him tomorrow. I can't think of any other way it could have ended, so I try to stop replaying the conversation in my head with slight variations and start projecting how tomorrow's conversation will look like.

I come up empty, but not showing up would be a bad idea, so I try to imagine what Berger might ask, how I could cheat a test if they give me one; I can't go into a police station with cupfuls of someone else's urine or spit. Better just go in like I have nothing to hide.

I turn on the TV, but there's only static, even after I hit it like ten times; still nothing. I open it up from the back, look at every circuit using a flashlight for light. This is the billionth time I had to do this; damn thing keeps breaking. The interior is filled with duct-tape and half-assed soldering everywhere, a piece of cloth is jammed between one circuit and the plastic frame because I figured it needed the pressure to make the connectors actually touch each other. After running through everything I start thinking there is nothing wrong with my Frankenstein-TV, so I put it back together and stop trying. I sit on the empty bed and look for something to do. I decide to read my mail. Not email, actual mail; yes, people still use it, especially law-enforcement and the legal system.

Already the first letter explains the death of my Frankenstein-TV. A letter from the city; they apologize for the inconvenience, but there will be road-works and infrastructure repair that might require disabling some services, like water and cable. Well...

great, no TV.

I leave the rest of the mail to rot; I already have what I wanted. I walk over to the kitchenette when it occurs to me that the letter also mentioned water, so I check to see if I still have that. I do.

After that saving grace I go and take a shower, I still smell like Jenny's vomit which necessitates this.

I have to use my hand soap as everywhere-soap and shampoo, but that just means all of me will smell the same, no separate smell for each part.

After the shower I smoke another joint and decide I need to eat. My fridge is kind of full since I was barely in this week, but to me, that just means I can't decide WHAT I want to eat. Pizza, burrito, chili con carne, chili sine carne (some kind of vegan crap purchased while drunk), Asian-noodle with powdered duck flavor, microwaveable fish-n'-chips, apple pie... The list goes on.

Random selection determines a beef and beans burrito as dinner and I comply with it, and shove the burrito into the microwave. It tastes stale and soggy, but after two joints and almost no food today, it hits the spot.

When I wake up, it's still dawn. The sun is just coming up and I keep trying to go back to sleep, but no such luck. Eventually I get up and make a coffee, having a beer until the kettle boils. I actually have one of those old kettles you have to put on the stove, which could take ages since my stove is electric; I guess that in a way it only means I have a slow ass electric kettle. My mom loves this kettle. She said my family brought it with them from England in the seventeen hundreds, but my dad just shook his head when she said that; her family came from Ireland and Poland, in the nineteenth century (Ireland) and after the Second World War (Poland). My mom loves making up stories, she is good at it. As a teenager, I hated that because I kept thinking of her as a phony, but afterwards, between school and the war I tried to see what those stories meant, WHY she had to tell them. At first, I just thought she was crazy, but then I thought of Joanna's mom... that was crazy... mine just wanted to be interesting, I think; and if that means she want to have an heirloom from a non-existent family from a country she knew nothing about except that their pudding is savory then so be it.

Good news! TV is back on. I watch the morning cartoons and then go to work. James is there, waiting outside before any of the guys are even there; he looks serious.

"Johnny, how are you?" When I get close enough he hugs me; not a little "sup?" hug, but a real hug, huge and warm. "Heard you're taking on the reigns after Jeff. I just wanted to come by and show some support, you know? It sucks about Jeff." How do I answer that? Thanks? Damn, James... I opt for awkward silence.

"Uhmm... You mind if I join you guys today? I need some extra cash and stuff." Ohhh... so that's why he's here.

"Sure, you're on waste and cleaning duty, stick to Brian over there and you'll be fine." No, I'm not blowing him off, or ignoring him, or resenting him for walking out on everybody and not contacting me in two months; I'm actually giving him an easy job.

"Cool, thanks." He gets it... he's still a good guy. James has always been a good guy, the kind of person even Stalin would get along with. He never gets any drama from anyone, which is why he is actually the best person to go to with your own problems; he is never burdened by his own shit. James also never changed, and if at all, then only for the better. Why I came back from Iraq he was the first to greet me, in the airport and everything. He drove me around before I got my car, he bought me drinks and Weed. James just knows when to take the backseat of his own story, and just be there for you.

I stay close to James most of the day; he shows me pictures of Joanna with different sized bellies, and bounces baby names off me. He is leaning towards Raphael for a boy or Danielle for a girl; Joanna want Hope for a girl or Philipp Jr. for a boy. I try to stay neutral, but both sets of names rub me the wrong way, kind of kitschy naming a girl Hope, or after angels... Raphael is my middle name, so it is, in a way, them naming a baby after me, and yes, they do know it's my middle name.

When we finish I say goodbye to James and we schedule to meet later for a few drinks. I haven't been to a bar in ages, and James is too broke for one, which means we'd probably just drink at my place.

I drive to the police station and ask for detective Berger, who walks in behind me; following me, I suppose. Within a few minutes we're in a small room with snot colored walls again with a table made out of the same indeterminable substance as last time, only this time, a cop in nicely pressed uniform is there too.

"This is Lieutenant Clark; he will be sitting in on our talk, okay?" Excessively polite; he's in trouble.

"Sure."

"Good, please state your full name."

"John Milaowic."

"Second name too."

"John Raphael Milaowic."

"May I call you John, Mr. Milaowic?"

"I prefer Johnny."

"Okay. Johnny, please tell us how you know Mr. Hunter."

"Jeff and I went to the same school, had mutual friends, and after I came back from Iraq we were introduced and became friends, he helped me find work." Stick to the truth as far as you can, that is how you lie.

"I see, and what about Mr. Pope?"

"I think Jeff knew him, I told you."

"Right, you were in the car." He is reading out of a dossier, where my breakdown is broken down to its useful statements.

"Yes, then we drove back to town, without Mike."

"Why?"

"He said he has something to do."

"More business?" I just shrug in reply.

"I need an audible response." He taps the recorder.

"I don't know."

"Okay, Johnny. Did you see anyone else there?"

"Yeah, some... unsavory looking folk." Time for some invention.

"Can you be more specific?"

"Four unknowns; two wearing hoodies, one green, the other gray; other two wearing jackets, one long and dark colored, the other a nylon vest-jacket; all four huddled together near the old fountain; all were talking to each other; several empty bottles around them; one had a dog at his lap. Specific enough?"

"Making fun of me?" The lieutenant makes a restraining cough at Berger's remark; he's on my side, or afraid of a law-suit, at least.

"I'm just observant."

"Okay, did you recognize any of them?"

"The dog; it's always there." I make a stupid grin; I just couldn't help myself. "Just kidding, sorry, I've never seen those guys before, I think, I didn't see the faces very well." I have to look like I'm cooperating, just enough so one of them buys it.

Berger looks at his superior and they seem to be consulting

each other over some cop-telepathy, eventually, Berger turns back to me.

"That's all for now, we might get in touch." They both walk me to the door and show me out.

I think I exceeded the amount of times one is allowed to go in and out of police stations before one gets the other junkies nervous. Jeff told us a story once about a friend of his from Huston, but Jeff said he lived in New Jersey, who kept on getting pulled over for driving violations, but people thought he was a rat, so they beat him senseless, and he's still in a coma. I don't know if I believed Jeff about that, but it does illustrate a point; Junkies are unreliable. Maybe that's why this story exists; a didactic myth to teach the young junkies the ways of proper Junkdom. I mean, I heard seven other versions for this story: in some it happened here, but a long time ago; in some it was in a different part of the country; in some it's a different drug... it goes on and on, name change, places, times, chemicals, and punishments change, but the upshot is always the same: stay away from the police. I'm not a rat. I thought that going to the police headlong just once will make them leave me alone; and it seems I was right.

I get home and take a shower before James gets there; I haven't seen the guy in months, this warrants a shower. I also clean the designated sitting area, and make sure the TV is working. When all is done I sit and wait, rather pleased with myself. Meeting James makes me feel like more of an adult; there's no drama, we actually CAN talk about complex and important things... he's the one who got away.

He arrives half an hour late, bearing beer, whiskey, and burgers.

"Sorry for being late, Joanna was on the warpath, and then some Trail of Tears and the need for attention." He sounds so... domesticated.

"No prob, have a seat." I let him sit on the good chair, the one with the upholstery, and we both start with a beer and burger. The beer is in cans, but has odd European names, in Czech or something; the burgers are those you can get in any supermarket, not frozen, just that they come in neat little nylon wrappers and are meant for a microwave, buns and all. He put them in a paper bag for the fast-food effect, though.

"What's that smell?"

"Orange soda... had a bit of an accident last night, it's in the carpets and stuff..." It's kind of embarrassing, and I normally don't get embarrassed, to be like this in a shit little hovel smelling of orange soda in front of this junky turned family man; he even owns a suit! (handed down to him by Philipp.)

"You're a riot Johnny. How's Jenny?" Like always, asking the big questions like asking for the time of day, this is the guy I need to be hanging out with.

"I" Actually...I'm not sure. Did she forgive me? Did she say I was just a costumer now? Oh God... What do I say? I have to show him SOME change, some improvement since last we met. "She's doing okay, has a new apartment, a new tattoo...'works' for Jake."

"Not entirely what I meant, but nice to know, except for her... employment under Jake."

"I knew you couldn't stand that fucker either!" I burst out laughing, launching tiny pellets of pickles everywhere from my mouth.

"Not that, though he is becoming increasingly 'Scarefaced', it's what he does, to people, or just generally. I hope you know what I mean."

"You mean dealing?"

"Yeah... Me and Joanna, we see things different, it's hard, but at least it's really us; and soon enough we'll have another human being to take care of." His tone of speech reminds me of Jeff's letter; they kind of have the same... well, tone. Joanna won't fail like Tammy, right? She can't, she mustn't. I start getting really anxious so I roll myself a joint and drink a little quicker.

"Do you mind? If Joanna smells that on me I'm fucked."

"If I open the window and let air in, and I let the smoke out there?"

"Well, it is your house." House... my mom's kitchen was bigger than this apartment.

I open the windows and light my joint, instinctively wanting to pass it on, but James just smiles at me and takes another big bite of his burger, though I do catch him taking abnormally long, deep breaths to take in SOME of the smoke.

"How is Joanna, the pregnancy and all?"

"She stopped working in the shop, doing only Philipp's paperwork, we get by... She's become very depressed, you know? About money, about raising a kid here, about being a mom." James looks like he could use something to relax him, but I want to be a good friend, and right now, that means letting him wallow in the sadness.

"I'm sure she'll be better than Tammy."

"That isn't putting the bar very high, is it?" He smile, the smile he always had, friendly and honest.

"I know, that stupid bitch... Poor Jeff... poor Samantha."

"Who?"

"Samantha, Jeff's daughter, you know... who died." I don't think he knew that. How could he not know? Is he so out of the loop? I guess he really had to cut all his ties to us.

"Shit... How?"

"Tammy was too busy with Junk to take care of her; she died

at nine months old." I think for a second of what else to say when I realize that this is why I invited him over, this is what I wanted to say, but I still add "Don't worry, Joanna will be better, she is stronger, the strongest girl I've ever met." He looks at me despondently when I finish talking, and opens the whiskey bottle, drinking out of a small cup he salvaged from a crate-functioning-as-nightstand.

"It's hard on her, she can't do anything; no smoking, no drinking, no toking, no nothing... she just sits around and cries."

"Remember in school how they showed us interviews with junkies, talking about how terrible their life is? They should've shown us interviews with people who quit, how shit their life is and how they don't even have anything to make it more bearable."

"Fuck, man... thanks." He laughs ironically and takes of his boots, finally getting comfortable now that I've shown him I'm still me; a little messed up, and the social equivalent of a land-mine.

I finish my joint and the burger soon follows. We head back to the sitting area where it's nicer but leave the window open; it's a nice night. We drink a bit in silence and start on our second burgers, I can't help but notice that James changed; skinnier, paler, there's less confidence in his movement, he even dresses different. A gray buttoned shirt and some no-color pair of cheap pants, yellow socks... who wears yellow socks outside of kindergarten? It all makes him look... either like someone who might eventually go postal, or just the dullest human being in the United States of America (England must have someone duller). His face is clean shaven as always, but it somehow looks different, cleaner.

I decide to shoot the elephant in the room.

"How is it, being clean?"

"Oh boy... Johnny, man, it's both the best and the worst." He looks as if I had really shot him, kind of drained. "Let's not bring it up, okay? I'm not judging, man, you have fun, I just want to stay away."

"Sure man, I get it... The misses will kill you." I smile like an idiot, trying to put James's mind at ease.

"Not just, I really am trying to quit, and well...it's like abstinence, it won't help if you talk about walking around in the damn Playboy mansion." He takes a huge swig of the beer and throws the can at the rim of the bin; we watch it bounce off and spill beer on the floor.

"Maybe I should get a pet to lick my floor clean." He laughs at my comment and opens another beer, imported. "Will you be staying with us for long?" I use my 'Boss voice'.

"Till the end of the week, if that's okay, chief. I really need the money."

"The paper industry not as lucrative as you thought?"

"Fuck man, it's boring and underpaid. Plus, we're closed for the month... No new orders coming in." He sounds like a... working man; an average Joe.

"Well, the de Silva job won't last forever, though we are stretching it on as much as we can, so I will need another job after... and without Jeff... I don't know how I'm supposed to find anything." We all got problems James, you have a wife and kid to feed, I have a heroin habit and a demanding girlfriend to satisfy.

"You'll be fine, you always are." We drink to that and carry on with our empty conversation, but I can't get this sentence out of my head. *I am always fine?* Me???? How am I fine? I am a murder suspect, I am an addict, I am... a fuck up, I lost my friend, I lost Old Jenny, I lost control.

I start crying in mid-sentence; we were talking about something completely different, but my mind was still there lingering on the word "fine", and how it couldn't be further off in describing my current or general state.

"She isn't going to forgive me, I know it, it's never going to be the same as it was in your shed." He has no idea what I'm on about; he's just drinking his beer.

"Here, have a little, it'll make you feel better." I take a big swig of the whiskey and I feel it in my throat and nose. It doesn't make me feel better; it doesn't even make me numb enough to stop caring.

"Fuck it, fuck all of it." I start punching myself at the thighs, over and over until I am certain their blue all over under my pants. James just looks at me in silence, the fact he doesn't look shocked or surprised at this outburst somehow validates the outburst.

"You're done?"

"Yeah." There's a nice, long, uncomfortable silence to follow, here, it's kind of a social requirement, I guess; both of us silently admitting this never happened. "Any progress with name picking?"

"Hope for a girl, Han Solo for a boy." He smiles rather stupidly again, the good, cheap beer having the desired effect.

"Why stop there? Java the Hutt." I raise my can but he just laughs instead of toasting to it.

"Where's the bathroom? Or do you piss in the corner?"

"You know where it is, the same place you washed your hands after getting my puke off you after I ODed." I just feel like reminding him where he comes from, that he is getting out, and hence better. Looking at his face, though, I think it landed differently with him than what I had in mind; he wants away from it. "I was just saying... You're better than me now."

"Fuck, man..." he goes and I can hear him piss, a steady, confident stream of what minutes ago was beer.

When he comes back we finish our beers and the rest of the whiskey bottle, and after another joint I make a frozen pizza for us, too. We don't really know what to say to each other now. It's been ages since we got drunk together, Junk was always so much more efficient, and I liked High James, but he is gone, hopefully forever.

"Listen, I told Philipp and Joanna I'd do it, so here goes: You should quit too. Here's a number of a group we go to, some psychology major is running it." He hands me the note, a little yellow post-it with a smiley, Joanna's writing.

"I'll think about it." I put it in my pocket after mock-wiping my nose. We eat the rest of the pizza and he leaves, leaving me with a few left-over cans and a lot of garbage.

I make a mental note to go visit Joanna soon and start cleaning the mess, putting the cans in the bin and same for the burger wrappers. When I'm done I try to sleep, turning the TV on very, very quiet. When that doesn't work I have a joint, after that fails I have a big hit, one to send me reeling for the night. A gram and a bit should do it. I avoid all my used needles, it's been a while and I haven't really cleaned them; they might be infected. I know this guy, he used dirty needles, and not only is he dead now, his death was accompanied, if not caused, by so many illnesses... Not just the cliché ones like hepatitis and HIV, but minor, more annoying ones too, like chicken pox. So, yes, I am trying to be careful and get a new needle out. Thanks to newly acquired muscle-mass, finding a vein takes only a second, and presto! I wait to float away into joy and from there to sleep.

The phone rings. I pick up and imagine it's Jeff, but that can't be so I try to focus harder.

"Johnny?" it's Bart from work.

"What, man? Why are you calling so late?"

"Fuck, dude, it's ten in the morning! Where the fuck are you? Me and your buddy James have been covering for you in front of de Silva, but, dude, what the hell?"

Shit, that never happened to me before, I could always wake up on time; in fact, when I know I have to get up, I usually wake up an hour earlier and then either wait an hour in bed, or half sleep until the alarm clock goes off.

"Oh, I'm a bit sick today. Let me talk to James." I hear the mobile changing hands, and then:

"Yeah, man, hungover?"

"Not really, just a bit sick, you know." I wait the appropriate time of awkward silence before I continue so he'll know what I mean. "I need you to cover for me today, I won't use tonight so I will be there early tomorrow, just help me out, man."

"Sure, don't worry about it, like old times, huh?" He hangs up and I can picture him turning around and giving orders, even though everyone already knows what to do, it just works in my little mental cinema.

Okay, so, two rules for a fake sick-day: Number one, do not go outside and be seen by someone who shouldn't see you, e.g. de Silva. Number two, Try hard to convince yourself you're sick by staying in bed and watching cartoons, that way, it sounds believable when someone calls you and you have to sound sick. I know, it's, in a way, like reverting back to being a kid, you know? When you had to trick your mom into thinking you are too sick for school. Oddly enough, this only gets harder when you grow up. You have to convince yourself, or your boss, you are too sick. Or in the army it's a real bitch to get downtime for illness. I know a guy who was like a magician, when you asked him how he did it, he told you the most farfetched thing in the world, like that pencil graphite can trick an X-ray that you have a broken limb, and stuff like that, so no one was sure if they should try it, because we were afraid we'd get caught trying to cheat our way to staying in bed.

I turn on the TV and have my coffee to Spongebob and Oprah, along with some pop tarts with chocolate. The chocolate is seventy percent fat; looking like an oil slick on the pop tart.

The phone rings again, and I start mustering my acting skills, coughing once or twice before answering, just to get this rugged tone in my voice.

"Hello?" Very well done!

"Hey, man, it's Gustav, you aren't coming in today?" It's de Silva, he uses his first name only when he wants to sound sympathetic.

"No, sir, I can't. I might go to the doctor later, if this persists." Involving doctors makes it sound serious, especially for the uninsured.

"Okay, feel better." He hangs up, a sign that James did his job superbly! He is not only taking care of the actual job, he also convinced de Silva I am actually sick.

I try to take a nap with the TV on until lunch time, but I can't sleep, between Oprah and the Bold and the Beautiful, there is something that bothers me. I eliminate the smell and the dense thick air in the room as possibilities; I've slept all night with those. I also don't think I already am in need of another hit either. It's boredom, and the need to do something.

I decide to finally do SOME cleaning, and what better place to start then the bed? I quickly realize I don't have any detergents, but I can't go outside to Philipp's so I call Jenny for help. She agrees to come over with some stuff, so I wait for a few minutes.

She arrives after an hour and sits herself on my bed.

"God, I haven't been here in ages, the place looks like shit. Mind if I smoke?" I nod my approval and she lights a cigarette and leans back on the headboard of my bed. I try to picture her like those old actresses, the ones, who looked super elegant smoking, Audrey Hepburn or Marlin Monroe, but Jenny just isn't THAT majestic.

"So, been drawing anything lately?" I ask as I scrub puke and soda from my floor, trying to cover the smells with a bottle of lemon scented acid.

"Not really, just a bit. Thought about visiting an art class." Wow, she still has plans. "At the very least I could find people to sell weed and LSD to." She tries to make smoke rings but fails so she sits back up and shoves a sandaled foot in my face. "Painted my toenails, what do you think?"

"Not bad, smells terrible, though."

"Fuck you." She smiles; she knows it was a joke.

"Why aren't you at work?"

"Sick day." I wink to let her in on my secret and she laughs.

"I used to do that to my dad all the time."

"Do you still talk?"

"No... but he is my emergency contact, also if I get arrested." Long pause to let her see that I get the gravity of her statement.............. and cue conversation:

"I talked to James yesterday, he and Joanna are doing okay."

"That's nice, hopefully they won't fuck up their baby." She seems even less than interested. Well, she never really liked anyone in that group, just as they barely liked her, she was there for me; I guess that sort of made me proud.

"I saw Jimmy a couple of days ago, he misses you." She met Jimmy? I thought he left town or something.

"Where?"

"He and his new girl bought some Crystal from me." She puts

out the cigarette in a coffee mug and leans over, sort of looking like the girl from Pulp Fiction. I try to get rid of that thought, because doesn't she die in the movie? From an OD or something? "She looked nice, Joy or something, right?"

"Joyce... yeah." So Jimmy is turning to a Meth-head, great.

"I liked her, and the story of how they met, almost romantic. They told me they had sex via notes, isn't that cool?"

"I guess." I've been more concentrated on a die-hard stain on my floor and been scrubbing it forever.

"Come on, I thought you were into that whole romance shit." She half-heartedly strokes my head from the bed, which I think was meant as a tease, but I kind of liked it.

"don't feel like talking about Meth-head love while I'm cleaning puke off the floor, that's all. You thirsty?" I finally decide to play the host and she nods both approval, that she is thirsty, and disapproval that it took me so long to ask. "I have orange soda, cherry cola, beer, and... that's it."

"Beer will be fine, unless it's that shit stuff you always get, with the blue can, fuck that." I bring her a beer from the same company as the blue ones, but the can is red, I don't think she'll know.

It's generic stuff, really; some own-brand of a convenience store chain that operates anywhere where people give homeless guys enough change to buy beer.

Jenny sits up to drink it, and shows little signs of having realized it's a really cheap knock-off of really cheap homeless-beer.

"Cool T-shirt." She is wearing a T-shirt that says ' Today may be a good day to die, but how would I know until tomorrow?'

"Thought you might like that, sounds like something a marine would say."

"I'm not a marine, a marine would fuck me up if I would say I was a marine." I start to laugh, almost abashed by her calling me a marine.

"Come on, I just mean it's something badass to say; like, he won't die yet because he has to go on fighting another day."

"Really? I thought it was more of a coward looking for an excuse to shirk the duty of dying for something..." We both just shrug in our disagreement and continue drinking our beers as I go on cleaning.

"I'm bored, let's watch TV." She turns on the TV and watches some daytime-drama about a female cop who spends half of the autopsy trying to see if her partner on whom she has a crush likes her too; totally unprofessional. After a while she starts to doodle on a notepad I had laying around and ignores the TV, which moved to our heroine checking out a crime-scene and pondering herself wasting her time on this crush over her emotionally scarred partner, and how hotter he is for being emotionally scarred, yep, I bet the ten pounds of muscle and chiseled face have nothing to do with him being hot.

The stain is gone, only the smell remains. A junky poem, by John R. Milaowic. Just kidding, no poem, but yes, the stain is finally gone. I finally stand up and stretch while Jenny draws me and frowns about me moving to an upright position.

"You looked better on your knees." I want to tell her that so did she, but she might punch me, or cut me off.

"Want a joint?" I start rolling before she answers, and she seems committed to toking with me. After we smoke our joint she leaves, says she has a costumer waiting somewhere for Crystal.

With the bed area quite clean I sit down all pleased with myself, but pissed at Jenny for being no help at all. She could have at least done something like taking the dishes to the kitchenette instead of just sitting there doodling.

I pick up the notepad to look for the doodle but notice she tore it out and took it with her, leaving only a tiny bit of it on the pad, namely the digit five and the letter J. Does J make Johnny? Does it make Jenny? I shouldn't obsess. The worst thing you can do in a relationship, sexual, romantic or otherwise, is to over-read things; to find meanings where that are none. So I decide to distract myself again with channel-surfing. Drama, drama, talk-show, reality-TV, reality-TV, cook show, cook show, news, drama, a Chuck Norris movie, a Charlie Chaplin movie, drama, football, baseball, basketball, basketball, golf, TV off.

I decide to give James a call.

"Yello, what'chya need my sick old chum?" I can almost hear him wink at me like a six-year-old.

"Just checking in."

"We've burned the house down."

"Well, I'm taking it out of your pay."

"Shit, boss... Everything is fine, man, don't worry. The guys wish you well." He hangs up, like everything was said, and what wasn't isn't important enough.

I start making an early lunch for myself, more out of boredom than hunger. It's frozen Fish'n'Chips today.

I finish my lunch and decide it's late enough for a hit, just a small one to kill a bit of time; the day is a waste anyway.

I only have half a gram anyway. I try to find filters, any remnants of Junk caught in the wonderful little specks of cotton that hopefully keeps weird stuff out of my bloodstream. I found one in the bathroom, behind my painkillers; the only actually legally prescribed drug in my apartment. I got it from an army doctor in Cleveland when I was there for a checkup last year. They never asked me to come to another one. It was a waste of time, an hour and a half drive there and twice as much back due to traffic, and all that for ten minutes of some guy telling you what you see in some vagina looking ink blot.

The filter I found looks a bit dirty, but I don't dare wash it because that would defeat the purpose, won't it? Just steal all that beautiful Junk down the drain and to the belly and brain of some fish in the bay, or even worse, a crab. So screw that, dirty filter it is. I try to wring the filter and get everything out onto the spoon and then use a second filter for this hit; I guess it kind of worked, but I wouldn't know until I push it down into the vein.

I think that last question hanging in my mind increased the anticipation for the hit, my brain is titillating with excitement as the plunger goes down the length of the syringe and time slows down for a second, waiting to see what happens next. What happens next is fairly simple: I feel happy. My arm jus drops down and my eyes start to flicker. I fall onto the bed and roll around for a bit to feel the sheets before they melt. Wait... What? I am going to melt, not them. Why? I kind move now, that is what I meant by melt. The mind. It melts. It can't work anymore. I. I am drooling. The bed is getting wet and I don't care. The day is dead. How could it get better? What is there left to make of this day? Eat crap, drink crap, and no more Junk. FUCK.

Phone.

Rings.

Let the damn thing ring.

Doesn't stop.

I try to bring my mind out of its afterglow enough to talk on the phone, but we'll see how that will go.

"What the fuck do you want?"

"Well hello to you too, Sunshine." It's Joanna.

"Sorry, kind of thought it was someone else, you know? Like someone wanting something, to bring me down. I don't feel like talking serious now, so I just thought I'd scare away any shithead that way, but not you; you're always welcome."

"Are you floating?"

"You know."

"Maybe I should call back later."

"I'd be passed out later, whachya need?"

"I just wanted to... ask you for something."

"Anything for you guys, your man saved my ass today."

"Yeah, he told me. Well, it's something big."

"Out with it!"

"Could me and James borrow three hundred dollars?"

Pause. Really long pause.

"Dude, I'm broke."

"Thought so, I'm sorry, we're just kind of desperate, we can't afford the move, you know... so... We thought you might be able help us out."

"Sorry, no can do. Bye now, There is a burrito with my name on it."

"Okay... Bye." She hangs up and I go to the kitchenette and nuke me up a burrito, cheddar and beans filled.

Aren't Joanna and James supposed to have their shit together? Why are they asking a junky for money? What makes them think I have any? Don't they think that if a junky would have money he would spend it on... Junk? It's kind of what we do...

Ding!

Burrito!

It got a bit mushy in the microwave, but it still tastes like a burrito, so I declare it a win for my culinary segment of the day.

I get back on the bed, it's rather disappointing, I'm not high anymore; Joanna woke me up. I actually do consider taking another hit, but... come on, one after the other with only half an hour in between? Too much. Besides… I don't have anymore Junk, and anything else I'd take would just ruin the cellular memory of the Junk I just had, so why leave the day with a bad note? Poor brain, it had enough for the day.

I call James again, see how things are going. Of course I have another couple of coffees before that in case he gives the phone to de Silva.

"You don't trust me, do you?" Again, I can hear him smirk as he speaks, again a confident man working with his buddy.

"Nope, word is you're a quitter." I hear him laugh, a real one, not some weird half-assed nervous laugh.

"Sure, ahh, well, we finished the last wall and now we are almost done with the floor, only that you're the only one who knows how to work the sander and the table saw." He's right, most of my guys are high school dropouts and general morons, except Bart and Omri, but they couldn't operate a toothpick without a ten days crash course.

"I will be there tomorrow… How long do you think we can keep squeezing that job?"

"Here's de Silva."

"Hey man, listen, I want this thing done, comprende? I could do the floor myself if I want, man, so you finish this thing quick, yeah? Your buddy here said you guys are almost done."

"Mr. de Silva, I promise you we will be done shortly, I just can't make any promises as to exactly when without seeing today's progress, I'll talk to you tomorrow, bien?" I wonder if it sounds condescending if I try a Spanish word here and there. I don't think I will feel bad to hear a word of English every now and again if I were to live in Mexico, but then again my Spanish sucks; trailing off again, concentrate Brain!!!

"Ok, just get the damn thing done! My wife hasn't seen her

home in a month, keeps telling me to fire you and get some hombres to do it in a day." I didn't know Mr. de Silva was married.

"No problem, we'll be out by next week, I hope." That was my best salesman slash contractor slash law abiding citizen slash boyfriend slash sober driver voice, if that doesn't exude trustworthiness, I don't know what does.

"Cool." He hangs up on me and I fall back on the bed. I pick up the notebook again, the one Jenny doodled on. A "J" and a "5", that's all that I see on the remaining paper, after that I see the following blank page. I try to continue a doodle off hers, a sort of continuation on the following page. The "5" turns to a face with a crooked nose, the "J" is for "Johnny", Johnny with the crooked nose; Johnny whose face is destroyed. Johnny who can't draw. I rip out both pages and throw them away, actually hitting the bin, but no one around to see my marksmanship.

I open a can of beer and watch TV. I wake up later and it's dark out. Seven missed calls; Two from Jenny, SCORE!! She was looking for me; one from James, I'll call him later; one from de Silva, I won't be calling back; one from an unknown number, also to be ignored; and two from Jake. Now this I got to see, what on earth does that dumbass want? Dial back.

"Yo."

"How laconic."

"Big word for a junky."

"Fuck you."

"Ok Johnny old pal, how are you?"

"In the words of Bill Clinton, I repeat my former statement."

"Great, got it out of your system?" He's no fun today.

"What do you want?"

"Here I am, with a position to offer, a job, paying money, and immediately thinking of my old friend from days of yonder, despite him failing me before, just because I want to give him a chance, and what do I get? Impatience."

"How indignant of you, what's the job?" I don't have time for his shit, but I do need money, the de Silva job is coming to an end.

"Not on the phone."

"Sure thing, Capone, when?"

"Fuck you, come by my new place up Old Avenue, number 79."

"New place?"

"Yeah, old one smelled of termites and my dad's armpits." Not a time for dead parents jokes, is it? He is offering me a job.

"Weird you moving away."

"Getting nostalgic Johnny?"

"No... It's just that... it's your house." You know? He fought for that house. After his folks had died he dropped out of school, nothing special, but he kept his sister in school, and found a job, albeit an illegal one, but still. Some of us thought him to be inspirational, some thought he was stupid, others crazy, but most of us thought he was a quitter. I know it sounds harsh, but he was our local dealer, and yeah, he still lived close, but provided for a new clientele. Just imagine that your favorite local neighborhood burger joint closes down and moves to a new, richer part of town as a upscale, upbeat, super-healthy, super-chic, vegan shit-hole; that's how we felt.

I head out to Jake's 'new place'. Old Avenue is called that because it was the first avenue in this little town, and then people built a new commercial avenue in town, and back then people referred to the place to 'go shopping' as "the Avenue" so you had to differentiate between the old one and the new one, conversely, there is no "New Avenue" it's called "Smith's Avenue" after the first bank to be founded there. The things you learn when you come to social studies class on weed and think everything is interesting.

It's a bit of a drive there so I turn on the radio, lots of news about the surging crime rate, but whatever, the music will be back on in a second.

Number 79 is a rather nice building. White, almost pristine in its hue, with big shaded windows that tell you that the people inside have so much stuff they'd rather people DIDN'T know about it. I ring at 'Cole'.

BZZZZZZZZZZZZZZZZZZZZZZZZZZ

I get it and go to the elevator; I swear I expected a doorman to greet me, with a nice little uniform like a schoolboy's, but no such luck. Seventh floor.

The apartment is nice, big TV, two computers and three game consoles, a nice kitchen, no microwave in sight, and three doors leading to mysterious rooms I am barred from entering.

"Welcome, man." Jake man-hugs me. It's awkward and weird, but I get what he is trying to do, reconcile as quickly as possible, or just show some new 'underworld generosity'; I don't really care.

We sit on the couch, black leather,, and I notice he had bought a LOT of new 'bling', an odd thick necklace, a big golden ring, and something that would qualify as an orbital station if it weren't stationed at his wrist as a bracelet.

"So, how's Jenny?" Small talk? Sure, whatever.

"Not bad, busy, but you know that Mr. Kingpin." I emphatically look around me, at the TV and expensive stuff a high school dropout shouldn't be able to afford.

"Yeah, great dealer, your lady; just that ounce of the 'let's get high together' about her eyes."

"Yeah, you talked about a job?"

"No time for the better things in life, huh Johnny?" He offers me a drink, bourbon, says it was really expensive, but worth it; he sounds like some Don Corleone.

"You know."

"I need you to shake someone up."

"Pardon?"

"Go all ninja on his ass." He comes closer. "kill him if you have to."

"What the fuck, man?" What did he just say, I find myself pacing the room like a lost sheep, or hound.

"He isn't paying up, he got the merchandise and kind of... disappeared, only I know where to, because he's an idiot."

"That isn't- "I keep pacing and trying to find words. "I meant, why do you think I will do this, that I can do this? you're just... Jake. Why the sudden violence?"

"Shit, man, look at this place! It's so small time. I can just come in and Scarface this town, pussies and all!" He has been watching way too much TV. "I know what you did, and even if you didn't, just the rumor, people would be scared if I sent you after them, my killer. Ten thousand dollars; for finding, threatening and bringing my man back in line."

"How do I do that? "

"With this." It's a Colt 9mm. manufactured 1990's by the look of it. 15 bullet magazine, one firing mode, steel, aluminum and plastic, made in the USA.

"I never fired one of those."

"Horseshit."

"No, seriously... M16, M203, M249 SAW... yes, that... never."

"Well, there's a trigger and a barrel, you know which part the bullets come out of." He pushes it towards me. Just the way he is handling it is all wrong. *These rule have been written in blood* they would say. *Finger off the trigger unless you want to shoot; weapon discharged unless you aim to kill; barrel to the air or the enemy.* He broke all of the above; I snatch the weapon and disarm it. "see? You know how it works."

"Where did you get this? Are you insane? This isn't Miami, this isn't the 80's, and I am already a suspect." The magazine was empty, his isn't that stupid, at least.

"Come on, man, this is our chance to go big-time. He keeps talking but I barely listen, I can only see the 9mm. It's shinning under Jake's stupid florescent light, crome on steel, I can smell the powder ingrained in the joints, between the parts. I see all the parts moving, grinding out the fire and the dust. I feel the heat all over again, the texture of khaki on limbs and the life's fluid's color on them. "Will you do it?"

"I need a drink."

"You have one dumbass" I down my drink, bourbon, it tastes like oak-shit, but it gets the job done and I relax a bit.

"I have to think... Help me out..." I can't really breathe, but I try to act cool. I light a cigarette, but have to ask Jake for a light, which he gives me in a most benevolent way, like a charitable Scrooge.

After the smoke I do relax enough to think; and it all boils down to this: ten thousand dollars, my reinstatement as one of Jake's dealers with my own spot of choice, and a gun. But isn't this a bit too much? This isn't Scarface, this is Ohio, 2013. I don't want to go to prison.

"Sorry, man, can't do it. I will do the one job, but no 'Scarfacing' . This town isn't a pussy waiting to be fucked; it's a shithole, waiting for nothing but Armageddon."

"Come on, man, you got the moves and shit, most people here like to think they're 'gangsta' but they don't know shit, you got it, like US army got it." He keeps shoving the magazine I left on the table my way, a sort of bait, but I am not biting.

"What do you mean? I had enough of this shit."

"You've seen things, man, most asswipes here only watched The Wire for their 'background' into this life, you and I could be on top, man!"

"And that means killing people?"

"You've killed."

I feel like I've taken a hit. There's a rush of blood, a ringing in my ears, a general confusion of who is where, or who is who. A hit of Junk, a hit from a mortar shell, Jamal once said he could barely tell the difference between the two, both took away your ability to feel yourself, or other people. He forgot to mention a hit of pure stupid. I think I said that out loud.

I think he punched me for it.

I am lying on the floor with a cold press on my nose.

Jake is on the couch, looking shaken.

"I'm sorry."

"Don't worry about it, I know all the war stuff fucked up with your head." He seems more understanding about this than about most things, lucky me. "I had to get you off me, don't be mad about the punch." I'm not mad, just confused.

"I'll do the one job, no guns, I just need the money." I don't really think I am in a position to make decisions, but I do need it; if I can just get back on my feet and show Jenny I can manage myself I might move out of my pathetic position, I need to regain control.

"Sorry, dude, but it's a package deal, can't have without the other, do this job for me, and stay as a dealer." He is sitting next to me now, acting all... fatherly. Does this crap work on his regular dealers? I mean, I've seen his dealers around, and they are usually really young, mostly still in school, so they might fall for this crap, but I know Jake since he was in kindergarten. "No need for violence, I mean, how many deaths did you hear about before that guy you killed?"

"I didn't kill him." I sit up and grab another drink he offers. It seems a moot point by now, but I didn't kill that Mike guy, it was the doctors who were probably too busy with their own shit to help him. I mean, I saw a whole bunch of guys beat the shit out of some guy for being an ass, a sort of an unofficial military punishment. They covered him with either a blanket or tarp, so he couldn't see the participants of the beatings, he broke seven bones and never said a thing, but more to the point, he lived.

"Take it, just in case." He shoves the 9mm into my hand and shows me the door, promising to send me a picture of the guy or tell me where to find him. It's the 'or' that bothers me, if I am honest.

I drive home with the second amendment in the glove compartment, like some other presence. I get home before noting Jake sent me away with a bottle of something-or-another . I try to unwind but the booze doesn't cut it.

I set everything up for another hit before realizing I don't have any Junk. I do a quick inventory of the place and find: eight hundred milligrams of painkillers, one and a quarter grams of Smack, one joint's worth of weed, half a gram of cocaine, and lot of booze. I decide on the Smack.

There are a billion pipes in my place, and I use the first one I find on the Smack. Normally, guns and drugs don't mix. If you ever start a drug-ring, don't let you users shot or your shooters use. I suppose this is a bit of an exception. I do not intend to load this gun, ever.

I watch TV to make time go by faster, but I can't help but oil the gun.

Spring, latches, catches, slides, and whole are new-looking, oiled, and well maintained. I start to wonder where Jake got this gun.

As I expected; the serial number is still there.

Dumbass bought it legally or stole it from someone who did; either way it could be traced back to Jake.

Does this mean I own Jake, or that Jake will own me? Will this put me back in charge with Jenny? *When in doubt ask your superior.* I know so many who are my superior, but narrowing it down it leads it to just one, sergeant Mahdi.

"Hi Jamal, you're busy?"

"A bit... What do you need, man?"

"Advice, sergeant."

"I'll be there in a minute." He means a sergeant's minute, which is relative. For him it could be anything from now to eternity, for us it means NOW, for him, it meant his own leisure. Jamal know that if I call him sergeant then something is going on. Last time I called him that they diagnosed me with PTSD and asked if I wanted medication. He said Terry could get me better stuff, and he did. Flash forward three years, and there is a 9mm on my table next to a Smack pipe... so... better?

He gets there after twenty minutes, which is the minimal time with traffic, so I am impressed.

"Okay, corporal, state your problem." He sounds very official, which means he is very worried. He isn't sitting, he just stays standing near the bed with a jeans and black shirt that makes him look like a black Vin Diesel. I don't know what to expect of him. I supposed it's like asking advice from any close friend; you already know what they are going to say. "Come on, out with it."

I show him the gun, no word required, he will know, that is

what sergeants do. They are supposed to take care of problems.

He says nothing, he just hits me with the butt of the gun, then with his fists. He kicks me, and pushes me. He throws varied objects at me, from little cans to chairs and even the toaster. I take it all. Even the violence the sergeant lays out is a kind of answer. Every action the sergeant makes is in itself to be translated into myth, a rite. So we were taught. Not low enough to be ignorant, not high enough to be an ass, the sergeant is the only real person you should be listening to; so his every action becomes a nuanced myth, meaning a thousand things. Even the way he eats.

Jamal gets tired of beating me eventually.

"What the fuck are you doing?"

"I don't know, that is why I wanted your advice." I don't think I am rude not offering him anything to drink, especially after his exertion of his strength, but I am a bit sore.

"Chuck it, and never look back." He leaves me with that, which might almost be mysterious if it weren't for the painfully obvious remark.

Morning does come, and I wake up on time for work.

It's a sad sight; the place is almost done. We have only a bit more tiling to do, by Friday, we are done, no way to push it longer.

"Sorry for being just too good." As douchey as that apology may sound, James just about covers it. Okay, so, seven and a half weeks of work, makes for two and a half thousand dollars after our little distribution at Jeff's death. Minus this, minus that... I get left with... two hundred seventy dollars, for seven and a half weeks' work.

The guys stare at me all day as I stand by the big power tools, scanning the bruises and marks and cuts, and when, for fun, I decide to work shirtless, one of the guys winces as he sees where the toaster landed and the mark it left. James doesn't ask, he just keeps bringing me food and water, and when de Silva isn't looking, beer.

The day is done and the bathroom is ready for use, of course we don't tell de Silva that and claim we need another day, which we will use for mostly cleaning, but he need not know that.

I choose to be the first to use the bathroom. I spend a while in there, basking in being the first to use the renovated lavatory. It's a weird and petty kind of victory to be the first to use something which isn't even yours. That is the true pride of the builder and laborer, to be the first in your house and take a shit in your bathroom, not the joy of seeing his complete work.

When we all disperse, James asks me about the bruises, I don't feel like explaining so I just tell him Jenny hit me and we both laugh, when he gets pushy as I drive him home, well, to Philipp's, I tell him Jamal was a pal and threw a toaster at me. He doesn't get it, but the group has always respected mine and Jamal's 'special dynamic'. When we used to take hits together at James's, me and Jamal would break off to some corner and... I don't really remember, Jenny told me we did that, and that Jimmy told her not to disturb us.

I drop off James and head back home, have a shower and lay down after a hit. I find a letter from Jake in my mailbox, big brown envelope with a picture of some guy. Asian, with thick glasses and dyed red hair, a sort of punk look, he looks shady through and through, only the picture is one of those machine booths pictures people take with their girlfriends, and he is with his girl there. She is really pretty; also Asian, dark, black hair, but pink lips that make her look innocent and lovely. I can't help to think about her and what she would do if she would catch me shaking down her boyfriend.

The back of the picture has an address on it, and a name: Roy Liao. Roy? Really? I expected something much cooler; maybe not Tony Montana, but something nicer than... Roy. Roy is the guys that serves you a burger, or who asks "how may I help you, sir?" at Costco, or something like that; someone whose life is sad enough as it is. It reminds me of that videogame James always played on the Playstation, Hitman; where you get assignments and stuff, but this is real life, which explains the disappointing name.

I spend a few moments considering the nuances of Jamal's beat-down on me, an advice in its own rights, and decide to do the job, but unarmed. I do need money, and rebuilding the bridge with Jake could bring in unlimited supplies of Junk and restore the balance of power, sounds fancy, doesn't it, 'balance of power'?

I google Roy's address and find it's miles off, next to where Jenny lives now. I sigh and sort of fall back on the bed. I need a hit. But I am still Junkless, so I settle for a few bong hits instead. I don't really own a bong so I improvise one with an empty soda bottle, water and a knife. I was told it's called a "bucket", I just call it "broke and desperate"

I wake up the next day and head over to de Silva's, all alone, and tell him we are finally done. That's right; I am unemployed. De Silva, or Gustav now, is very gracious, he doesn't know I took a shit in his new bathroom. I get the money all right, every cent, and for a moment, I feel rich! That is until I think of how it needs to be distributed. Gustav is all hugs and all, his wife is there too, beaming about having her house back. My Spanish isn't good enough to converse with her, but I think she is thanking me. I hear some "Gracias" and such, I try a few "De nada"s for good measure but she just looks at me. They cordially invite me and my "significant other" to dinner tomorrow, some authentic Mexican food, maybe that would excite Jenny.

To be honest, all I know about Mexico is from the news or Terry. You constantly hear about stuff, like illegal immigration and stuff, or drug cartels, who apparently can't bring enough product up here, but not enough about their food. Terry always talks about stuff his grandma' used to make, but it mostly sounded terrible.

I'm not trying to put down Mexico, I owe a lot of my highs to them, and probably a bit of money, I just don't understand how a human being, or any organic life form, can live off beans, rice, and lava-like sauce. I've only been to Mexico once, when I was fifteen my dad took me there. It was a father-sons bonding thing, a bit awkward. It was supposed to be a little trip through some desert, into Mexico City, from there to the beach, and back to Texas, and from Austin, home. Well, Michael ended up with the shits, me too. Our dad said, we were too out of it to remember, we were seeing things, and that I saw a horse trampling my luggage and running away. Only I always think that a fifteen-year-old boy should have very different hallucinations, ones you can't tell your mom about. Thinking about it, maybe that is why I may have MADE UP the horse thing, to cover up more embarrassing truths. Michael was seeing spots and stars, like in the cartoons, only he saw them for real. Well, I've been avoiding Mexico and their food since then.

My dad tried to convince us to go again when I was eighteen, but we both clutched our stomachs and screamed like we were on fire, that put him off it. I don't think my dad was misguided or anything by trying again, he was probably thinking we were becoming men, and soon, bonding trips might be off the table. I invited him to base once, to see what I do, but the drill sergeant refused him entrance, so we ended up just sitting outside the gate and eating ice cream.

This is what is going through my head as I get into the car: the shits, and my dad. I drive away and just pass through some commercial area with lots of graffiti in Spanish. It's mostly the nice kind, not the gang kind. Jenny calls it "Street Art," but it's just letters and colors, and something that looks like a Disney character or something. Getting home is a drag, traffic is stuck in every street and I have to pass the time somehow, so I have another look at that Roy guy's picture.

I decide to call Jake, tell him we are in business, but he won't answer, that shit. When I get home I try again, still no answer, so I settle down on the bed and watch TV for a few minutes before making a joint and getting a beer. There is nothing really on, so I start texting with Jenny:

"Hey babe, you cool?"

"Yeah, just got out of the shower."

"Still naked? Just kidding... wanna come over?"

"Nahh, not 2day, I feel like shit."

"Sick :(?"

"You know... :)"

"Yeah... btw. Did you hear from Jake 2day?"

"Yeah, he was here 4 a few, then went somewhere."

"Great, ttyl."

"Ok, KOTL."

No idea what that last one means. Jenny always was one of those girls who used cutesy things like that and those text abbreviations, I never did. Why can't people just use words, isn't that what they are for? I'm not really one to speak as an official idiot, but still, at least I know the difference between a letter and a number.

Since Jenny is busy, or simply high, I guess my day just completely opened. Things are going to get pretty boring soon without me getting another legit job. I really do think that in the modern age, people invented job just so they'd have something to fill up their day. Making money can be done in an hour if you're smart, so why work nine to five? So you won't have to sit around like a jackoff and do nothing from nine to five. Think of Philipp. I doubt he works that store seven to eight in the evening because he likes it. He has savings, he can probably get money from the army or something. But no, he gets up at six in the morning, stacks cans and frozen lasagna and stands at the cash register for a billion hours a day; because if not he'd just sit in his crummy apartment and think of his dead friends.

That reminds me, I need to buy more beer and stuff.

I get back to the car and drive to Philipp's. James is there with Joanna, who looks HUGE! They are restocking some shelf and James keeps grabbing her tit when he thinks no one is looking, she only gives him a slap on the wrist for it, but smiles. I tried grabbing something of Jenny's once in public, she gave me a forty minutes lecture afterwards about her feelings and about "a time and a place."

I grab some beer and ice cream that's on sale, toilet paper, cotton balls, cue tips, rolling paper, filters, frozen chicken-parm, instant noodles, some chips, and socks. Yeah, sometimes Philipp gets stuff like that, cheap socks or underwear for men. I say hi to the two love-birds and they get up, coming up to me Joanna pushes James like he were a little kid, shy to talk to an adult.

"Hey man...listen, I was going to ask you something."

"Can't get you any more jobs, need one myself."

"No, not that. Can you help me and Joanna move? We'll get you pizza and beer in exchange." Move?

"Where are you guys going? Did you find something cheaper?"

"Not exactly cheaper, but better. Cleveland."

"Get the fuck out." I can't believe they want to move to

Cleveland, it's shit. Ok, it's shit here too, but at least they have Philipp here, and friends. Oh… The friends are the problem. "You need to get away, huh?"

"No, no, no… I got a better job, and there are more cheap doctors in Cleveland, and it's nice to raise kids there… Just, you know…"

"Adult stuff." He sounds like an awkward scene in a movie, when they don't want to let the loser know they think he's a loser; he always figures it out, though. Then they fall out, there's a big fight, and you see parallel scene of both parties and how they miss one another, but pride keeps them apart until they both realize they've been jerks and simultaneously apologize. CUT.

"Parent stuff." He looks grim, like he were consoling me about someone passing; hand on shoulder and everything.

"Yeah, sure, when?"

"This coming Monday, at three?"

"My schedule is wide open." I give him my best 'it's all good' smiles and pay for the stuff, despite Joanna giving the frozen chicken-parm a very poor review, but James says her taste buds went crazy last month.

Home looks the same, I should move stuff around, spruce it up a bit. I make the chicken-parm and see no problem with it, so I guess James was right. After my little lunch I decide to go visit this Roy guy. I try eight outfits before going. I spent less time trying out clothes before my first date with Jenny. I try to look threatening, but not so much that I would be an immediate suspect if someone calls the cops. Jeans and a wife-beater shirt, no; army fatigues and a wife-beater shirt, no; Cheap pulp-fictionesque suit, no; Khakis and a T-shirt, maybe; jeans and a T-shirt, no; Jeans, wife-beater shirt with an unbuttoned plaid shirt on top, yes. I don't have any jewelry like the thugs on

TV or the news, so I do without. I also don't take the gun, but I do take a small metal chain I had in my toolbox.

The drive is short now that there are fewer cars on the road, and I reach the address in ten minutes or so. The building is nice, like Jenny's, but older. A quick scan of the names on the mailboxes tells me Roy is on the fifth floor. I wait for someone to come out and just get in to the building, trying to attract the least attention to myself as humanly possible. The fifth floor smells like soy sauce. I know it sounds racist, but the apartment where the smell is coming from is my first guess as to where Roy is. I knock.

"Yo?" Really? A 'yo'? Are we in the nineties?

"I got a package here for a Mr... Liao?" The mailman trick... oh yeah... I spend so much time congratulating myself I forget I don't look like a mailman and that I am not holding anything that looks like a package.

"Hold on, my man."

The door opens and he is there, half naked. I push past him and stroll through the apartment, like in Pulp Fiction.

"Ahhh... Where's the package, dude?" He has such a strong accent, it's bordering on annoying.

"You're pretty slow, huh? No package. Sit down." He complies. This might turn out to be the easiest shakedown ever. "I'll cut down to the chase, you owe someone money."

"Oh... Jake sent you. It's cool, I'll pay him tomorrow, ok? Good, bye now." Is this guy for real?

"No, no. You don't understand." I sit down next to him, he looks confused like a kid, not at all like I imagined this would go. "You owe money, I can't just go and tell my friend you'll pay like a good little boy, can I?"

"So... What now?" He lights a cigarette, and actually offers me one, which I take. Waste not, want naught.

"Ahh... Good question." There's a knock on the door, probably the girlfriend. He goes to get it, I give up on him.

Within two seconds five cops are in the apartment, shouting "Clear!" "Left! Left, clear!" "Perp on the right, headed out the window, go go go!" And I am out the window, running down the fire-escape and jumping to the street below. I make a run for an old used cars' lot and hide in one of the cars. There's a lot of noise outside, radio talk, lots of "Suspect last seen headed west on Vine, wearing a plaid shirt, mostly red in color, not considered dangerous." Fuck, it was a bust, I walked into a bust.

Back in Iraq, when the guys were out looking for people it could last for days, house-to-house shit, I doubt any cop in Ohio is going to invest more than one coffee break on little old me. I decide to wait it out in the used car, hoping for tired cops and impatient DEA agents. It only take three hours, but the coast is more or less clear and I get out of the car, sneaking my way back to my own car, which has a ticket on it for overdue parking meter, crap, great.

I am not an idiot, I left the plaid shirt in a dumpster, far far away from my car. I manage to drive away past the uniforms left at the scene and park near Jenny's then walk home. There's a store next to Roy's apartment, I can claim to have went there from Jenny's and back if anyone saw my car at the scene, and Jenny would back my alibi simply for me needing an alibi; even if she would hate me, which she doesn't, she would lie just because a cop asked her the question.

Junkies would usually lie for one another in front of cops, it's like an unspoken bond we share. Cops are the Gerries, the Charlies, the camel jockeys, the enemy. Even if it's someone you hate and skimped on you or sold you shit stuff, you'd still lie for him or her; I'd even lie for Jake. Which leads me to a question... did Jake set me up?

It wasn't my first thought, but the more I think about it the more it makes sense. He's getting me out of the picture entirely, the little turd! Why else would the cops try to bust such a fucking retard like Roy? Like he's some kingpin... Damn it! I was set up.

Phone keeps vibrating in my pocket.

"Hello?"

"Johnny, holy crap, they locked down my entire street! There's a damn manhunt out there! Please come here, there might be a killer out there." It's Jenny, and yes, she still needs me.

"Sure thing." I was only half way between her place and mine, so I go home to change first and decide to take the bus to hers. There are cops everywhere again, some are in civilian clothing, but you can recognize them by their walk; the walk of a man with a gun. One stops me and asks where I am headed, and I told him the truth: to my girlfriend's place.

Jenny opens the door and runs back to the window, checking out the cops as they pretend to work. She is eating something that smells of cheese and sodium out of a big bag and smokes self-rolled cigarettes, not weed.

"What do you think happened?"

"Don't know, some guy trying to make a buck and corporate America trying to stop him? The outbreak of the zombie apocalypse? Aliens? We will never know." I make myself at home and take one of her cigarettes before raiding her fridge. She has fancy cheeses with French names, and some chocolate alongside a half-eaten pizza and a lot of wine. I take the pizza and eat it cold; I feel so hot from the day, with the running and the walking that I actually enjoy cold pizza.

"Get back here! Look, they're talking to the news! We can watch them on TV live!" She turns on the TV, and indeed there's a bald, aging cop talking to a young blond reporter with Jenny's building in the background.

"Yes, we have our man, whose name I cannot reveal right now."

"And what is it this man is charged with, captain Kassel?"

"I can't give away too much detail at this moment, but I will say that he faces charges to do with his involvement in the local drug business, a business which the citizens of this fine town have been seeing growing under their noses. This is the first in a wave of arrests meant to cripple the rising surge of drug offenses in my town!" If he were ten years younger, a little more in shape, and had any look of decency in him, it would have sounded like Bruce Willis giving a speech before going off to kill Jeremy Irons.

"Looks like your first guess was right, just some guy wanting to make a buck." She sits next to me and finishes another cigarette. "Thanks for coming."

"I was in the neighborhood..." Yes, because this is a nineties movie, and that is how people talk.

"Sure you were." She's not teasing, I think, but I can never tell with her anymore. She used to be really light on both makeup and sarcasm, now they both made me lose track of what she says and thinks.

"Whatever babe, you got anything for the two of us?" She knows what I mean and starts looking. I think she learned too much from Jake, her stashes are separate according for whom they are to be sold or given to.

"Here babe, it's from my 'samples'. It's just Smack, but decent."

"Nahh... I meant some 'wonder powder'." I give her a strange grin, thinking I look super clever and mysterious.

"What's with the name? pfff..." At least she's laughing.

"Come on, I had a shit day."

"Fine... But I don't have anything as a sample. I have to take some money."

"Forget it, I'll take the Smack." I look offended, maybe even indignant, even though I'll admit that it's all free, but I want the good stuff.

She gets me a relatively generous ball of Crack, we share, of course, and start watching TV, but can't concentrate on it, so we end up having sex. It takes forever to get it up, but when we get started it's amazing. She doesn't stop moving the entire time, I can barely keep up with her; if it weren't for the Crack I would probably pass out before we're done. When we are done she gets dressed and lights a smoke, going back to the window to look at the cops.

I join her after a few seconds, still mostly naked. We instinctively dive down from sight when a cop looks up, though I think one of them caught sight of my ass. We have some wine and keep watching the cops, who eventually leave and the street returns to its normal hipster-trap it always is. I wake up at three in the morning without noticing I fell asleep and unconsciously check my phone. I have a message from Gustav,

"Hey man, so you and your girl up 4 dinner? Da wife wuz askin."

Should I send him a message now? Or is it too late? Nahh, he probably has it on silent.

"Have to ask my girl first." And send.

I try to fall back to sleep but can't, so I go and have a beer, the last one she has in the fridge. I sit on the couch and turn on the TV on mute. Night time TV is dumber than daytime TV. It's a lot of reruns and infomercial. They are trying to sell a thing now that will revolutionize the way I cut cheese, no pun intended. In a moment of boredom I notice Jenny's stashes, still on the floor next to the couch. I take a quick look through it, just to see. It's a big crate divided into little sections, the smallest of which is labeled: "High End." It looks like Junk, the kind Jenny gave me for my birthday. I am not a thief, so I won't touch that; she probably sells it at college parties and makes good money, I'll take something else. There's a thing labeled "75/g" which probably is just the price, but it looks and smells like Junk, so I take a tiny bit. Every dealer skims, and every supplier knows it, so Jenny won't get into trouble with Jake over a few grams of missing cheap Junk. I get back into bed and Jenny is there sound asleep. She looks just like the Old Jenny when she sleeps; quiet, pretty, comely. I lay next to her until I fall asleep and the sun wakes me up at ten. Jenny isn't there but she left a note:

"Hey babe,
I have a doctor's appointment today at eleven, so I had to split, but I'll be back by noon, I think. Feel free to hang out or go home.
Kisses, Jenny."

Kisses, not as good as "Yours" for a signoff, but still. I make myself a platter of cheeses and some toast. The cheese is terrible and I throw it away and settle for the toast and some butter. Her coffee is excellent, though, and I take some in a bag before I go home. Only in the car does it occur to me to call Jake, so I do.

"Yo, dude, what the hell?"

"Happy to hear from you too."

"It's all over the news, this Liao guy was arrested, and you, holy shit." I think the gravity of the situation got to him, no more 'scarfacing' for him. "We stay down low, or people might start thinking I set this up, come over to my place tonight."

"No can do, boss-man, I am just going home, besides... If he got arrested, don't you think they're coming for you next?" I hang up, thinking I scared the shit out of him. He does call four or five times after that, but screw him, I want to go home and shower, and stash my new stolen Junk, or try it out. When I get home I take a shower after texting Jenny about dinner, hoping she would answer by the time I am done in the shower.

My hope is vindicated and I get a text back, or five of them. The first just approves of dinner with Gustav, the others...

"Babe, Jake is livid, wtf?"

"Johnny? Are u there? Need to talk."

"Babe, call me, now!"

"If u don't fucking pick up the phone and call me I will fucking kill you!!"

I think I should take her seriously.

"Hey babe, I was in the shower, what's up?"

"What's up? Jake's been arrested, the cops are probably coming for me next, I am going to get the fuck out of here for a while. If I find out you had something to do with this, you are fucking done!" She hangs up. I was expecting something like it, but you know what? Screw her too. I guess dinner is cancelled. I decide to try some of my stolen Junk, and you know what? It feels better now that it's stolen.

It's really cheap crap. I can't believe Jenny was charging seventy five bucks for this. Yeah, it got the job done, but it smells, it took forever to liquidize, and even through a filter my arm burned after injecting it in. But the high. The high was there, and with a vengeance! It was like a long lost brother I rediscovered. It's been too long since I took good Junk. It was, in a way, like going for a piss after you had five gallons of soda and then had to hold it for the whole day; the liberation! The exquisite freedom of mind and body, it all melted. I had no more body, I had no more mind.

I got to throw up.

I do it on the floor, the bathroom being too far away. Chunks of pizza and cheese and bread fill my floor with a mirage of color and stench. I pass out.

I wouldn't exactly call this waking up. My phone rang and I answered it. I am practically still asleep. I can hear De Silva talking, but I treat it like work talk, but I think he is talking about food. Did I volunteer to cook for him? No, dinner, right, yesterday, didn't show up. Excuse? Jenny was sick, yeah, that works. I should tell her to get well, of course Gustav, huh? Raincheck? Sure, maybe next week, we'll see.

Uhh.

I need to eat. Holy crap, I have actual meat in the fridge, mutton. This was planned for my birthday, I was going to cook something for everyone. Since I bought it things changed, though... Jenny hated me, Jimmy disappeared, James and Joanna couldn't hang out, Jamal and Terry took the backseat to knowing us... Man, whatever. I am going to have mutton tonight. It is night. It's going to take the mutton forever to thaw, so fuck it, frozen lasagna it is. It's actually quite good, and easier to make. When I left home, my mom gave me a million recipes, it was weird trying to tell her the US army would be making my meals for me for the next couple of years. I do have a 'one size fits all' kind of recipe for a pot roast, which was what the mutton was for. Other helpful recipes include chicken soup ("For when you're sick and there's no nice lady to take care of you," yes, my mother had no faith I would find someone to take care of me, or me taking care of myself.), Mashed potatoes, which is the most useless recipe ever (take potatoes, mash them, done), banana bread (useful, but hard). Well, I never did have the discipline to learn to cook, besides, what for? the stuff I buy is good enough and tasty, and every now and then I do have some veggie soup to get some vitamins, so, yeah, I'm a-ok.

That really hit the spot. I wash down the lasagna with some beer and then water. The phone rings and I answer without checking who it was.

"Hey, dickwad, I need a lift."

"Fuck you, where from?" From really hating Jake I moved to a more friendly plain of swearing at him, like old navy buddies who are too homophobic to say they like one another, though I wouldn't want to be stuck with him on a boat for months on end, I might kill him.

"Police station, yeah, they figured out I had nothing to do with anything, so I'm sprung." I get a distinct feeling there's a really angry old cop standing next to him, listening in with frustration as he is forced to let the town's only kingpin go.

"Ahh.... Can you wait like... an hour?"

"Shit, man, are you" Pause for dramatic effect "*unwell?*"

"No, well, a bit. Whatever, I'm coming, hold on." I hang up and down two cups of cold coffee from the coffee maker, which tastes like yesterday's socks. From the car I try to call Jenny, but her phone's dead. She's smart, she probably had a 'how to disappear in five steps' plan; I'm just glad that letting me know was one of those steps. She's bound to surface again, though, seeing nothing really happened to anyone except that Roy guy, but he had it coming for being that stupid.

I get to the station and all eyes turn to me, like I'm Batman or something.

"I'm here for Jake Cole, also known as a complete and utter jackoff." I try being funny with the lady cop at the desk, she probably remembers me, though, from my little breakdown and she ignores me, and then calls someone on the intercom. "Cole, someone for Jake Cole."

Jake is brought to the reception hall flanked by two skinny looking cops, both in uniform and both look new. They look reluctant to let him go. In a way, the entire station always seems reluctant to let people go. When I was brought in for the first time ever, at seventeen, it was like in Star Trek, space seemed bent when you entered. It was as if the station was its own gravitational anomaly, or maybe more like in those weird horror movies where the house wants you dead, but not to leave.

I see familiar faces looking at me, jotting it down that I was the one to pick up Jake. We leave the station in silence besides the pens and burps.

We get into the car in continued silence and I start it.

"Where to, boss?"

"Get me home." He sounds odd. "On second thought, drive over to New Lexington. I have someone to meet there."

"You're pitching in for gas, right?" I put the car into gear before he answers, guessing he's in no mood for levity. "Look man, this turned into a shitstorm, obviously you don't have to pay me." I decide to be diplomatic, maybe even preemptive, I know being interrogated isn't fun, so he is no joking mood.

"Whatever man." Again, silence.

This is like a family trip, you know? All nice and amicable, until somebody gets pissed off, then there's shouting, an argument, and then silence and driving. After that everybody just waits for someone else to start a conversation and make it nice again, but no one wants to be the first, so the stalemate continues. It was always Michael and me who did the fighting at first; we always knew how to press each other's buttons. All I needed to do was act like a big brother and know I know better and tell him to shut up, and that would be the shit shot expertly thrown at the fan of family vacation. Sometimes I did overdo it, and when he was young our mom sent him to a child therapist because I overdid it, but still.

Jake is still quiet, so I turn on the radio.

"I was made for loving you, baby

You were made for loving me.

And I can't get enough of you, baby

Can you get enough" Jake changes the station without asking.

"For whom the bell tolls

Time marches on

For whom the bell tolls."

"Who's that?" It sounds heavy, neither mine nor Jake's style.

"Metallica." It speaks!!

"Didn't know you're a fan."

"I'm not, it just sounded cool." The song is over and we are out of the city. The radio tells me about traffic and Jake turns off his phone. "Pull over, I need to take a whizz." I do as asked and Jake gets out and pees for like ever; how much did they make him drink in lock-up? Did he drink his way out of being water-boarded, or something?

I remember just after coming back from Iraq, when I still bought directly off Jake, he asked me if I had water-boarded anyone. He didn't believe me saying "no" and started to 'cite' articles about "what really goes on" there but oddly enough he didn't care much for the opinion of someone who actually saw things there, only for those of bloggers. Jake was always into conspiracy theories, but to his credit, not the real wild ones. He approached this topic with method, some research, but was still more willing to accept the opinions of internet-forum yahoos rather than those of established professors, not to mention witnesses or common sense.

I get tired of waiting and go out to have a piss myself. A few seconds after I start I hear Jake walking towards me.

"Johnny, I have to ask, did you rat me out?"

"Fuck no! I think you're a crazy dick, but I did not rat you out." I turn to face him and my face explodes with pain. It gets warm and gooey and I can feel a loose tooth.

"Are you sure about that? It's little wonder that a day after I tell you to get Roy he gets his ass arrested, and another day goes by, " Jake hits me again, I think, he isn't enjoying it as much I would have. "and I do!" Now he kicks me in the stomach, God he has a heavy shoe.

"They tried to get me too! I split and hid, that's it."

"I don't know Johnny, you've become so... unpredictable." He has a point there. "I can't trust you anymore at all."

"If you'd kill me, they'd trace it back to you, you were the last to see me alive."

"I'm not going to kill you; just tell you that you are done. No one is going to sell you jack shit here." He gets into my car and drives off. I somehow feel vindicated not having invested half a cent into that car that wasn't necessary to make it run, mostly, it went on duct tape.

There isn't much for me to do, I guess. Reporting my car stolen is useless or counterproductive. I can't afford a cab. I just sit up and light a cigarette, then get up and finish that piss I started. I spend the next hours smoking, walking towards town and trying to hitchhike.

The phone rings– de Silva.

"Hey, so when are you up for dinner?"

"How about tonight? Jenny isn't up to it, but she insists I don't be rude." Free food!

"Sure, eight o'clock? Bring some wine, will you?" He hangs up. I walk the remaining way and within two and a half hours I am home and in need of a hit. I find some smack in the kitchen stash behind the fridge. I smoke it; it tastes of lint, but I start to feel better. Things come back into focus and my face barely hurts. I lay down, but I feel restless so I get up again after a second. I try calling Jenny but it's dead; after the third time I get pissed off and chuck the damn phone to fuck knows where. I start looking for it after a minute and find it nice and snug under the fridge, which remind me I'm hungry. It's half past six, which is late enough for me to wait and eat at de Silva's but do I want to do that? I am so starved that I decide to make myself a snack. It's a BLT sandwich, with stale bread and no L involved. There isn't much of a T either; it's basically two pieces of bread, ketchup and bacon. I have a couple of beers with it to feel truly satisfies and wait an hour till I have to go. My car is there, a little bent out of shape, but there it is. I didn't notice it coming in, but I knew Jake wouldn't be that much of an ass to really steal it, he was just pulling my leg. I get in and find a note from him taped to the wheel:

"Dear asswipe,

I couldn't think of anyone stupid enough to give the car to except back to you, so here you go. If you try to buy anything from my guys, I will fuck you up.

Have a great day, Jake."

The drive over to de Silva's is weird at this hour. I got used to driving from there in the evening, but not there. I ring the bell and realize I had forgotten the wine; too late, I hear footsteps coming to the door.

"Hey! Beunas tardes! Good to see you." Gustav, or de Silva, however he'd like to be called. He gives me a hug, like, a man-hug.

"What happened to your face?"

"Just a little accident, that's all." I step inside and everything smells amazing. "oh shit! With everything that happened today, I forgot the wine!" Rule #1 to getting away with social misconduct: be the first to mention your misconduct, politeness will oblige others to forgive you.

"No worries, we have plenty, see?" I am led to a table laden with goods, Mexican and pseudo-Mexican, yes, I know some so-called Mexican dishes are actually American inventions, but Gustav saw it right to serve some of those. Gustav's wife is like a fast-forward-play after the Super Bowl match, moving in and out in fast-forward speed. Taking over the hosting duties was Gustav, who moved in a bunch of new things since we finished working on the house. A bigger TV, a Blu-ray player and surround-sound. I sit there as he demonstrates the abilities of his new home which I built, or at least its shitter.

We sit down to eat and it's amazing. A small part of my brain prepares my ass for a difficult night, one has to be careful.

"My wife, Catalina, makes the best Mexican food in fucking Ohio, you just wait; your woman is stupid to miss out on this." Fuck him for calling Jenny stupid, in reality, she is very smart for disappearing when things go south like that. A true dealer has to build a system on trust, but it's all a matter of self-preservation. As much as you need to make sure your clients think of you as one of them, you have to take care of yourself, that's why Jenny split. I am sure she'll be back soon. To be honest, I don't kid myself thinking I'd be a reason to risk coming back for, but there's still a lot of money to be made here; it's a small town so you won't see a big task-force here in some anti-drug effort, but a lot of people with both money and contempt for their life, the perfect drug-users.

"Yeah, she's just has a lot on her mind right now, and is a bit sick." I assure the couple in between spoonfuls of some kind of bean soup, feeling a bit self-conscious about slurping. They both sort of stare t me with what looks like awkward bewilderment.

Dinner is excellent, but de Silva's long stares and weird attempts to make conversation reminds me of those people who just sit around with you when you get high, not to share the experience, but to get some free stuff, like sloppy seconds, which activates my junky-senses, he wants something.

"So, what's in this...ah... whatever it's called?" I'm too drunk for Spanish names right now.

"Pork and chili, mostly. They're called Empanadas." Catalina answers me, and I think I insulted her by not knowing the name. "Oh, well, good thing Jenny didn't come, she's Jewish, doesn't eat pork." I grab another piece and stuff it into my mouth before she'd ask me a question.

"How did you two meet?" She's indifferent to the pork-juice dripping from my mouth and asks about romance, I like her.

"At a party. I came back from Iraq rather recently, well, couple of years, and a bunch of people from my old school organized a party, albeit a year and a half later, but they said it was for me, and she was there, the rest is history." She still looks like she'd rather be anywhere else, but fuck it, she's a great cook, so I like having her there.

"I will leave you men to it." She goes off and carries away more dishes than inhumanly possible and leaves me with her husband, who in the meantime managed to procure a bottle of tequila, two glasses, and some lemons from somewhere.

"Here you go." He hands me a glass, not a shot glass, a proper glass, full of tequila and a lemon before raising his 'tequila-kit' for a toast. We clink glasses and I try to down the drink, maybe

Mexicans know what they're doing, if it weren't for the lemon, I wouldn't be able to keep it down. De Silva seems unaffected, but I suppose his drinks this often enough to have lost all sense of taste.

"Thanks, man." When I say it in this context, now, I sound like one of those TV-teachers, trying too hard to be cool by adopting the kids' lingo, I come off with a pseudo-Mexican accent. "Not used to drinking tequila, wow, strong stuff." I feel like an idiot. I had Heroin this morning, but tequila is too much for me? Fuck that, I empty the rest of the glass in one gulp.

"Easy there, hombre." He laughs, I think it's endearing, but I don't know if he just thinks I'm a shit-head.

"Sorry, not used to being beat by booze."

"No worry, just don't hurl." He pats me on the back and laughs. "Shit, I don't have beers, I'll go for a beer-run. Be back in a few."

"Hey, there's like, this awesome store, friends of mine work there." I realize I don't know what's Philipp's store is called. I've been visiting it since before I knew Joanna, from, like, the nineties, when I was ten. How can I just forget something like that? "It's only a few blocks away, on Memorial Street."

"Sure, I'll go there. They have canned?"

"Yeah, trust me." He leaves and I am left with an empty room and some food. I stuff some food into my pocket before realizing I could probably just ask to have some. I call out to see if Catalina didn't run away entirely. She comes back in a night gown, blue and yellow. She is younger than de Silva, but older than me, I would guess thirty two to thirty five, dark skin, amazing black hair, and now as I look it's like a porn-video and she is about to seduce me.

"Yes?"

"I was just wondering if I could have some of your wonderful cooking to go, I didn't want to wake you later so I thought I'd ask now, didn't realize you are getting ready for bed." In my head she assures me it's ok, but she is feeling lonely in bed, and wants me to keep her company there. In reality she goes to the kitchen to bring tin foil and wraps some stuff, leaving it there afterwards for me to take it later. She even marks everything like they do in a deli, and I can't decide if I like that or not. She goes back to bed, alone as she prefers it.

De Silva comes back and we go on drinking, like he was never gone. He bought imported beer, he is a man of the finer things, he says. After a few more glasses of tequila and more beers he gathers the courage to tell me why I am actually there.

"So, listen man, the bathroom turned out great." No, that's not it; that is the introduction. The bigger the bad thing people want to say the bigger the compliment they open with. "And you know I know some people around town, maybe I can get you another job." Not what I was expecting. "My brother-in-law wants to build a deck, and maybe like, a brick housed grill, you up for it?" What's his game?

"I don't know, how big? What's the schedule?"

"Why, you busy?" He kind of bumps the tequila bottle into my forehead, but the bottle is almost empty so I didn't even feel it.

He gives me a number before I leave, the rest of the evening is mostly comprised of de Silva talking about his various money-making schemes, like The Honeymooners. I don't really know what he does for a living, I just assumed it's to do with food, or smuggling workers into the country.

"So, you'll give Carlo a call, right? I promised the wife, she was really happy with the bathroom."

"Yeah, you got yourself one hell of a wife, not a trace of old porn movies in her." I leave it at that and go. Only halfway through the

185

drive home do I realize how ridiculous that sounded without the context of the bullshit that went on in my head. I do sometimes wish I could transmit my chains of associations to peoples' heads, but most of the time that would probably get me arrested.

I get home a see it's four in the morning, and tomorrow I have to go help James and Joanna move, load up the truck and shit. I decide not to go to sleep at all. I have a giant coffee and try watching TV. I do fall asleep

I wake up and look at my watch, not too late. I take some leftover Coke and get in the car and drive off to James's, which is actually Philipp's. Truck's already there and so are Joanna and James, they looked pissed and sad.

I get out of the car and grab a box to load it up into the truck. James grabs my arm before I do.

"You're early." What?

"Huh?"

"We only really expected you to get here at four, come on, we have time, say hi, relax." He hands me a beer and I give Joanna a big hug. She's crying. I hate seeing a girl cry, and in her current state, Joanna's a mess. It's not like I don't understand, she's leaving, she's quitting, she's pregnant; of course she's a mess. I hug her back and we sit there reminiscing about stuff that we've known for a while never actually happened that way, it's just the accepted myth we keep rehashing. About how James and I stole a car, which was actually abandoned by his parents, or about that time we broke into my own house to steal my dad's premium whiskey. It's not really breaking in when it's your own house, but we said it is because it was after curfew AND I brought people whose house it wasn't. After those they want to start reminiscing about really hard stuff, but I am too Coked up to allow them the pleasure, they are quitting, and that is the last thing Joanna needs.

I start loading the boxes when James asks me why I'm getting so restless, but isn't that what they invited me for? I start loading up till I get tired, and it's getting dark. I have no idea where James and Joanna went to, I find myself with Philipp, loading up the last boxes; DVDs and kitchenware.

"Corporal, you're a good friend to those two." Oh no, I don't do emotional crap very well. I can't deal with someone dumping on me very well. "here you go, I know you are used to stronger stuff, but come on, indulge me." He gives me a beer and a joint, I accept both. The Coke has worn off, and I feel exhausted. We sit on the hood of the truck and all is quiet for a while, which means this is going to be bad. I think I just have one of those faces people feel comfortable talking to, like a shrink or a priest, I would have made a great spy.

"Thanks gunnery sergeant." I accept and take a big toke, preparing for what is to come. Like most veterans, Philipp doesn't have a lot of friends, and the last few months he went through a lot. His daughter got married, pregnant, she is moving away. There was a murder in town, Obama withdrew from Iraq, there's just so much to process, and Philipp doesn't really have a way to do that. I'm lucky, I have Junk, I have Jenny, I have that part of the wall I punch to feel better; Philipp only has Joanna and now she is going to be there for another man, a man who never knew the horror Philipp knows. I start to cry for no reason, I hug Philipp and tell him he is a hero, which he just accepts with the stoic dignity of a gunnery sergeant, and that tells me how much that means to him.

Civies often think discharged soldiers are cold and distant, but no, like other cultures we simply have a different way of expressing what we feel. Like with Jamal, it's a nuanced, intricate maze of sarcasm and stoic silence.

"Corporal, sit up." To translate, this means 'I know, I appreciate this, but gather yourself, please'.

"Sorry, gunnery sergeant, it's the shitstorm." To translate, 'oh, my God, that's embarrassing, I'm sorry'.

"I know, here, have a minute." To translate, 'I feel the same, there's a lot going on'.

"She's leaving." I venture into direct speech, since this isn't covered by the more nuanced lingo of people who share what we share.

"Yeah, my little girl is leaving, damn good." Unbelievable. That is why he is a gunnery sergeant. He not only gave me this break from our established grounds, he was ahead of me in there in essence.

"James is going to take care of her."

"Fuck, corporal, she could take care of herself, and him if she had to. That is not what I am worried about."

"What then?" We pass the joint between us. Even though it's very weak for me, I know it's a lot for him and that he probably only made it to make me comfortable.

"You know." Wow. He is depressed. To translate: 'things are so bad there are no words to describe it, and giving a detailed list would just take up too much time'. "World's gonna just keeps spinnin'." To translate: 'I feel helpless, like the world is passing me by; we don't belong in this world anymore.'

"C'mon." I give him another toke and pat him on the shoulder. "Suck it up." To translate: 'I know it gets rough, but all you really can do is fight on, against life.

He sits up on the hood and looks at the streetlights.

"Corporal, a sergeant is only is as good as his squad" Oh my Lord. To translate: 'I don't know what to do now without those around me, I need you.' He took a big swig of a little flask he had at his side. It smelled like whiskey. I thought he was off the wagon. It was his drinking after the gulf war, the first one, that drove him to beat his wife, Joanna's mom, and eventually drive her insane, according to the lawyer who represented her after she tried to stab him and kill the then ten-year-old Joanna. The trial was a local fiasco, a meal-ticket to all anti-interventionist politicians, the returning soldiers after a senseless war with all that burden... to me, it was just like Rambo, the first one, which is the good one.

"We've got you covered." To translate: 'I know this is really hard for you and I am trying to show support, I just don't know what to say right now.'

"Ok kid, time to work." To translate: "I knew it, fuck all of you people. I'm just gonna do my own thing.'

We finish packing up the truck for the next day when they will be off, and we head inside. Philipp hides his flask, I volunteer to take the fall if Joanna finds it, obviously she is a bit sensitive about Philipp drinking.

A bunch of people are there for a small farewell; James's work friends, Joanna's non-junky friends, and a bunch of people I don't know. I try to mingle but everybody is talking about either baby stuff or work stuff, and I can't really discuss my failed shakedown attempt or drug dealing. I gravitate back towards Philipp who sobered up again and is looking really tired.

"Gunnery Sergeant." I hand him a beer, thinking it's non-destructive enough for him.

"No thanks." He keeps drinking his Sprite.

"Lots of civies here." I try to revive our earlier conversation. As much as I don't like being dumped on, I prefer being dumped on by a gunnery sergeant over talking about reality TV with a civie any day.

"Did you expect anything else Corporal?" He seems colder than before.

"No, sir. I just don't know these people, and am probably out of place here."

"You're here because my little girl wanted you here, so suck it up." To translate: Shut up and take it, neither of us is here of their own volition.

"Sure thing, sir." I walk back into the sandstorm of the party, and try to find something to latch on to, a mention of Weed, a morsel of army-talk, maybe even a slip of the tongue about the economy. I get nothing, so I stay on the periphery of conversation James gets into all evening, slipping in a word of general agreement with someone while offering to top off anyone's drink as an excuse to get out.

Joanna, of course, doesn't drink and is trying to talk to everyone at once which looks funny and sounds ridiculous. She's acting like some gracious hostess but is at the end of her rope as she can't 'float' from clique to clique due to a life form in her belly. James is more or less out of commission, just kind of hovering in the room with a glass of something in his hand. Philipp decided to leave and is in his room, leaving the love birds to fend for themselves.

I decide to try and help Joanna with everything and start serving drinks and moving the food about a bit, offering people from the uneaten bowl of mush Joanna called flan. At some point James abducts me again for some small-talk with people I don't know and he doesn't like; I think they are Joanna's friends from school. They talk about their husbands and wives, and how one of them, who isn't present, but standing next to the flan looking rather disheveled, had a miscarriage, and maybe will get divorced. I get reminded of those soaps Jenny used to watch when we would just stay home and smoke all day, getting high bit by bit. There was always something massively wrong with those not present, and all the characters took turns in not being present. The only thing I really found disquieting about those shows was that they all looked and proceeded the same, even when they were in Spanish, I always knew what was happening, because I saw it on the other shows, it was like one mega-show that never ends, if you missed your episode, just watch its equivalent on another show, you'll get to the same point; that someone is cheating on someone, and it's someone's evil twin.

I lost all trace of the conversation, so I retreat back to nodding and "He did what?" when a space between two sentences presents itself. Eventually I get to go to the bathroom, where I have a small smoke of some weed I found in my pocket, great thing I didn't wash these pants. Going back to the party, I finish what is left of the flan, I felt sorry for it, and its ginger and mint goodness, so I ate it. Miscarriage-girl is there, having upgraded herself to guiltily staring at some vanilla pudding. I try to make conversation, but she isn't interested in talking to someone who can't swallow his flan before speaking, so she excuses herself to the bathroom, but actually going for the front door.

I lean back on the table and look at the room. It's odd how many new friends James and Joanna have since leaving the group. True, I'm here, but most of the room are still strangers to me. I understand why they didn't invite Jenny, even if you could, or Jimmy and Joyce, but it's still weird. Don't get me wrong, I am super happy for them moving on with their lives, getting married, having a baby, moving to Cleveland, I just don't like losing my best friend, you know?

"Hey there international man of mystery." A cute girl starts talking to me. I think she's one of James work friends, don't remember the name, though.

"Hey there, you..." Smooth as always.

"Hahaha, Brianna, with two N's."

"Is the extra one for good luck?" I think I heard that line in a movie, a crap one with Hugh Grant.

"No, funny man, it's so my parents feel special."

"Are you sure it's not so YOU feel special" She smiles and pauses.

"Aren't you a charmer."

"I do snakes, too." Great, double entendre for: I have sex with snakes.

"Ok, I am going to forget you said that." Thank you, lady.

"You work with James, right?"

"Yeah, I do the ordering management, how exciting!" She is seeping with sarcasm it's almost attractive. "You?"

"No, I know James from school."

"I know, dummy, if you'd be working with him, I would know you from work too, genius. What do you do?" Sell drugs, fail at beating up idiots, get beat up, fix some guy's toilet, and just generally nothing.

"This and that, you know how the market is..." This never fails.

"How vagabond..ish? Is that a word?"

"Not really, but if you get enough people to use it, it could be." My ninth grade English teacher taught me that after I had invented over seventy words in one essay!

"You can be the first. Could you mix me a drink?" The booze is just spread around on the table, gin, vodka, whiskey, beer, rum, wine, and some juices too, I take a random pick and mix us both something that comes out a sort of gray whirl of drunken flirtation.

She's very cool, Brianna. She hates her job, and thinks James is the only cool coworker she's had in seven years of working there. She started out at seventeen, as an assistant, then they paid for some night classes for her to get proper training, and now she manages all the orders the company gets. She and I leave the party and head out next to the truck to smoke and after a few minutes I realize that it's my second and last joint we are smoking, I think she noticed immediately. We get into my car and she starts kissing me, I try to tell her I have a girlfriend, but I'm not sure I do. She lets me touch her, but stops me when I try to take off her shirt.

"Not that kind of girl, Johnny." I can respect that, which is why I decide that now that things cooled off I should tell her about Jenny.

"I kind of have someone." Good solid start.

"What?" I don't know how, but she already has her coat back on. "You asshole, were you planning to wait until I'd fuck you before telling me?"

"I was trying to say something, but your tongue kept distorting my words."

"Shut the fuck up, get out."

"Ahh... It's my car."

"Real classy, you were going to cheat on your girlfriend in your car, great." She opens the door and gets out.

"Listen, I'm not even sure we are still together, you know, she left, and I can't reach her."

"Real heartbreaking stuff, go back to the party, maybe there's a bimbo there drunk enough for that to work on her." She slams the door and goes back to the party, which, I suppose, means I can't go back in there; James will understand why I split.

I start the car and drive home, which at first glance looks like someone had trashed the place, looking for something, but then I remember that's how I left it. Between getting drunk with de Silva and rushing to help James on Cocaine, I fucked this place up good. It's too late to tidy up now, and I am so far down I don't think I'll ever be able to get high again, so I fall asleep on the pile of dirty undershirts decorating the bed, my head comfortably resting on my belt buckle from my Beating-Up-Roy outfit.

I wake up late, I guess. Turning on my TV before even getting out of bed. The news is on and there have been more arrests last night, I see a mugshot of Jimmy in the report, with the headline, "Addicts resist arrest, now complaining about police brutality." I never had much stoke or trust in the news media, but I can totally picture Jimmy resisting arrest, biting off an officer's ear, again.

The rest of the news is depressing, more talk on getting out of Iraq, economic crises, fires in California... The only thing missing is a couple of zombie outbreaks and presto! The Apocalypse; according to the news at least.

I don't have any milk and Philipp is closed for the day, driving the love birds to Cleveland, so I don't have anywhere to go buy milk either. Not that I would have even if Philipp were open, because A) It's too early, or at least it is for me, and who ever goes out to buy milk BEFORE drinking his coffee? And B) Don't want any questions from James and Joanna as to why I vanished last night, and why Brianna seemed pissed all night.

My coffee comes out pretty strong and I have a smoke after it, along with some pop-tarts and honey. And... God, I have absolutely nothing to do today. Ever had one of those realizations? That you woke up, got yourself (more or less) together and... nothing? There was no actual day to begin? It's both nice and shit. I start rationing my remaining Junk and drugs of all sorts, barely enough for two or three days. I do this more out of boredom than necessity, to be honest, it would have been better not to do that, it just made me see in what sorry state I am. It'll probably just annoy or depress me, so I kick off my day with some weed. I have quite a bit of that left, so there's enough to go around. More relaxed, I sit in front of the TV again, at least now the news is over. There's nothing really on now, just the general babble of some panel about how horrid something is and how someone should do something about it.

I make myself some toast, more out of boredom than anything and start looking through my phone in case Jenny called. Of course she didn't, she thinks she's on the run like the fifth member of the A-TEAM, ready to... sit there and see if anyone wants to get high. She will eventually see it's pointless, and she will come back. I keep browsing through my phone and read every text I ever sent Jenny, I've only had this damn phone for less than a year, so there aren't that many messages anyway, so it only takes an hour or so to look through them, I skip most of the drama messages, of course, having less energy for the drama of five months ago than for the current dramas.

Eventually I get to the last few weeks, and the messages get less and less personal. That is when Jake got into her head, and now he said he's cutting me off completely; that fucker. Jenny, in a way, is my last hope to score here, so either she comes back, or I move somewhere else; maybe I can ask James about Cleveland, not that I think he'll look people up, but a junky's a junky, he'll be able to see around him, like a police dog. The police should hire junkies to sniff out drugs; who better? Just cut one off for a few days and he'd be five times faster and more ferocious than a sniffing dog.

Which makes me realize, time to face the music.

"Hey man, how are you? Nice party last night, on your way to

Cleveland?"

"Sure thing, dude. Where'd you disappear to, man? You were supposed to help clean up." I don't remember volunteering for that, but I can't refuse James anything.

"Long story."

"Ok." 'nuff said', as they say.

"How's Joanna?"

"Asleep, barely shut an eye last night, crying; she gets emotional lately."

"Poor bastard." He laughs a bit. "Take care, you two."

"You too, stay in touch."

"Sure thing." We both hang up and I go back to the TV, he presumably to an exciting game of I Spy against Philipp, undisputed champion.

So... now what? Without having to go sell, go build, or go bug Jenny, I am left essentially without any reason to get out of bed, which means getting back to bed for me. I take my first hit of the day. It's a strange and rather sad feeling to prepare my works in absolute silence. It's not the first time I've used by myself, no, but usually the noise in my head provides some background, some sense of urgency and purpose. By 'noise in my head' I don't mean voices or anything crazy like that, just the regular white noise between the ears, like after a busy day or Jenny-drama. Now, I don't need to go anywhere, I'm not taking it to make something bad go away, I'm just... it's like lunch, you know? It's a part of the daily routine.

I finish cleaning the works first, needle is new, so no need to work on that. The syringe has been with me for a while, though, and there's some congealed blood and a white kind of crud inside, so I clean it with steam and vodka. I don't really drink vodka, ever, but when people come around for a drink they always bring some, but no one drinks it, so I keep the bottles for disinfection. I also like to think that it gives the high a special boost. Like in those movies where the old sea captain puts whiskey down the engine of a ship; my dad loves those movies. He was a big fan of navy stuff, wanted to be a sailor, but they said he can't on account of his physical fitness, so he showed them and became an engineer and came back to fix their boats, feeling a bit smug when he got to tell a captain the ship isn't sea capable.

With the cleaning done I look for a lighter, and when I find one it's so low on gas I have to light a candle and do everything over that. It's my last bit of Junk, so I plan on savoring it. I wait a bit longer before releasing the strap, let it really build pressure. It's in. I feel out of breath and full of life. I can't stop blinking, it's so fast, so impelling. My neck falls to the shoulder and my head rolls around like a traffic cone being run over and the noise is back. Static and currents run between my ears and I just let them stay there, they are better than the quiet. Now I turn the TV back on to the Discovery channel, where monkeys are fighting over dominion of their little charred looking tree. The narrator is on about evolution and early civilization, but fuck, it's just monkeys, and one tree is as good as another, isn't it?

I have a beer during the commercials, it's a different show now, actually, it's a different channel; don't remember switching, maybe I sat on the remote. I get back to the couch and watch some stupid cartoon. I feel out of breath again. I probably didn't get enough sleep, my head hurts and my eyes feel dry. I decide to take a little nap.

Shit. It's dark again. Ok, more than a nap. No use going to sleep again, I'm awake as I've ever been. I go outside and get into the car, just to anywhere really and end up driving to the library. Yes, it's late and it's closed. I am just curious to see who's selling there. It's obviously one of Jake's guys, so I won't be able to buy from them, call it a professional call. Like a head chef going to eat out somewhere, or a retired architect hanging out at construction yard, which I guess they don't do, but that is my analogy nonetheless.

It's some weird skinny kid, being way too obvious as a dealer. God, where do those kids buy clothes? Not that I have a developed fashion sense, but at least my pants don't fall under my waistline and my hoodies aren't ten times my size. He looks about as bright as a blacklight, so maybe I should try and buy a bit, still have some money from the de Silva job.

I get out of the car and walk up to the kid, he looks barely eighteen. He gets up, trying to look 'gangsta' and spits several times in the five seconds it takes us to narrow the gap between us. He also keeps rubbing his nose, so either he just did some Coke, or he watched way too many cheap action movies.

"Yo, man, you got beef?" I really have no idea what that might mean.

"What? I'm just looking to score." Okay, I'll admit, rookie mistake coming off like that, but God damn it, this idiot is going to be completely incomprehensible.

"O'yeah? Watcha want, man?" His accent is a mix of Mexican and Down syndrome, but by his complexion I would guess... Irish American.

"Something to while away the time." Let's see if he has the IQ of those monkeys I saw on TV.

"Wha?"

"Okay you little genius, I want what you're selling."

"You a cop?"

"Don't you think the cops are either all tucked away nicely in their donut bibs, sleeping?"

"Answer the question." Finally, English!

"No, I neither am, nor have I ever been a police officer."

"How much you wanna buy?"

"Three hundred fifty's worth." I might as well stock up as long as he is willing to sell me.

"Hold on." He takes out his phone and looks through it, probably for the calculator. "No can do." Fuck.

"Come on, man. I came out all this way."

"I'm not supposed to sell you anything." He actually looks sorry, even a bit sympathetic; fuck it, I don't need some asswipe junk's sympathy.

I punch him in the face and kick his shin, really hard. He goes down screaming, but there's no one around. Shit. This was stupid. Now I gave Jake a reason to actually come after me, not just cut me off. By the time I realize that he starts getting up, so I kick him again and look through his pockets; he's smart enough to have hidden the stash elsewhere. I sit on his back and try to think what to do with him. He will tell Jake. Can I scare him enough to get him to leave town before he does? No, I am not that scary. Shit!! Luck strikes!! He has a bit of LSD on him.

I put a shitload of LSD in his mouth and wait for him to start tripping, when he does, I get off him.

"The fuck you do to me? Get that thing off me!" He's preoccupied with whatever it is he is seeing, which gives me time for a quick search of the area for his stash, and a short SMS to his boss from his phone.

"Sorry, man, tripping balls, I'm out for the niiight." That should sour any 'testimony' he might give Jake about me.

I can't find his stash, and he is making so much noise I decide to scram, taking nothing else from the guy or he might suspect something. This was a pointless drive, but at least I got some exercise, which might help me fall back to sleep.

When I get home I lie down until I get so bored and hungry I just decide to stay up all night and just have something to eat now. I make microwave hamburgers, with some fries that I actually do fry, like, in a pan. It tastes nice, and goes very well with my late night TV shows, or better said infomercials. Someone who seems overly excited about a vacuum cleaner is cleaning everything in the studio, even his own pants! God, who is dumb enough to call and order those things, who besides insomniacs even watches these commercials? Well...

I stay to watch this crap until I can't take it any longer and turn off the TV and turn on the computer instead. I watch some senseless YouTube videos, but that gets boring too. In the end I switch to the most time tested method of entertainment, reading.

"Though she never before noticed, but always knew, she found the sun to be the most beautiful sight in creation. Today, a day of rebirth, was now to her a pure and insurmountable achievement and victory; she even managed to shed a tear. After the night of terror and captivity ended, and her captor dealt justice, she was free, and the sun was to be the ever-emphatic reminder of her victory."

Wow, so many words wasted on basically nothing. I throw the book aside and stare at nothing in particular for a second. I used to tell people who asked me that if I would go to college I would study literature, I even told Nathan that, but I doubt I would have had the patience to start dissecting poems and shit. I don't know why I said that to people, or why I didn't go to college, I had okay grades in school, the whole army thing just seemed right. My mom thought I was crazy, my dad had the most typically 'him' reaction to the idea: he just asked me "You know you actually have to do stuff in the army, right?" and left it at that. I guess I just went for it because he seemed to presuppose I won't be able to; big, stupid mistake.

Either way, the result is the same; I am sitting here with nothing to do. I decide to have a smoke and watch TV again, anything but the news. There's a TV show on that shows a guy trying to shoot another guy with a bow and arrow, and the other guy has to dodge it; people would watch anything. Just a few hours before sunrise, might as well stay up and watch it, isn't that all the rage in literature, the beauty of sunrise?

I light my second cigarette and it feels too light, so I roll up a third in advance. The drowsiness is taking some toll on my motor skills and it turns out the worst cigarette I have ever rolled, which makes me rather happy not to have wasted any weed on it. Eventually I decide to shut my eyes for a few minutes.

I open them to find a shitty bright morning. I get up from a sweat stained sheet and have a morning beer. Fuck. On the bright side, seven missed calls and two messages; people remember I exist, hopefully not all death-threats.

"To hear the first message, press one." A calm nice voice of a potential psychologist who decided her voice would be of better use telling people they are needed. ONE.

"Two thirty, call me at my prepaid, Jenny."

Oh YES!! She's back! What time is it? Whatever, I call anyway, still with sleep in my voice.

"Hey babe."

"You moron, I told you two thirty, it's eleven." I woke up early, it seems. "Listen, I forgot something important in my apartment, very important, I need you to go get it."

"What is it? How do I get in? How are you?"

"You'll know it when you see it, key's hidden behind that ugly Jesus painting, and I'm very stressed." She's all business today.

"What do I do with it?"

"Dispose of it." Quick answer. "Johnny, has anyone been looking for me?"

"No." Well, it's true but also a lie, not like I've been keeping my ear to the ground, for all I know there's a huge manhunt going. "They let Jake walk, you know. But Jimmy's locked up, again."

"He's a moron, tried to sell Meth to a cop, they couldn't ignore that, and speaking of which, go to my apartment and get rid of the thing." Ahh, ok.

"Sure, can I have breakfast first?" She laughs, all Old Jenny like, like when people look at embarrassing pictures of themselves from the fourth grade.

"Not your mother, Johnny, just get it done." I think it was mock resignation, but she did hang up. I do have my breakfast, she isn't the boss of me and I am hungry. I gulp down some pop tarts and drink a black coffee, not because I'm hardcore, but because my milk's spoiled, the fridge was open, who knows how long. I dump the cheese looking milk down the drain, when it fails to flow down, scoop it up and dump it in the trash, making a note of emptying it before the flies come in for a taste and sue me for giving them poisoned food.

I drive up to Jenny's apartment, and this time I do check around for people with an earpiece standing around checking stuff out. I don't expect for it to be weirdos reading newspapers with eyeholes cut in it wearing trenchcoats, but if you know what you're looking for you can spot them. That is truly an area where junkies and US soldiers meet in their standard of excellence. A junky always has to be aware of possible police stings, an arranged meeting could turn into a bust in a second, so when you arrive, you need to know how to find the undercover cop's backup, suspicious vans for stores that don't exist, workers not doing any work, thin, well-groomed construction workers, that kind of stuff. Soldiers in the field need to be able to see who's a civi and who might be carrying a weapon, or acting as a spotter, and there are always tell-tale signs, you just need to be sober enough to spot them.

I think the coast is clear so I get out of the car, and run into the little girl from a while back, she doesn't recognize me, because last time I was thinner, high, and unshaven. She opens the door for me and I climb upstairs. Man, that is an ugly Jesus painting.

I get into the apartment and am surprised to see it in more or less perfect order, well, Jenny's version thereof. The sofa and coffee table are a bit messy, but only with ashtrays and smokes, there is nothing on the floor besides an imitation oriental rug. The only stain in sight is that weird one on the floor from the wine I spilled a while ago on the sofa while pouring Jenny a drink; back then I covered it with my ass.

I start looking around for anything incriminating Jenny might want me to get rid of, and find quite a few things. Seven grams of Junk, ten of Meth, almost ten grams of weed, and some good vodka, or at least the bottle is nice. Yes, I know vodka isn't illegal, but technically, Jenny's underage, so it's illegal for her to have it, so I 'confiscate' that as well. I put everything in a bag and water Jenny's plants. Going back outside, I call Jenny again, but there's no response, so I get into the car to 'dispose' of my find.

At home I get everything ready by cleaning a needle and spend ten minutes digging out a clean spoon from the kitchenette. Eventually I make a compromise with the kitchenette by cleaning the spoons before using of one. I barely have the patience to do it right, I start getting sloppy, almost forgetting the filter. I notice I didn't tie up tight enough, I barely am willing to wait for everything to liquefy. But I am not stupid, I know it's better to wait, better to do things right, the rewards are better. When everything is ready I push down and wait a second for the Junk to come, which happens very slowly for some reason. I feel it first in my nose of all places, like a bad sneeze decided to rebel and take hostages in my left upper-nostril. Then it move up to behind my eye and lands on the front of my brain. I think that's probably how brain surgery feels like, something crawling up the inside of your skull to come in and make you all better.

A few seconds more and the eagle has landed, it almost feels like a slushy melting into my brain, cooling it down from the dangerous work of everyday computations. I fall back on the couch/bed and take stock of the day, week, month. I had some ups and downs, but I think things are alright now. Jenny's back, and that can only spell good news.

I feel the bubbles of euphoria floating in my head, popping here and there with a soft gush of air like a secret fart you squeeze out at dinner parties with your girlfriend's mom. I walk over to the fridge and break something on the way underneath my foot, I think it was my syringe which kind of sucks. I want to eat something, but can't find anything so I close the fridge again and storm the pantry, find instant noodles, and get the sudden urge to lie down. I walk back to the bed and all but collapse on it; shit Junk. I start heaving, and my head almost explodes as more and more of the bubbles of euphoria become brain-farts. I start throwing my head left and right as that seems to help alleviate some of the brain-farts.

I think I passed out. It's dark out and there's some vomit on the bed. I don't remember vomiting, so I must have passed out. I go and have a huge drink of water, and wolf down several empanadas that de Silva's wife gave me. My sheets are full of puke now, great. I try hand washing them, but the smell is still there, so I decide to soak them in water and soap overnight. As for the mattress, well... This isn't my first rodeo; knowing I could hurl anytime I take a big hit I use a nylon cover over my mattress. It kind of feels like being a bed-wetter, and Jenny thought it's the weirdest thing she ever saw when getting into bed with a guy, but hey, at least my mattress isn't full of puke.

Now I am really hungry, and eating cold empanadas isn't going to do the trick, so I do go for those instant noodles I found earlier. My head still hurts and so does my arm, which is weirdly blue at the track mark. I guess it means I have some infection or something, but I feel fine, so I just take a bit of antibiotics I have left over from being sick last year and go on with eating my instant noodles, with an emphasis on "instant". It definitely isn't enough and I find myself looking for more to eat, so with my incredible ingenuity in the kitchen(ette) I combine the goodness of bread, ketchup, and some cheese to create a sort of mini-pizza.

Me and Michael used to do that all the time when we were kids. I am the older brother, so I was sometimes responsible for feeding the kid, so I just shoved one of these babies into the toaster oven and waited for the cheese to melt. Michael didn't really have an actual pizza until he was seven, so he had no idea that my little improvisation was so far off the mark. My other culinary inventions included microwaved potato (sometimes even with butter), 'whatever salad' comprised of any seven ingredients I found in the fridge, and pasta with tuna. I think I was a good brother, I mean, it was hardly home cooking, but what do you expect a six-year-old to make? Fillet mignon?

I finish my make-believe pizza and decide to go outside, walk off the headache. The neighborhood is lit well by streetlights and passing cars, with stupid teenagers 'carpe dieming'' hooting and yoohing until their lungs might burst on their ways to silently and inconspicuously trying to sneak into a bar or club. I reach Jenny's parents' house and stop for a second, not weirdly or to stare, just for a second. I really thought it was funny back then, when we first met at that party, that I knew her since she was ten, but never really knew her. She was just another girl in the neighborhood, well, in a slightly better side of it, until we kissed. Before that she was background, her mom was a center of attention for some of the boys, Jake included, but not Jenny. By the time I think of this I walk past the house, past the neighboring house, and past the gas station at the end of their street.

A police car drives by and I think the cops are checking me out, but they look too tired to bother with me; I try walking with a bit more purpose, like I'm late somewhere. I eventually reach Craig's, which is a sort of bar which pretends to be a restaurant. That tells me I walked almost four miles. I go in and sit at the end of the bar, looking over the menu.

"Beer please"

"Care to be more specific?" It's Laura, she's been working here forever. She has the patience of a coked up squirrel, but everyone loves her, because the sight of Laura is the sight of coming alcohol.

"The cheapest you have." She walks away and murmurs something about my ass and cheapness, but I try to ignore her. The place is only half full, all those teenagers from the road don't come here; they go to bigger towns with more upbeat, hip bars, with music released after 1984. I get my beer and drink very slowly, I can hardly afford to spend a lot of money.

"Hey, what time is it?" A thought occurred to be.

"Nine fifteen." Laura answers me before even looking at her watch, she knows how long's her shift and she counts the seconds until she can get rid of all these morons here and go home to her TV and beloved four cats. I don't really know how many cats she has, if any, but I guess it would be four.

At any rate, nine fifteen isn't too late to call someone, and de Silva did suggest a new job.

"Yo, this is Carlo Vasquez, if you're not the IRS please leave a message after the beep." BEEEEP.

"Hey there, Mr. Vasquez, my name is Johnny, I fixed your brother in law's toilet, and he said I should give you a call, so... ahh... call me back on this number if you still need that deck done." Shit. I hate phone calls, so I wanted to get it over with as fast as possible. If he does have another job for me I could take that money and move, or get Jake to go back on the whole boycott thing.

I get bored and leave after my beer, my head still hurts a bit but my arm looks better, by which I mean it is no longer discolored. When I get home it feels really late, but it can't be. I sit down on the bed and look at the ceiling, then I pick up the remains of my syringe from the floor, where I stepped on it. I can't really throw it away, who knows who might see it. I put it in a little plastic bag with the other old syringes and plan to take it out tomorrow to... somewhere to dispose of safely. Call it paranoia if you like, but after the last few months, I am not going to take chances.

I call Jenny again.

Beep

Beep

Beep

Beep

"Hello?" She sounds high.

"Hi there sweet cheeks, how are you?"

"Sweet cheeks? Since when do you call me that?"

"Don't know...Thought you'd like it. I went to water your plants." Wow, that was clever, I feel like a spy.

"Oh, right, wait, do I have plants? I suppose..." She sighs very deeply. "Listen Johnny, I think I might be gone for a while. Did you throw away those things?"

"So to speak."

"Good." She is interrupted suddenly.

"Ms. Levi, if you would just sign here." It's a male, husky, formal voice, like that of Josh... exactly like Josh's! It's Josh!! Josh used to hang out for a while, he was one of Joanna's admirers, but also completely captured by James's charm, so he was just 'biding his time' until Joanna would notice him. Oh, and he was the first ever Smack dealer I ever met. Oddly enough it was a family business, his dad started the operation and then took the fall after a DEA raid, Josh has been working at the Plaza Hotel Ohio ever since. She is staying at the PHO... wow, that is like a five minute drive from here.

"I'll be right there Ms. Levi." I like that she took on an alias, goes well with my current super-spy vibe in my head.

Indeed I am there in six minutes (traffic) and sit in the lobby on a big leather couch and look at an embarrassed Jenny. Josh is at the reception desk looking unhappy and sober.

"Yeah, I know, not exactly Bonnie and Clyde material, but it's the only thing I could think of, so go ahead."

"I think it's cute."

"Fuck you Johnny."

"Don't be like that. You panicked, wanted to split, didn't know where, and found yourself here, I get it." I probably would have tried Canada, do they send you back? I don't know.

"Anyway... Thanks for taking care of business for me." She lights a cigarette, and puffs real slow, like you would expect a trucker to do. "I took most with me, but I was in a hurry. Jake told me about your...talk." What the hell? It took her like almost a week to call me but she had already talked to Jake? "Don't take it personally, he's under a lot of stress. He is actually a great boss, and doing very well, but his guys keep fucking up. A couple of days ago one of his guys took all the LSD he had for sale and tripped all night, made a lousy hundred dollars; Jake is afraid to lose control of what he has built." They seem to be cozy together, real snug and friendly. Don't pick a fight, Johnny, don't pick a fight.

"Well, I am just happy to see you again." She smiles at me, I guess mentioning that guy wasn't an accusation; they really don't know I gave him the LSD. My super-spy vibe is back now; it almost feels like I should be wearing a cape.

"You're really very sweet Johnny."

"So now that the jig is up are you coming back? I guess you never really left, but, I don't know."

"If you can find me anyone can."

"Wow, thanks for the vote of confidence." I wish I had a drink in my hand to make that remark sound cool, like Sean Connery or something. That just sounded like a whiny kid.

"I suppose I will go back home now, but keep the 'goods' at your place for now, for selling Johnny." Wow, she must really trust me if she's using me as storage.

"Sure thing." But that does mean I can't use any of it. What good is this? It's like going to a kid's room, storing all the cookies there, but forbidding the kid from eating them, you are asking

209

for trouble.

We leave the hotel together and I drive her home, she wants to go alone, but seeing her struggle with her 'sample bag' I help her carry everything up and she feels obliged to invite me to stay. A small part of me wants to decline and go home like a gentleman, to show good will and decency. Another part of me misses hearing her breathe at night, and playing with her hair when she sleeps. Another part misses taking the gamble of touching her at night, hoping she'd reciprocate.

She showers and goes into bed, but I'm not tired yet, so I do the right thing and leave her in peace, with a little note on the fridge:

"Dear Jenny,

You were too tired for company, so I thought I should leave you to sleep like you wanted. Hope you had great dreams, I will call you.

Love, Johnny.

P.S

You're out of orange juice, milk, cream, sugar, eggs, and apples."

I get home and start laughing as soon as I walk through the door. It was so ridiculous of her to hide in one of the three hotels in town. It isn't Manhattan, not exactly a lot of choice here; if the cops were after her, they would have found her on the first day. I don't think I will ever say that to her face, not to mention laugh to her face, but I think she knows it. That's probably what threw her off her game tonight. She worked so hard the last few months to build up the image of an expert drug-dealer, and supplier, and here she was, proving she's still a rookie; and a self-deprecating one at that. She was genuinely afraid of what I might think, and

I did think it was cute. I guess that upset her the most.

I look around me while dismantling my outfit and reverting back to my house-clothes, boxers and T-shirt, and I see Jenny's 'goods'. She said I am to act as storage. That means I need to leave it alone. But here is my problem: I am more or less broke, Jenny is the only dealer in town that would sell me anything now, at least that I know of, and here I have her merchandise... for free. Logically, I should have told her I had disposed of it, but I didn't. However, she does know I used a bit in the time between her telling me to get rid of it and the time she told me not to, but she doesn't know how much, ergo, anything I use before she sees the current state of the stores will be attributed to that in-between-time, for which I cannot be held accountable. Or said plainly: Anything I use now, I use with impunity! So stock up!! Thank you Jesus for this blessing of free Junk!

I set to work immediately, feeling like a bit of a glutton. First I roll a joint from fine weed and smoke it at leisure, then I get ready for the big guns. I taste the stuff this time to measure how much I need for a good hit, since last time made me pass out, which was weird.

I rarely use a scale. I go like the great chefs of Europe, by feel. But I was not used to this 'brand' of Junk so it hit me in some of the wrong places, this time I will be fine.

I get a new syringe out and clean my needle, taking extra care because it was on the floor. Then I grab a candle and a spoon. I reuse an old filter because that is all I have left; it floats around like a turd in the pool, a golden pool. I fill up the syringe and handle it like it were gold, or explosives; precious cargo. I take a few seconds in finding the damn vein, seeing my arm is weird and discolored again. Wait, no. It's discolored now. I'm done. Why couldn't I find a vein? I lost the sense of time. Or touch. Is time a sense the way hearing and sight are? I digress, not important. It feels even weirder this time. No up-traveling fart bubbles, but I feel like I am in a constant state of throwing my head back, like I were making backflips with just my head, but I am not moving. Then it comes. I start blinking fifty times a second, watching the world like in a club with those flash strobes. It makes it look as if the world didn't matter, my room isn't real, isn't fake, it's just a place. I'm on the bed now, rolling around and punching the pillows. This is strange. I need to snap out of it. I start to panic in my head, but my body is lagging behind and is still in a state of utter bliss and cosmic indifference. I walk over to Jenny's bag of wonders and grab some Coke, not a lot, I will try to do a control descent back to planet earth.

The Coke doesn't snap me out of it entirely, but I feel much better. Man, Jake is selling some weird stuff to people. I decide to try the Smack, just to make sure it's good. I know Jenny would feel bad selling people an inferior product.

The Smack is good, very good even. I 'wash it down' with another joint to relax and land smoothly. My brain needs a few hours' break so I go to bed, thinking I have not taken so many drugs in one night in ages.

There is a clear difference between an alcohol hangover and drug hangover. One big difference is the fact that most adults with an alcohol hangover would often utter the phrase "I will never drink [that much] again," no junky in his or her right mind would say something like that. Oh, the alcohol people don't mean that either, not really, but the thought does make sense to them at that moment, not so for junkies.

I don't even bother trying to get up, that seems like a total waste of time and effort. My phone reveals two things: one, it's noon. Two, I have five missed calls.

I try falling back to sleep but get a phone call, Jenny.

"Hey babe, thanks for the shopping list." She is like a robot from the future who never learned how in inflect their tone for irony or sarcasm, so I never know what she means.

"Glad to have been of service." I sound terrible.

"Rough night?"

"Yeah, had a crazy foursome with some girls, how about you?"

"Had a wonderful monogamous experience with my pillow." I thinks she finds my inability to understand her charming, lucky me.

"Anyway, can I come over?"

"Sure." No need to stress, I know how much I used, and it isn't too much, and besides, I am in the clear thanks to my amazing plan and reasoning. I think this will be just the motivation I need to get out of bed.

I get up to make coffee, if all else fails, caffeine is your salvation. I make the worst breakfast ever, which consists of some jam and cream cheese that tasted like cottage cheese. After that I start cleaning up a bit for Jenny's sake, I am a little proud that there's no puke anywhere, and that that sheet hanging out to dry looks like I'm trying to set a mood.

Jenny comes in and throws her purse on the chair next to the door. It isn't next to the door for any particular purpose, I was just changing a light bulb there and left the chair. She sits down on the bed and looks around. She has a paper bag in her hand and she throws it in my general direction. A bagel.

"You never have a proper breakfast."

"I know, it's part of my irresistible charm, isn't it?"

"So is the cheese on your cheek." She gestures with her hand to her left cheek, suggesting subtly that I brush off any unwanted dairy goods from mine. "God, I've actually missed this place." She would always say she hated here, but actually saw it as a refuge from her parents, she would always come over unexpectedly and just hang out.

She is sitting there, trying to take off her shoes and look good doing it, her hair falls down to the left of her face in this kind of wild way, so I guess she does look good doing it. She has pink socks. I cannot see pink socks without smiling. It just reminds me so much of kids, how many adults wear pink socks? The rest of the outfit is really mature, maybe even a bit too much so; a skirt down to the lower thigh, in black, and one of those very loose gray shirts that shows her bra to the world, albeit a sports-bra which reveals little, but is still sexy.

"So, can I have my stuff back?" She gets to the point.

"I took a bit when you said I should get rid of it."

"I am sure that will be fine." I go to get the bag of wonders and it looks much emptier than it was last night. I almost throw it into the air when lifting it, expecting it to be much heavier. I bring it to Jenny feeling a little bit like standing in front of a customs agent after coming back from Mexico, nervous and a bit afraid even if I know I did nothing wrong.

"A bit? There's like, four thousand dollars' worth of merchandise gone!" I just stare at her speechless. I have no recollection of doing even a quarter of that amount, but I look in the bag and it is somewhat lighter than it was yesterday. I still don't believe it's four thousand dollars' worth that's missing.

"Don't exaggerate, I didn't take that much, besides, you were willing to throw it all away." It's starting to look like she isn't up-to-date with my plan. I am sure I can make her see things my way. "I stopped using as soon as you told me you want it back. "

"Well, I thought I lost it all, and then you said you didn't throw it away, and you can't have used to much, so... where is it? Did you sell it on? Where's my money?" I think she means to sound threatening, but it completely misses its mark with her squeaky voice. She gets all red in the face and I begin to think she means it; she never gets this mad. One time I mentioned to her that I had had a crush on her mom when I was a teenager, before I met Jenny, and she got angry, but not really, just a bit jealous. "You are just the most fucked up person I know, you know that?"

I honestly fail to see her logic. She went from losing all of what she had to losing all but four thousands' worth, how is that not good? If I had told her I had thrown out everything, would have made everything better in some way? I decide to go on the attack, Cheney said that is always best, or maybe it was Sun Tsu...

"Listen, you said get rid of it, I just thought I'd enjoy it while I do as you ask, I was taking all the risk!" I raise my voice, I don't ever raise my voice, at anyone. I find myself yelling as though it's blown through a horn far far away, the words are just spittle flying through the room, some landing on Jenny's bangs, some on her shoulder. I push her down to the bed, and slap her hard, she kicks me in the nuts, slaps me right back. She shoves something in my mouth, a stamp of LSD, before storming off and yelling something back, but I can't hear her, there are explosions everywhere, the dunes around us are full of blood. She took everything and drove off. The Humvees are broken but she got through, the Major is telling us to get back, find cover.

The mortars aren't getting past the bed; the kitchenette is the safest dune around so me and three others from the tech-team make a run for it. He's hit, but puke comes out instead of blood, but it's from me. The floor is covered with it, but the two of us carry on. I fall down, clutching the microwave for dear life, but I only end up taking it down with me, another casualty in a war that never made sense except as a way to piss off my dad.

"Get me out of here!" I yell out in the comms, but there's only static, masked by the more immediate sounds of fighting over the dunes by the front door. A no-man's-land of sand, blood, and dirty underwear cover the short distance between me and my fellow soldiers; the other tiny American flags in the yellow sand on someone's map.

I throw up again, an acidic taint fills my nostrils and perception. It's over.

I find a piece of paper on my tongue. It tastes of Jenny and LSD. Everything hurts and everything smells of puke. There are four knocks coming from the left wall; the agreed sign that am being a loud prick, so I shut up. I have to wait a while for the sounds of gunfire to subside, for the sand to disappear. I sit up against the pantry and cry a little, seeing as there is nothing to distract me. Then I resume my attack and go for the enemy headquarters.

The street is empty, which was a standing order that something is about to go majorly wrong. The camel-jockeys are afoot. The hard brick tells me of the fortifications done on the place. Hard walls and a system of internal tunnels, guards at the front, locks and possibly manned machine-guns at the top. No, no machine guns. I am not in the desert. But the place is on lock-down.

I don't bother with pleasantries and break the front door's lock to get in, not expecting too much resistance. A short burst of protests from an elderly black lady does little damage and I go on, climbing the stairs to Jenny's apartment. I bang on the door, and all the noise inside stops and becomes an oblique, telling silence. The silence of an ambush. I bang on the door again, three times.

Bang bang bang.

Bang bang bang.

Bang bang–

Jenny's there holding the phone.

"I have the cops, they're listening." I push past her and get inside, all the while with my hands up, making a show of being unarmed. Of course, I am unarmed, but history tells me it always pays off to make it clear that one is. She doesn't seem to be too alarmed by my entering, so I try to project calm. I sit on the couch and wait for her to join me in the living room, which she does, phone still in hand, but not next to her ear. She sits opposite me on the floor. We stare at each other for a while, but I don't think it's too awkward.

"Thanks for the LSD."

"Thanks for making it clear where we stand." That sounds scornful, hell hath no fury. "I was unsure if you're still worth–while, but I guess you are just a fucked up junky; a junky who owes me four thousand dollars."

"Come on, give me a fucking break. I should have just told you I had thrown it away."

"No one uses that much in twelve hours, you are either still stashing it or you sold it on without giving me a cut." That's her business voice, all analytical and cold; so sexy.

"I don't have that much money."

"Oh, you will pay me, you know why? Because I am the only one who would sell you anything, so you need me. Jake won't sell you anything, neither would any of his guys, it's me or no one, and let's face it, you're too much of a chicken–shit to go anywhere else. Oh, and you get nothing before I see some cash." Okay, we made it to the negotiation stage, if I can keep my wits, I think I can come out on top. "Oh, and if you ever touch me again, I will kill you." She gets up and walks away to the kitchen; no way I let her win like that. I start following her, she just extends her hand to let me see her phone with a ringed finger ready to press 'dial' to 911.

"Jenny, don't be like that, I'm sorry."

"Not yet, you're not."

"I brought your stuff, it's in my car."

"Good start Johnny, bring it up, I'll open for you." I have to admit it, a big part of my brain is telling me to take the contents of the bag and run away, sell anything I won't use and settle into a network elsewhere. Maybe Chicago, or Seattle, I could try something more modest, like Maryland, do they do drugs there?

I reach my car and look into the trunk; there, next to some work tools and a few DVD covers, is Jenny's bag of wonders. It's still a bit heavy, I really do think she's overreacting. Okay, I shouldn't have slapped her, that's a given, but she shouldn't have drugged me without my permission. Walking back I wave for her, she's at the window watching me. She disappears as I approach, presumably to open the front door. The climb upstairs seems Sisyphean, like she might ask me to go back downstairs and bring up the car, and then a reckoning for all my sins.

I do reach her door and it only opens up a slit, a hand reaches out for the bag.

"Come on." Another hand is extended with a phone, 911 flashing on the screen. "Fuck you, Jenny." I drive back home and beat the shit out of the mattress and a cupboard; neither stood a chance. I scream at the walls and they respond with a polite knocking telling me to be quiet or they would call the landlord. I throw some stuff around in a more or less silent protest.

I can't stand waiting. I can't stand standing around impotent as to what to do. It's a funny word, isn't it? Impotent. It comes from Latin. 'Potens', able, can, power. 'In', as in the Latin negation of any verb, together with a 'P' that makes it into an 'Im'. Impotence, unable, powerless, weak. It's amazing that this word for being powerless existed for so long; as long as the feeling. And just by its modern context you can see what the extra factor has always been: a woman. Unable to take a woman, rendered powerless by a woman. Fuck Jenny; that ungrateful bitch. Another piece of household appliance flies through this hovel of mine. How did I let her win this?

She was nothing before me. She was just a good little girl, hating her dad and fearing her mom. Now she is the biggest deal in the world in her own eyes. I'll put her in her place. She thinks it was bad I took her stuff last night? She has no idea. Where the fuck is it?

I rummage around, under dirty socks and boxer shorts, behind empty doritos wrappers and broken syringes, I find what I was looking for. Jake's pistol.

Always control your weapon. Know your enemy. Only your superior has the authority to tell you when to shoot.

All fucking bullshit they teach you in training. None of this crap matters in the real world. Those people don't know the desert, they don't know junkies.

Cocked and loaded. I missed the smell of an oiled barrel, it feels so sure of itself. It knows its purpose. To unload, it has just these charges, fifteen lives to spend and launch it into a fellow human. I was always fascinated by the short life of a bullet.

I reach back to Jenny's and open the door by force. A woman is there to protest, some old black lady. Does she spend her whole day there just complaining to people? She sees the gun and shuts up, starting to pray voicelessly.

I climb up and break Jenny's door before she manages to even dial a nine. I drop her to the ground and she starts begging. Now she begs. She never begged before, too proud, I suppose. I grab the bag and throw the Meth at her, I am screaming something but have no clue what, and my hand hits her with the butt of the gun, but she just gets angry and scratches my brow with her left hand, which I break. She screams, very loud. Her neighbors are at the door, which makes her look almost smug under all that pain and Meth. They are saying something, but she is too scared to answer so I say something which I mean to sound calming but the voices get louder.

"Johnny, please..." She is crying and I can almost see Old Jenny past all the makeup and Meth, but no, she is too far gone, she isn't my Jenny, she left me, she hates me, she is beyond my reach, she abandoned me.

I kiss her forehead and shoot her; five slugs to the chest. That got the conversations outside the door reignited. The voices out there are warning of the impending knocking down of the door, and officer sounding most serious and convincing.

He comes in and I salute him. He is a lieutenant and I am but a Corporal, I have to. I surrender my weapon, he will take it to the armory, Slate will file it in with the returns, I was never supposed to be there anyway, they will have to file it away in a different name. The officers won't want to take responsibility of putting someone in the line of fire who was never supposed to leave the FOB.

"Erfaa' yadayk!" No, that isn't what he said... he said "hands up." I am confused. "Put your fucking hands up! NOW!"

"John Milaowic, Corporal, ahh... no serial number."

"What?"

"That's what I'm allowed to tell you, name, rank, and serial number."

"Fuck you, jerk off! Hands where I can see 'em, you are under arrest for the murder of... this girl. You have the right to remain silent, anything you say can and will be used against you in a court of law. You have the right to an attorney, if you are unable to afford one the state will provide one for you. Do you understand these rights?" His tone is somewhere between auto-pilot and confused. My hands are put into handcuffs, which looks rather pointless to me.

"Dispatch, I have one gunshot victim, female, around twenty, perp is in custody, mid-twenties, male, found with murder weapon in hand shortly after the shots were fired, please send back up, and forensics, and... and some uniforms to control the crowds, they are raining a shitstorm on Hailey." The cop is looking at another uniformed cop trying to restrain a large group of unruly elderly women, looking for the latest reason to complain about the town.

"I can help."

"Shut the fuck up."

"She's twenty, you're very good at estimating ages."

"Why'd you do it?"

"You know the market." That always works, right? As long as it's accompanied by a shrug it's a sure excuse for anything. I'm too poor, I'm too weak, I'm too stupid. I was too high. There are more uniforms there is about ten minutes time dispersing the crowd of elderly women and teenagers drawn by gunfire. A city coroner is moving Jenny's body. Her body.

I killed Jenny.

I killed Jenny.

I killed Jenny.

I killed Jenny for Junk.

I

I .

I don't know why.

I chose her death. I didn't choose Junk over Jenny. I just chose for her to die so I could maybe get Junk.

Jenny is dead.

I killed Jenny.

"Is she okay?" That question was less than dumb.

"Mr. Milaowic, you know better." It's him, detective shit-for-brains, only I suppose his brains were a lot more equipped to understand me than people gave him credit. "Care to take me through this?"

"I came here, I... found her like this?"

"Are you asking me or telling me?"

"Don't know." I think I start crying again but he doesn't seem to care. I can't stop, though, it isn't a show this time. I try to wipe my eyes but the handcuff behind my back make it impossible. "I want to see her."

"Guys, hold on." He motions to the coroner guys to stop and they do. They lift the black nylon from her face and there she is. She lies there motionless and angry. I expect to be thrown back. I await some kind of flash to scorch my brain beyond the jurisdiction of men, into some limbo that only me and Philipp and countless others share. But I remain to stare at her eyes; her beautiful green eyes. Like she knew all such things would build a case for temporary insanity and guarded the corpse from such acts; lawyer's daughter.

I am then taken to the station, from there to an evaluation of some sort in the hospital, which might be to my advantage, so I don't resist. Let them take blood, MRI, scans, play with my balls, until they get too friendly.

I feel rather lucky. I get the top treatment, Morphine, and lots of it, is in constant supply.

"Is Jenny okay?" I don't know whom I asked. I just get the sensation of a head nodding a negation. I know she's dead, but that doesn't mean she isn't okay, the rest are okay. Buried with a flag and the love of millions, why wouldn't she be okay too?

I can see all the machines, administrating drugs, monitoring heart-rate and such. The evaluating doctors are all a sort of bland repetition of the last.

I sit at attention as colonel Hearts walks in, a representative of the US Army Corps.

He looks at me and sits down next to the bed, reviewing a big binder, which probably has a much better image of me than what he sees, hospital food must have deteriorated me over the late few... I don't know.

"Murder, that's bad press." He's still reading, like he hasn't done so on his way over, like most brass. "But drugs plus murder, that's real bad press, like Ozzy Osbourne press." I like Ozzy. I know he has a bad rep, but he's a good musician. "Corporal, what happened?"

"I don't know."

"That's not an answer." Isn't it? It's a reply to a question, which, by definition, makes it an answer. "Let's try again. Why should the army help you?"

"Because I was there for my country?" I know how weak that sounds, kind of like how I am feeling. I think he chose just now to come, just after my sedative administration. He wanted no part of my all-so-famous meltdowns. I tore out two retraining belts and beat up one doctor. I apparently also scared one of the nurses half to death by calling her Jenny; and she knew what happened to the last Jenny; it is a small town. I also threw five puddings at my nurses, two chicken-breasts, and something they call a Tapioca-surprise at a certain Dr. Frank, of whom I have no recollection.

"Corporal, how are *you* feeling?" He sounds like those cartoon shrinks, making a mockery of those hacks on TV, trying to get into your head. "We will need a spin on this."

"A spin?" It is all about PR, I know that, I'm not stupid. Can't have Uncle Sam looking like he's destroying lives. "I just killed a girl."

"Well, that is a spin, 'addict kills girl.' But the news people are bound to exploit you being in Iraq and such to get their ratings up." He's right.

"What should I do sir?"

I can't see anything because of the tears, but that's okay, there's nothing much to see. Besides, even if I could see I would only see a bunch of degenerates staring right back at me, but that's where the difference lies: I would know they are looking at me. I don't want to be seen.

To my left, Dr. Cahani is mock-coughing to get my attention, and I become self-conscious of crying. I wipe my eyes and apologize.

"All I'm saying-"

"You've had said enough for today Anna, and this last thing was less then constructive." Dr. Cahani comes to my rescue. He's a good doctor, and if I have to go to this 'group thing' I'm happy it's his group. He's a Jew from Washington, divorced father of two. He always lets you talk, but doesn't let anyone babble on for too long, he has a good feeling for when the group victimizes someone too.

Anna, on the other hand, is a first class man-hating bitch. As an addict, her dealer used to rape her, often, so she decided all men are bad. She is also very argumentative; at first I sympathized with her, but now...

"I was just saying that he's the only one here to have killed someone, and surprise surprise, it's a woman. And here is *Uncle* Sam, saving his sorry ass by putting him here with us like some repentance, how symbolic that the system would do that." Anna didn't take the not-so-subtle hint and just keeps talking. She sits there, hands crossed over her chest, and stares at me like I am the embodiment of patriarchy.

I get up to leave, I can't take her shit today.

"Johnny, sit. Remember what we do when we reach our limit? And you Anna?"

She drops the tough-girl act and surrenders to the doctor's voice.

"I'm sorry Johnny."

"I'm sorry Anna." We say as we hold hands in a private mini-circle of made up togetherness.

We are technically allowed to leave at any moment, but I am here under certain circumstances that would be very much frowned upon by certain people, people with handguns and badges.

"Good. That's all for today, Barry, you make sure Johnny and Anna don't fight now, okay?" Barry nods at the doctor. Barry is the doctor's pet patient. He's been here for six years, comes to group every week and boasts, if that's the right word in this context, about being clean for that long. I don't really get along with him, but that isn't because he's the pet patient, it's more because he's one of those people who would smile at anything, just sickeningly optimistic.

Barry comes over and gives me a coffee, and does the same for Anna. There's always coffee at the sessions. I think it's for two reasons: one, it's cheap, just water and powder. Two, caffeine is the only drug we can have now. There are also some stale cookies on the table, but I am sure that they're the same ones that were there last week and the week before that and so on. They really do believe in recycling here; recycled people get recycled cookies.

I get through the painful pleasantries with Anna and Barry and get home to my little empty hovel. The police really ran a number on this place during the trial. I gave them the location of all my stashes, even my emergency stash, though that one is still at large with a very happy looking, and probably the wealthiest, garden gnome. Most of my stuff is still in the evidence hold in the station. I often have dreams of detective Berger diving in a pool of those things like Scrooge McDuck while singing an opera. Whatever, I confessed almost everything, pleaded what I was told to plea, went where I was told to, cried when I was told to. I was much more comfortable having someone ordering me around and giving a direction. Trouble is, I can't find anything now. My day used to consist of fridge, bed, stash; now, I just sit around and stare at the computer.

I see that I have two email. One from Joanna, the other is from an address I don't recognize.

"Dear Johnny,

I hope you're well, your letters make me worried sometimes. Little Rose wants her Godfather out of rehab and in one piece, got it? Things in Cleveland are fine, the city isn't all that big, but James still found a job quick enough after the last one turned out to be a dud. He's still doing menial office work for just slightly over minimum wage, but we get by. I'm thinking of finding some work from home too, but Rose is only two months old, and very demanding :-) I just don't know if I'd find the time to breathe. The whole 'being a housewife' thing isn't for me, though, I can tell you this much.

Here is a picture of the little darling (in the attachment, genius), she is my life now, she and James.

I know you too will be happy like this soon, you will. You are doing the right thing, quitting. Best thing me and James ever did. I don't know if you're doing it right, but the group thing is very good for you; you shouldn't be alone in this. I'm sorry we can't be there for you (physically), but you are a strong guy :-) you'll make it.

All the best, love, Joanna, James, and Rose Stevenson."

She isn't saying anything about the bigger issue. Jenny. That's a name that hangs between me and everyone. They all know, but no one dares talk about it, except Anna. James and Joanna moved a while ago, about three months ago, looking for a better life. Joanna was instrumental at helping me find a job, with Philipp at the shop. The jobs simply wouldn't come after my face was plastered on the paper as a murderer; though in all fairness, I am. The money isn't great at Philipp's, but I get stuff almost for free, and Philipp is great fun to work with. He still calls me Corporal, and I mock salute him, at least I started when I noticed he stitched stripes to his work-shirt.

I'm open the next email, and my eye catches the signature before anything else: Michael. It's an email from Michael. I haven't heard from him since I got kicked out of the house. He and I always had a special relationship, which can only be characterized as typically fraternal. We fought a lot, but out of caring for each other. I don't know what to expect and have five beers before I gather the courage to scroll down a little bit; past the little familial "dear John." I pick and match words before I read, "Army", "mom", "grown", and "dead" all make their mark on my consciousness. I'm still too anxious to read it so I have another beer, and delay by eating something greasy that, for all intents and purposes passes as chili con carne. I open the computer again after it became impatient and gave out, and I start to read.

"Dear John,

It's hard to find a way to start this email. I guess I should start with... How are you? I heard from James you're in some kind of self-imposed rehab. I wasn't aware you were taking drugs. My first reaction when I heard you were on drugs was wanting to come over and kick your ass, but I guess an ass-kicking isn't what you need right now... You need help, which is why I am writing. Mom and dad might not want to help you in that, but I'm not them. You still have family.

You probably don't know, but I joined the army too, artillery. I'm on leave now until next week. Mom and dad aren't happy about it, they were worried (that's right, worried) when they got that letter saying you got hurt in Iraq, they didn't know you enlisted, and now they are worried about me. It's nice to be back home, it might not be our childhood home, but I've grown to love it since we moved in. Mom and dad are fine, just nerve-wrecked.

Dad is close to retirement and mom doesn't have anyone to take care of anymore, so she is a bit lost.

I would want to tell you about training and everything, but as you know, I can't in an email, so let's meet. I also want to know what you've been doing, but I suppose not... everything.

Missing you, Michael."

I read the entire email in his voice in my head, and a lump in my throat. He's a soldier now too? Well odds are he's not going to be deployed anywhere, I hope. I can't imagine him in uniform, skinny little kid, well, not so little, he's much taller than me. I remember one of the infantry guys assigned to escort me, Jamal, and a few others, he looked just like Michael, but with slightly darker hair. He died. I really want to smoke now, but when I quit, I quit everything, Cocaine, Smack, Acid, Weed, Junk, cigarettes... everything. So I can't smoke. The first three weeks were hell, and I still get muscle spasms from going cold turkey; Dr. Cahani says it's psychosomatic.

Today, I am sober for sixty eight days. Yes, I count days.

I sold my car because I don't make much and I walk everywhere now, or take the bus. It fills the time and I feel less and less like using. So now, instead of rejecting thoughts or avoiding them with drugs, I use other thoughts, like now. Dr. Cahani taught me to catch myself doing it, when I'm ignoring an unpleasant issue and try to run away from it, like now. I don't want to have a family again, I was doing fine without one. *No you weren't*, fine, I wasn't, but I don't want him, my brother, to judge me. He would say he won't, they all do, but they all judge. "once a junky, always a junky." And a junky is dangerous.

I really should answer, I should meet him, my brother. I'll ask Dr. Cahani. Is this enough of a reason to call on his time off?

Should I wait for group next Thursday? Surely Michael can wait a week...

I sit back on my bed and fall over as there is nothing to lean on. I try to remember my last conversation with Michael, but I don't really recall it. It had something to do with video games that I elevated into an allegorical goodbye, encompassing love and hate, peace and war, family and solitude; in fact it was about the latest Resident Evil game. I find myself unable to get up and look at the screen again; I don't know why, it won't change, it's an email, as static as a letter, but more ecologically friendly. It's true that getting bad news is hard for me these days, but good news are a challenge too; maybe it's just news that are the problem. I just find it hard to deal with anything these days. The doc say that is normal, and I gave up on arguing with him, so I take his word for it. As for families he says they are both the greatest help, and the biggest challenge. We are to seek support from them, or get as far away from them as possible. People simply nodded obediently and did both simultaneously, like the good doc was some prophet in a cult whose contradictions were proof of his genius.

I try to formulate a response for Michael, but quickly give up and decide on a practice run by formulating one for Joanna.

"Dear Stevensons,

Haha, you're called the Stevensons like some 1950's family comedy. Sorry. I'm fine. I don't really know what to say. I miss you guys.
Love, Johnny."

God, that is pathetic. I delete it and decide to sober up before trying again. I guess this is the major change in my thinking since quitting. Instead of relaying or waiting on or for stuff to take over the mind, I wait for it to dissipate so I could think more clearly. I remember sitting down, a needle at hand, or a stamp of Acid, or whatever and having something completely override my mind, an uncontrollable need supported by the moment, a moment demanding to be expanded and experienced, Carpe Diem as the imperative written in blood. No!

"Hello?"

"Dr. Cahani, sorry, I know it's too late, but I'm getting it again." He sighs deeply, it's the fourth time I'm calling this week.

"Johnny, breathe deep. Where is your buddy?"

"How the fuck should I know?"

"Because that is who you are supposed to call first. Okay, never mind, do the breathing thing. Remember why you quit." Because the colonel told me to, because I had to or go to jail, for a PR thing for the army, I quit... I quit because that was the next step in the plan, after the press conference. I start sobbing to the doc on the phone.

"Jenny, is she okay?"

"No, she isn't. Do you remember why?" Of course I do! Why the fuck do they all think I ask that? I'm not looking for new information, I'm looking for the current one to be replaced.

"She's dead. I killed her. I shot her five times in the chest and abdomen. I killed her." I hang up, there's nothing more to gain from this conversation. The doctor is great, but his approach is more oriented at me doing all the work and him asking questions in an all-knowing tone. In many ways, he is like some kind of witch doctor or priest. Using some kind of social magic, calming like some kind of acoustic balm.

I want to try writing an email again, but I have to get to work. Philipp changed his format into a convenience store, twenty four hours a day, only Sunday off. I do most of the night shifts, Philipp does the days. He pays me enough, and again, it was good publicity; veterans helping veterans. The whole deal was brokered by the colonel, along with his entire PR team. We all went to the press, took a few pictures of my rehabilitation, my new uniform in the world of retail.

I take the bus to work and relieve Philipp who goes straight to bed without a word. He was the first to have my back when the trial started, like we all had his back when he was charged with domestic abuse. I get my ass behind the counter and wait for anything to happen. I use the boredom as an excuse to actually do something, like stock a shelf of shampoo, but time is still refusing to move forward, so I use Philipp's WiFi to answer the emails, trying to find a better formulation for Joanna.

"Dear Joanna,
Ah... Wow. I'm glad to hear you guys are okay. I'm fine. I'm okay too, surviving. I really love working with Philipp, I don't know why you've been complaining about helping him out all these years.

I miss you guys, to be honest, I haven't really been able to meet any new friends. I am restricted to only be home, at work or at group; and besides, people aren't that excited to pal around with murderers ex-junkies.

Little Rose is adorable, and getting big already, is that normal? . Looking a lot like you, and a bit like a pink stuffed animal. I wish I could join you guys, even just for a short visit, but... I would be sent to prison if I left town. Things in group aren't great either, I told you about that Anna girl on the phone, right? Well, she's really busting my balls. And Barry is a suck-up, and Abdullah is basically there to advertise his business to junkies.

The only person I really have to talk to is your dad." So far so good, I think. It's not too pathetic, and not too distant, and very honest, I think. "I'm trying to go back to school, get permission to move somewhere else where I wasn't on the news, but that'll be for the court to decide. I'm still living in the same shitty shithole. I know you said I should move, but I can't afford anything else, and people aren't too happy about giving me a place to stay, especially if they would be my roomies." I'm still dancing around the issue. "I can't stop thinking about her." Nope, can't write that. Need to show a stiff upper lip, whatever the hell that means.

"All the best, Johnny."

Not my best work, but it's for Joanna and James, and in a way Rose, so they won't hold it against me. I press 'send' and imagine the little bits of ones and zeros flying through the wires all the way to Cleveland, where James would be too busy pretending to 'accidentally' touch Joanna's boobs to notice he has an email, yes, they have a shared email account. This is what I think until some kid takes me out of my reverie and forces me to pass two packs of chips and a beer over the barcode reader and politely tell him "five dollars sixty, please" in a way that would make Tutankhamen seem lively by comparison' yes, I know who that was, I've been reading.

I read Michael's email again, and try to formulate an answer in my head, but give up and just start writing without thinking.

"Dear Michael,
Dear idiot,
Hi,
I wasn't expecting to get an email from you. I missed you guys Why didn't you write sooner? Haven't you been watching the

new? I'm almost a local star! I hope you haven' been watching the news lately, like... in the past two months. I'm fine now, been good, I swear. Odd to hear you're in uniform... but does that mean I get to call you Private now? Anyway, I got a sweet gig as a vending machine with feet at Philipp's, you remember him, right? He told you candy's poison when you were five. Well, he's a good yet quiet boss. How are mom and dad? How's the family? How are things at home? Mom and dad managed not to go insane of boredom? I should come visit, but don't know who would be glad to see me, so... maybe your idea is better, just you and me. Are you free tomorrow? Saturday? Sunday? Someday next week?

All the best

Love

See you

Till then, John."

I press 'send' before I lose my nerve and back away from the laptop as if it were a conviction. I get myself a beer (Philipp says I can have one every two hours as long as it's not an imported one) when I get back to the counter there's another costumer there complaining that the place is understaffed and it took almost five minutes before she was served; she bought five cigarette packs.

I spend the rest of the night playing cards with myself and obsessively checking my email for a response from Michael or Joanna. It became a real rare joy to have any kind of human interaction. I obviously don't go out partying at night, and after my face was on every paper for a month, I became, in some way, famous; the word should be notorious, but that seems to be a word reserved for fun, respected criminals like Billy the Kid, Al Capone, Butch Cassidy and the Sundance Kid, God I hate that movie. Junkies who popped their girlfriends aren't notorious;

they don't deserve that word for being inconsequential.

Four and a half hours after the last costumer for the night leaves Philipp comes to relieve me. He's a lot more talkative in the mornings. We do twelve hours shifts, so obviously we're tired when they are done, which is why we don't talk much. I do try, however, to at least be civil when he comes in. He returns this favor by making (very good) coffee and bringing donuts. I tell him I sent Joanna his regards, which is a blatant lie, but he won't find out about that. If asked, of course Joanna would say yes, and besides, who asks that?

At home I just sleep until some part of my brain says it's time to eat. To be honest, that is my favorite part of the day now. I did gain some weight since quitting, but the doctors say it's normal. The state has me checked once every two weeks; part of the deal. The doctors all say, including Cahani, that a routine will help me get through the day without feeling the need to use; obviously, they never tried Junk. I suppose it does help a little, but the need IS there. It makes itself known anywhere and at any time. I can't get rid of it, and the doctors admit that this is also normal, so all I can do is distract myself.

I open the computer while chowing down some yogurt, that's right, something healthy, and see an email from Michael.

"Hi there,

Glad to see you're still alive and responding. Let's meet as soon as possible, I'm on leave so I got all the time in the world (until next month, at least). Mom and dad are fine, keeping busy. Dad's practically rebuilt the house out of boredom, by hey, to each his own. When do you want to meet?

Private Michael Milaowic"

I see the little joke, adding "Private", I don't know if it's funny or not, but it does make me smile a little. I still have a few hours before I have to go to work, so I try to reply to the email, but to no avail, so I decide to draw some inspiration from TV.

Michael is trying to be very earnest and sincere, which feels a bit awkward; this is the kid I used to ambush and fart on. It's the kid I used to shoot tiny rubber-band crossbows at. It's the kid who was convinced lollipops are poisonous if you don't swallow the stick as well, which did lead us to taking him to the hospital once. But I remember what Joanna told the school councilor once when she was asked about staying with her dad: "Family's family, if you can't forgive them, who's gonna?" So maybe I should talk to Michael, maybe I should have done a while ago.

"Dear dipshit," To start things off on a lighter note.

"How about you come see me at work? I'm there every night from eight to eight in the morning, and there's barely anyone coming in on a weekday, so we won't be disturbed, often. Just come whenever.

See you, John."

Again, I escape my computer after sending the email and eat another yogurt to calm myself. It isn't nearly as effective as Weed, but desperate times call for desperate measures. I try to get lost in creamy, strawberry goodness, but the TV ads keep intruding into my thinking "It's good for you!" "Now with more probiotic bacteria!" "It both regulates my digestion, and prevents fat!" Who the fuck knows when something regulates their digestion?! Does the lady in the commercial feel tiny microbes floating around her belly with a whistle and handcuffs for all those bad molecules that make farts? Yogurt was never going to be the solution.

I have a beer and scan my phone. Michael doesn't know my phone number, but I still check in case he phoned. There are a few missed calls, but none of them seem important. I still get calls from former clients, or dealers, still trying to keep the Junk flowing. I told Dr. Cahani about it but he said it's fine, that it keeps me on my toes. I think it's counterproductive because said toes belong to the foot that is still inside that whole mess. I still have to kill the time, so I do what the good doctor told me; write what I am thinking.

"Dear thingy,

I wrote Michael today, again, and I think he will come to meet me." Fucking shit, that sounds like something a sixteen year old might write in her diary, except the "thingy" part. It really isn't a diary or a journal, just a random collection of notes I have scattered around the apartment; a collection of fragmented days and thoughts. The first one I wrote I was so deep in withdrawal that it just read "is Jenny okay? Yes, she is okay." Which Dr. Cahani asked me to read out in group and Anna proclaimed it is a patriarchal attempt to control the mind and image of women after their death to twist the perception of them for posterity as servile objects. I just didn't realize she was gone. That was my first fight with Anna, who apparently gave me a whole two days' worth of "benefit of the doubt" because I was too far gone to actually have been any fun to pick on, but at this point I was responding to outside stimuli; especially when said outside stimuli called me a "chauvinist pig," and many other creative, and less creative derogatory terms.

When it's finally time, I head out to work and settle in to my little comfy corner at the counter, next to the security camera, but still close enough to the Twizzlers. It's the weekend so I expect more movement tonight, young people coming in to get booze before going to a place where the booze is expensive. Philipp has a strict "don't ask don't tell" policy when it comes to selling booze. If I don't know they are too young, it's their fault. Technically, I know that isn't true; we'll get into much bigger trouble than any kid who buys alcohol here, like losing Philipp's business license, but he says I should use my head. I suppose he can see the advantage of having a former junkie on board, it means I can spot a cop a mile off, and that if push comes to shove he can blame it all on me and my weakness. I can't really blame him for that, if I'm honest.

I do find myself selling quite a lot tonight, just sold my last bourbon ten minutes ago, and had to get more out of storage between checkouts. The town has a lot of teenagers, and they all want a drink. In fact, I see it as a sort of community service. If they think of alcohol as the cool thing to get without permission, maybe they won't feel the need to go get Junk as the new thing. Who knows? It's rather optimistic, I know, but I have to explain all this somehow.

At three in the morning it slowly dies out and I get a minute to check my emails; none. I refresh myself with some milk and vodka. Philipp doesn't like that but he does understand the need to unwind on weekends like this, especially when I am nervous. I keep looking to the corner of my eye in case I find Michael there, but that stretches my sight ever more to the side and I end of turning in circles.

"You okay there?" It's a costumer. She looks at me like I were Mork, and I try to brush it off like I was just trying to scratch somewhere hard to reach.

"Yeah, all good. How can I help you?" She then looks at me rather embarrassed.

"Uhm… do you guys carry condoms?"

"Sure, at the back behind the milk, if you see chicken-wings you've gone too far." I try to be funny to relieve her embarrassment. I never understood way people get embarrassed when getting condoms, which they do. It's like saying 'I'm gonna have sex!' I would scream it from the mountain tops! She disappears among the products and comes back after a few minutes with several packs of condoms and cheeks so red they radiate heat. She put them all on the counter in a neat little heap and I scan them one by one, which turns her even redder.

Ribbed for her pleasure.

Extra thick.

Cola flavored.

"Cola?" That makes her reach to take it and almost run away without paying. Instead, she dumps it all into her handbag and keeps her silence. I take the seventeen dollars fifty three cents and let her go on her way to the lucky guy who will have a cola-like after-taste. I have to admit to be a bit envious of the guy. She looked very cute, but in my current state I would say that about most girls. She comes back after a second to buy some candles, scented ones, she has class.

"A special evening 'mam?"

"I'm going to lose my virginity tonight." She seems half excited and half terrified, and a bit embarrassed.

"Very exciting." She also smells of cheap rum and weed. "Are you sure you should?"

"Yeah, I love him."

"How old are you?"

"seventeen. Most of'm'ffriends 'ready did't." She is slurring more than I thought she would, much more than earlier.

"Well, have a good time." Who am I to judge? She's old enough to make decisions, and if she made a mistake, it's her job then to learn from it.

Nothing of any note happens until morning, though to be honest I did sleep between five and six thirty. Then Philipp shows up to replace me and make me coffee. He looks very cheerful in the morning and I tell him about the girl from the night and we both laugh.

He says that when Joanna lost her virginity, he assumes I know when that was which I do, she crept back into the house and spent half an hour in the bathroom to clean herself up, and waking him up in the process. He then wanted to shoot James for it, but she begged and cried and then promised to do the cooking for a month so Philipp ended up not shooting James. I didn't know that part of the story, only that Joanna was pissed for a month and didn't hang out at lunch time.

I go home and try to sleep, but my work-time nap was enough for a while and I can't fall asleep so I play on the computer. That gets tired after a while so try the TV only to get bored and fall asleep, getting woken up by an alarm clock I never set, which turns out to be the TV on a Schwarzenegger movie; apparently, it is imperative they get to the chopper.

I go and make toast before noticing an email on the inbox with the subject "sorry" in bold.

"Sorry for not coming to your work, I didn't remember Philipp's to say the truth, plus, I didn't see your email on time. I met up with a couple of guys from school, Dennis and Jay, you remember them? Well, Jay said he's met you, which I suppose means I should stop hanging out with him, right? Well, I thought maybe you can stop by tomorrow, at home. Mom will be happy to see you, no throwing shoes at you, promise.

Love, Dipshit :-)"

Jay went to school with Michael? I though all the screw ups were out of the system by then. Michael was hanging out with Crack dealer? I have no idea how I missed that, probably because he wasn't a Crack dealer when they were in school, but still I like to think I could have noticed it. Michael used to come by with his little friends all the time and wanted to include me in their little games. I sometimes did play with them, mainly to make Michael happy, but sometimes just because it was fun to be the one everyone agreed was cool.

I run around the email with my eyes before I land on the quintessence of it, he wants me to come by the house, the old house, my family's house, though, they did move there after I left, but for them, it is the family house. When I say it like that it sounds like the scene of a horrible murder where the ghost of the victims still traverse and avenge themselves on the living fools who dare wander there. In fact, it's just a small house in the suburbs, with a green fence, and blue blinds, and something that was going to be a shed but ended up being a lump of lumber; number of casualties, zero, well, one hamster.

"See you Sunday."

That's the most I can do for a reply, and I start getting my stuff together for work, knowing I will be too nervous later for any kind of a so called 'decent decision'. I kill the rest of the time by standing around and trying to write in my not-diary but am doing a poor job at that, but since Dr. Cahani said I have a way with language I try to do something else, I try my hand in poetry.

"When times are near, and the mind is blind with fear
Let loose your cheer, and make your soul austere
For there are forces there, so do beware,

Of minds a twist, and kissed missed"

It's terrible. Even I know that. I remember what I wrote when Jenny was there and tear this shitty excuse up. I start tearing up. I know why. I told Dr. Cahani why. I wrote poems for her, and any new ones would remind me of her. I wrote from a place of pain and uncertainty, I can't just call it up again. There is still pain now, yes, I'm not dead inside for the most part. It's just a different kind of pain now, and there is nothing inspirational about it in its current form. Back then, it was as if everything that happened became a whirlwind in my head and was vented out in huge gushes of verbal steam. Now, it's only a deafened thud in the dark core of my head, echoing against padded walls. Wow, those are shit similies. I give it another try, though, because the doc said I should.

"Oh how I miss the days of crystalline death

When all trouble was far and I in my own mind was safe

For no thought, nor image, nor Memory's wraith

Can through this smoke penetrate my depth." I think I have a solid start and I managed to kill a few minutes till I have to go to work.

I leave early for work and spend two hours just hanging out with Philipp, who is happy to have company. We eat burritos and talk about football, and other stuff we know nothing about.

"Corporal, why don't you try going to school or something? Or do you enjoy selling vodka to under-aged kids?" He finishes his burrito and throws the wrapper in the can, and this little gem of a question at me.

"Too stupid." I decide to act mysterious yet honest.

"In many ways, yes. But seriously, you can study something, engineering or something, you're good with your hands." I hate sincerity. Cynicism is so much easier to respond to, but the

Gunnery Sergeant is not letting this go; he is doing what sergeants do, solve problems, and in some cases, that means whole persons.

"That's what she said." I try raising an eyebrow to give the joke an extra kick, but despite what medical science knows about the human anatomy, I manage to get a cramp in my eyebrow. "Come on, do I look like someone able to pay attention to stuff? Or learn?"

"You look like you're trying to fix yourself, and that may help you, give you structure."

"I have structure: Sleep, sell vodka to under-aged kids, sleep. He isn't amused and looks like he might throw that packet of bubblegum he is tossing around in his hand.

"Have it your way. I'm out early since you're here." He just hangs up his proverbial smock and heads out. I put on said proverbial smock and set up the counter and shelves for tonight's shift. It's Saturday, so there will be even more kids in need of booze, and responsible adults wanting to pretend they're not so responsible. I stock up the booze and cheap snacks shelves and put Robocop running on my laptop.

After one hundred fifty seven "Thank you, have a good night"s I get to go home after locking up the store and putting the key in Philipp's mailbox.

I get home after an hour almost because the busses run differently on Sunday, and by differently, I mean stupidly. The number three line doesn't stop at the station next to the shop, but at the one three streets down, and instead of taking it all the way to the street parallel to mine, I have to change to the number ten line and get off ten minutes away from home, or end up heading toward the town center.

I take a quick shower and try to sleep, but can't. I find myself staring at Jenny's sketch. The one with the two images next to the two Jennys. I don't know which one I am, the mean one or the nice one. I would like to say it gave me some weird epiphany, but I am just staring. She wasn't a good artist, but how do you define a good artist? Is it just having the right technique for representation of reality on canvas? Or is it more likely the ability to capture and represent your own view of reality, and how you find yourself a part of it. People will pay for a nice painting of a bowl of fruit, but they would stare in awe at the strange little clocks, melting on a branch in what might be a river, or might be blue sand. See? Told you I've been reading.

"See you tomorrow." That's what I told Michael. And now I know why I was staring: I'm stalling for time. I know sleep would be a better way to do that, but I can't sleep, and besides, that would be a productive thing to do, in a way, hardly a form of stalling.

I go to my fridge and find a closed bottle of red wine, that's a thing people bring to stuff, right? Anyway, I grab the bottle and set out to take the number three bus, then realize it doesn't stop there today, so I turn around to take the number ten, which goes in the wrong direction, but I can change to the number one bus and then the number two for five minutes and then the number four.

My folks moved a long way from the neighborhood, I went back after I had come back from Iraq, because it was both cheap and familiar. Their new home, which is over ten years old now, is in the south part of the city. It's one of those fancy modern developments which makes the place look like Bel Air in the brochure, but in reality, it's all crummy, cheaply built wooden frame houses.

The number two bus is twenty minutes late, so I start walking in the direction it goes just to not feel the time passing. As I walk

I miss one bus, and when I get to the next stop I have to wait half an hour for another one. A part of me is happy about the delay, and another part of me is embarrassed to be standing around a bus-stop with a bottle of wine in my hand. A cop drives by and stops to look at me, decides my day is crappy enough as it is and gets back into his car and drives off. I was never afraid of cops, they just made me nervous, but now, I think I've seen the worst they can do, and have reached to peak of what they can get out of me, so I have nothing left to be nervous about around them; now I just feel resentful next to them.

I get on the bus and sit next to a black guy with a huge ring on his middle finger. I think he caught me staring at it because he puts his hands in his jacket pocket. He also avoids looking at me, but seeing as I am almost a local celebrity I understand why.

"Nice weather, huh?" I try it anyway.

"Sure, sure."

"I'm Johnny, by the way."

"Frank, nice to meet you."

"What do you do, Frank?"

"I'm an attorney."

"Fancy... I'm a clerk at a convenience store..."

"That's my stop." He gets up five minutes before we even reach the stop and waits by the door, looking back at me in case I chase him to continue our idle chit-chat. I don't.

I don't really talk to a lot of people these days, so I merely thought it would be nice to have a conversation with a complete stranger, who will not patronize me with recovering-junky-talk.

I get off the bus at Lincoln Drive and look around. Jake lived here, he's 'at large' now. Whatever that means. The number four bus comes after a minute and I sit next to a lady this time. She's also African-American. Looking like she's on her way to church. I know it's a bit presumptuous to assume that simply because I associate well-dressed African-American women with going to church, but she is carrying a bible. She looks too busy for chit-chat so I leave her without trying to start a conversation.

I reach New Spirit. New Spirit is both the neighborhood, and the huge shopping center around which it was built. I suppose the plan was to get as many middle class retirees to live there, and then give them a place to go and spend their money and waste their time. They do have a few good restaurants, though.

Number nineteen.

Knock knock knock.

I hear someone coming and have to fight the urge to run away.

"Hi mom."

"John? Where have you been?"